JASMINE HERNANDEZ

The Legend of Rosa

MORPHO BUTTERFLY PUBLISHING LLC

First published by Morpho Butterfly Publishing, LLC 2025

For information contact :

(Jasmine@morphobutterflypublishing.org)

https://www.morphobutterflypublishing.org/

Author website: https://bit.ly/aboutauthorjasminehernandez

Follow Morpho Butterfly Publishing, LLC on Instagram: https://www.instagram.com/morphobutterflypublishingllc/profilecard/?igsh=YnkxaXdicGd3amM1

First edition

ISBN (paperback): 978-1-969620-06-5
ISBN (hardcover): 978-1-969620-07-2

Editing by Lindz McLeod
Cover art by Alrun Art
Illustration by Alrun Art
Proofreading by Morpho Butterfly Publishing, LLC

This book was professionally typeset on Reedsy.
Find out more at reedsy.com

"Spreading wings one story at a time."
Morpho Butterfly Publishing, LLC

Contents

Acknowledgments

A huge thank you to my editor Lindz McLeod. You took my novel to the next level, really pushing me to think about my characters and the meaning behind all of the magical realism I had infused in this story. Thank you for your honest feedback and challenging me to expand on my chapters. I honestly can't thank you enough for taking my superhero novel to the next level.

To my cover designer and character artist Alrun Art, your talent and creativity have truly exceeded my expectations, perfectly capturing the essence of my protagonist. Creating a superhero from my imagination has been a dream come true, and your artwork has made my vision a stunning reality. Thank you for your beautiful work.
I'm excited to continue working with you both in future literary projects!

Dedication

To Guy Williams, the ingenious actor who embodied Zorro's spirit with unparalleled charm, wit, and valor. Your iconic portrayal of Johnston McCulley's legendary hero inspired generations with cunning, bravery, and heroism, forever etching the character's essence in our hearts. Your enduring portrayal inspires "The Legend of Rosa," paving the way for a new 21st-century Latina hero, forged in the spirit of Zorro's timeless heroism. This book is dedicated to you, reminding us that the greatest superpower lies within our mind and heart.

Author's Note

The Legend of Rosa has been a decade-long passion project, born from a spark of inspiration that ignited in my early twenties. As I began my career as a paralegal, I found solace in the world of Rosa, pouring my heart and imagination into her story. My fascination with the iconic character Zorro sparked the idea for Rosa's bravery, cunning, and unwavering commitment to justice. Now, after a decade of dedication and growth, I'm thrilled to finally share this thrilling tale with you. I hope you'll join me on Rosa's epic journey.

Content Warning

This book contains content that some readers might find triggering such as:

descriptive scenes of torture
gore
violence
dark themes
arson
murder
attempted sexual assault

Read with care

1

Chapter One: A Glimpse of the Past

As Judge Elizabeth Garcia called out her name, Florence Avila stepped onto the stage, her heels clicking on the polished floor of the Stetson Law School auditorium. She walked up to Judge Garcia, who smiled warmly and extended her hand.

"Congratulations, Florence," Judge Garcia whispered, her voice filled with genuine admiration as she extended her hand.

Florence's eyes met District Attorney Xander Reyes, who stood beside Judge Garcia, his tall frame and broad shoulders commanding attention. His dark brown eyes seemed to bore into hers as she smiled, shaking his hand as well.

"You deserve it," Xander said, his deep voice low and sincere.

As Florence accepted her Juris Doctorate degree, the warm glow of the Tampa auditorium lights highlighted a triumphant smile on her face, illuminating the sense of accomplishment that radiated from her. The rustle of the graduates' robes and the scrape of chairs created a subtle background hum, punctuated by the occasional burst of applause.

Then Judge Garcia's voice emerged over the auditorium.

"As you graduate from Stetson Law School today and take

your first steps into the justice system, remember that justice is a complex and multifaceted concept. It is not always black and white, and it is often shaped by the perspectives and experiences of those who seek it. As lawyers, your role is not to decide what is fair, but to advocate for your clients to the best of your ability, even when the outcome may not align with your own sense of justice. It is in these moments of tension and uncertainty that your skills, your compassion, and your commitment to the law will be tested."

Florence's eyes drifted to the front row, where her boyfriend Kevin sat, his eyes shining with pride. She felt a flutter in her chest as their gazes met, and for a moment, the world narrowed to just the two of them. The chill of the auditorium was suddenly more pronounced, and goosebumps rose on her skin, a physical echo of the exhilaration and joy coursing through her. The applause swelled around her, and reality gradually came back into focus. Florence admired Judge Garcia, who was thorough, fair, and witty, and her lectures on critical thinking had impressed all the graduates.

Sitting behind Judge Garcia was Melissa Ramirez, Xander's legal secretary, her dark hair cascading down her back in loose, sultry waves that seemed to hint at a life beyond the law office. Her eyes, a piercing brown, sparkled with a knowing glint, as if she possessed secrets that no one else was privy to.

Florence had interned over the past two summers for various law firms, but her dream was to work for Xander Reyes at the District attorney's office. She had applied multiple times for a summer internship, but his secretary Melissa couldn't seem to locate Florence's applications every time she inquired about them. Despite these setbacks, she had been drawn to Xander's courtroom prowess. While attending court cases as part of her requirements for law school, Florence had watched and admired Xander's skill and confidence in the courtroom, securing successful outcomes for the cases he prosecuted. When she finally received a job offer from his office last week to join their team, she hadn't hesitated to accept it.

"Congratulations, Class of 2015!" Judge Garcia announced over the speakers.

Flying caps filled the auditorium while Florence pondered Judge Garcia's final words of her commencement speech. The auditorium erupted into cheers and applause, the sound echoing off the walls as parents celebrated with their children. Dads patted sons on the back, and moms beamed through tears as they handed bouquets of flowers to their daughters. Florence felt the weight of empty seats where her parents should have been, her heart aching for the parents she had lost far too soon.

"Congratulations!" a voice from behind said, the familiar tone sending a warmth through her chest.

Kevin, a charming news reporter from the Tampa Bay Sun-Times, had a knack for facetious remarks that added humor to every conversation.

You're always putting your nose in other people's business, she'd teased him, but deep down, she adored his inquisitive nature.

As she recalled their first meeting, a smile crept onto her face. It had been during her first semester of law school, and she'd been buried under a mountain of case briefs. Desperate for a break, she'd escaped to St. Pete beach, only to have a shadow cast over her notes.

"Excuse me, can I help you?" she'd said, her stress evident in her tone.

However, Kevin's smooth voice had melted her frustration.

"What are you reading on such a gorgeous day?" he'd asked, his eyes sparkling with curiosity.

He was handsome, but Florence had been too busy for handsome. "I'm studying, do you mind?"

Instead of taking the hint, he'd charmed her with his smile and his words: "Such a beautiful girl like you should be enjoying such a beautiful day like this."

Florence's cheeks had flushed, and she'd quickly shaken off the feeling, but she couldn't deny the flutter in her chest.

"Look, sir, you're distracting me from my studies," she'd said, trying to sound stern.

"My name is Kevin Vega," he'd replied, his voice low and smooth. "Nice to meet you, Miss…?"

"Florence," she'd answered, her voice barely above a whisper. "Florence Avila."

From that moment on, Kevin and Florence had been inseparable. Their relationship had lasted for three marvelous years, filled with laughter, adventure, and a deepening love. Kevin was different from anyone she'd ever known – kind, genuine, and respectful. As Kevin approached her with a bouquet of white roses, his eyes shone with love and admiration.

"Thanks for the roses, Kevin, they're beautiful," Florence said, smiling at the bouquet.

"Hey, did you know white roses symbolize new beginnings?" Kevin said, a bright glint in his eye. "Perfect for a future lawyer, right? You're starting fresh, and these babies are like a blank slate – minus the thorns, of course. Oh wait, they do have thorns… kind of like the justice system, huh?" He chuckled, clearly pleased with himself.

Florence rolled her eyes good-naturedly, her smile widening at Kevin's dorky joke.

"You're such a fact nerd, Kevin," she teased, laughing.

Kevin knew exactly how to fill her heart with joy; a bouquet of a dozen white roses were her favorite. So delicate and pure, like the life of an innocent person. Florence admired how such a beautiful flower could contain thorns at its stems to pierce through even the softest touch. *What a marvelous defense mechanism for such a precious flower,* she thought.

"I want to take you out to dinner to celebrate," Kevin said.

"I'd love to," Florence said as she wrapped her arms around his neck for a kiss.

"It is no wonder I love you so much," she said aloud.

Florence pressed her lips against his and for a moment all her worries dissipated.

"Looks like we finally dug up your application," Melissa whispered as she walked past, her voice dripping with venom."I suppose it's no surprise Xander would hire a pretty face over actual brains. You'll make a perfect addition to his collection of courtroom eye candy."

Florence's eyes widened in stunned silence, the words cutting deeper than Melissa could have possibly intended—or maybe exactly as she'd intended. As Florence turned to face Melissa, a spark of irritation flared within her, fueled by the venom in Melissa's tone. Melissa's eyes blazed with a fierce intensity, her gaze darting between Florence and Kevin like a challenge.

Or a warning.

"Hey, Melissa," Florence said, her tone cool and detached.

Melissa's lavender dress swirled around her, the delicate fabric rustling softly as she moved. A sprig of fresh lavender was pinned to her dress, its subtle scent wafting through the air, mingling with the distant tang of perfume. As Melissa stepped closer, Florence felt a strange, almost palpable shift in the atmosphere. Kevin's hand slipped from hers, his fingers trailing away as his eyes drifted toward Melissa. His gaze held a far-off quality, as if he was lost in a dream, his thoughts tangled in a web of his own making. Florence's heart pinched with a sudden sense of disconnection.

"Melissa, I'd like to introduce you to my boyfriend Kevin," Florence said with a hint of unease, her eyes narrowing slightly as she watched Kevin's interaction with Melissa.

Melissa giggled, extending her hand to Kevin, who took it with a charming smile. As he placed his lips on her hand to greet her, Florence felt a pang of discomfort, her gaze fixed on the scene unfolding before her.

"It's a pleasure to see you here," Kevin said, his voice smooth and courteous. Florence's mind flashed back to the countless times he'd greeted her with similar charm, but something about the way he looked at Melissa made her feel uneasy.

"Congrats, Florence!" Xander's booming voice interrupted her thoughts, his face lighting up with a warm smile. "I'm thrilled you accepted our job offer. You've got a bright future ahead of you as an Assistant District Attorney. I'm looking forward to seeing the impact you'll make in our office."

As he spoke, his gaze flicked towards Kevin, who was gazing at Melissa, and for an instant, a fleeting shadow crossed Xander's features. The sudden change in tone and atmosphere was a welcome relief for Florence, shifting the focus back to her achievement and future career.

Melissa's lips curled into a tight, hostile frown as she rolled her eyes at Xander's words.

Kevin's eyes refocused, and he smiled, his voice warm."Would you like to join us for dinner, to celebrate? Florence and I were just discussing our plans for this evening."

Florence's eyebrow arched slightly, her gaze meeting Kevin's, but he didn't seem to notice her skepticism. " You want to invite her too?" Florence muttered under her breath, her words barely audible.

Melissa's response was swift and decisive. "No thanks." Her tone was light, almost flirtatious, as she added, "I'll be spending the evening with my boyfriend, Vincit Omnia." Her fingers brushed against the lavender pin, and Kevin's eyes locked onto the movement, his face softening into a smile.

"I'm sure he's lucky to have you," Kevin said, his voice low and smooth, his eyes never leaving Melissa's face.

Florence felt a pang of annoyance, her gaze drifting toward Xander, who stood watching the exchange with a polite, slightly puzzled smile.Kevin's gaze finally returned to hers, and he smiled, but Florence couldn't shake the feeling that his attention had already wandered elsewhere.

"I need to return to the office and prepare for trial," Xander added, his eyes crinkling at the corners. "Work never ends."

"Thank you again for everything," Florence said to Xander, deliberately tuning out Melissa's presence.

After the graduation ceremony, Florence and Kevin slipped into their car, the silence between them thick with unspoken tension. Florence's mind replayed the encounter with Melissa, and she couldn't shake off the feeling that Kevin's gaze had lingered on her a bit too long. The silence in the car seemed to grow heavier with each passing mile, until they finally arrived at the restaurant. As they were seated at their table, Florence's discomfort only intensified. There was something about the way Kevin had looked at Melissa that had really bothered her. She tried to brush it off as mere politeness, but the jealous feeling lingered.

As they enjoyed their dinner, the soft clinking of silverware and the murmur of conversation from other diners created a soothing background hum. The centerpiece on the table caught her attention—a delicate arrangement of white rose petals and lavender. She lifted the vase, inhaling the sweet fragrance of the roses and the subtle scent of lavender. As she looked over at Kevin, she noticed he seemed lost in thought again, his eyes gazing into the distance.

"Hey, what's on your mind?" Florence asked, trying to bring him back to the present.

Kevin's gaze snapped back to hers, and he smiled, but Florence could sense sadness behind his eyes. She watched as he mechanically pushed food around his plate, which was unusual for a man with such a healthy appetite. Kevin's gaze drifted off, and Florence felt a flicker of irritation. What was he thinking about, anyway? He seemed lost in his own world, like someone nodding along while texting on their phone, pretending to listen but clearly tuned out. The air was filled with the sweet scent of lavender, subtle but persistent. He did this sometimes, slipped away into his own world without warning, leaving her feeling like she was grasping for a hand that wasn't there. Would he ever be fully hers, or would there always be a part of him that remained elusive?

"Nothing, my dear," he answered, his voice low and rough, as he forced a smile that didn't quite reach his eyes.

As they finished their dinner, the waiter appeared to ask if they wanted dessert, but Kevin's gaze flicked to the check, and he nodded curtly for the waiter to bring it. The scent of lavender from the centerpiece on their table lingered in the air, a subtle reminder of the evening's tranquility, but Florence felt a growing sense of disquiet. Kevin's sudden urgency to leave seemed to pull the evening's warmth out from under her feet.

Kevin and Florence returned to their apartment. Their home—an ocean view apartment that overlooked Tampa Bay—was filled with love and photos of the three beautiful years that they'd shared together.

"I love sunsets," Kevin admitted as he pulls over the living room curtains."Especially viewing them near the ocean. It's like an eternal promise the sun makes with the ocean each and every evening."

Florence rested her head on Kevin's shoulder as he gently caressed her hand. "And what eternal promise is that?"

Kevin smiles at her and kissed Florence on the forehead.

The reflection of the pink sky exposed his dirty blond hair. Florence marveled at how soft it was when she ran her fingers through it. Kevin pulled Florence toward him softly kissing her lips.

Florence held him as she noticed the sun was beginning to set into the horizon, leaving behind a pink and orange sky. The fading light seemed to stir something in Kevin, and he walked over to the balcony, sliding open the door to let the ocean breeze fill the apartment. He stepped out onto the balcony, Florence following close behind, their fingers entwined. Together, they stood at the railing, admiring the sunset's warm glow as it dissolved into the horizon.

"You know, I've been thinking a lot about us lately," he said, his voice low and sincere. "About how much you mean to me."

Florence looked up at him, curious. "What do you mean?"

Kevin smiled, his eyes crinkling at the corners. "You're always there for me, Flor. You're my rock. My parents love you, and I love the way you make me feel when we're together."

Florence's heart swelled with emotion as she listened to Kevin's words. She felt the same way about him, and she loved the way he made her feel like she was home.

"I love you, Flor," Kevin said, his voice filled with conviction.

"I love you too," Florence replied.

They stood there in comfortable silence, gazing out at the breathtaking view as the sun dipped below the horizon. The sky was painted with hues of pink and orange, a serene backdrop to their tender moment. Suddenly, the ocean breeze picked up, carrying the sweet scent of saltwater and the faint tang of seaweed. The wind rustled through Florence's hair, sending shivers down her spine as it danced across her skin. The air grew cooler, and she felt the fine hairs on her arms stand on end.

The ocean breeze carried with it a husky whisper: "Amor… vincit…omnia…nocte… sequenti." The words seemed to seep into their ears, soft at first, but growing louder and more insistent. Florence felt a shiver run down her spine as the phrase repeated, the syllables weaving a sensual rhythm. "Amor…vincit…omnia…nocte…sequenti…AMOR… VINCIT…OMNIA…NOCTE…SEQUENTI…"

The chant pulsed with a dark intimacy, the words echoing through the air like a lover's caress. Florence's skin prickled with goosebumps as she turned to Kevin, her voice trembling.

"Did you hear that? It's… it's freaking me out!"

Kevin's expression was distant, his eyes fixed on the horizon. The chant continued to build, the words repeating over and over like a heartbeat.

Abruptly, Kevin turned to Florence. "I have to go."

Florence nodded, assuming he was off to work on a new investigative report. "Be careful," she said, but Kevin was already heading out the door.

She shook off the unease and walked into the living room, where she turned on the TV. A news report caught her attention, the news caster's voice filled with fear and concern.

"Recent developments in Tampa have brought to light a disturbing trend:witchcraft is being practiced in various parts of the city. Police have confirmed that rose gold tarot cards have been discovered at crime scenes, and investigators think they are linked to..."

The report trailed off as Florence's mind began to wander, her thoughts consumed by the haunting phrase still echoing in her mind: *Amor...vincit...omnia...nocte... sequenti..*

What on earth did it mean?

2

Chapter Two: New Beginnings

Florence Avila stood outside the Hillsborough County District Attorney's Office, her heart racing with excitement. Today marked her first day as an Assistant District Attorney. At 25 years old, Florence boasted an impressive resume, having graduated with honors from Stetson Law School and acing the bar exam on the first attempt, showcasing her exceptional wit and legal powers.

Memories of late nights spent studying for the Florida Bar exam flooded her mind. Between law classes and briefing cases, she had carved out every spare moment to prepare, determined to pass. The memory of the moment she found out she had succeeded still brought a smile to her face. She had been cozied up on her sofa, a welcoming change after three years of intense studying. But she couldn't stop learning, and instead of vegging out in front of the TV, she was immersed in a book on Egyptian history, fascinated by the story of Tutankhamun, the nine-year-old king who had ruled Egypt with the counsel of his elders. There was something about the golden light of the pharaohs that had always resonated deep within her, and she found herself drawn to the complexity of ancient Egyptian politics. She was amazed by the complexity of his situation, a child leader navigating the intricacies of ancient politics. Just as she was turning the page to a new chapter, Kevin had appeared beside her, a letter in his hand.

"Guess what came in the mail?" he asked, his eyes sparkling with excitement.

As she unfolded the letter from the Florida Board of Bar Examiners, her trembling fingers tracing the official seal, her eyes scanned the page until they landed on the words, *"Congratulations, you have passed the Florida Bar Exam."*

A rush of excitement had coursed through her, and Kevin swept her into his arms, his lips crashing down on hers in a joyful kiss.

"I knew you could do it," he whispered, his voice full of pride and adoration.

Afterwards, she'd glanced at her phone, where Facebook posts from her classmates filled her screen. Some had been jubilant, while others had been eerily silent. She had hesitated to post about her own achievement, knowing that not everyone had been as fortunate. The comments from those who hadn't passed still lingered in her mind, a sobering reminder of the exam's difficulty. Kevin poured two glasses of champagne, which he had bought weeks ago, anticipating her success. Florence had been skeptical at the time, thinking it would be a bad omen, but now she was glad he had been so confident.

"To you, Attorney Avila," he said, his eyes sparkling with love and admiration.

As they clinked glasses and took a sip, Florence felt like she was on top of the world. Today, she stood tall, ready to take on her new role.

The glass doors swung open with a soft whoosh as Florence stepped into the District Attorney's office, her heels clicking against the polished marble floor. The sound echoed through the sleek lobby, announcing her arrival. A young, thin paralegal with big, thick, round glasses like Buddy Holly walked towards her, a warm but guarded smile spreading across her face. Despite her pretty features, the glasses gave her a slightly awkward, nerdy appearance, which endeared her to Florence immediately.

"You must be Florence, right? Congratulations and welcome to the team! I'm Alexia, and I'll be your assigned paralegal. I'll be showing you around today and helping you get settled in," the woman said, extending a hand.

Florence's eyes sparkled. "Thanks, Alexia."

Alexia led Florence through the bustling office, where the hum of computers and the soft murmur of conversations filled the air. Florence's attention was caught by the faces around her—the paralegals and secretaries seem to be going through the motions, their expressions a mix of boredom and frustration. Some stared blankly at their screens, while others mindlessly copied and scanned legal documents, their faces scrunched up in concentration. The occasional glance up as they pass by was fleeting, with eyes quickly returning to their work. Smiles were nonexistent in this part of the building. The overall atmosphere felt heavy, as if everyone was simply counting down the minutes until the weekend.

They approached Melissa's desk, and Florence noticed the woman's eyes narrowing into slits, her lips pursed in a tight line as she looked up from the stack of files in front of her.

"This is Melissa, Xander's secretary," Alexia said, nodding

toward the woman.

"We've met before," Florence added, her tone carefully neutral.

Melissa's expression shifted from annoyance to a smirk, her eyes glinting with memory. She seemed to recall their previous encounters, specifically Florence's inquiries about her summer application, which Melissa had "misplaced" despite Florence's repeated requests. Florence glanced at Melissa, noticing a delicate pink rose quartz necklace shaped like a heart resting on her chest. Her gaze then drifted to Melissa's tidy desk, where a peculiar glass jar caught her attention. The jar contained a mixture of symbolic ingredients, including red rose petals and lavender, which seemed to be sealed with a piece of rose quartz similar to Melissa's necklace.

Melissa's face twisted in a scowl. "Excuse me, I am his legal assistant," she muttered, her voice dripping with venom, as if the title of "secretary" was somehow beneath her.

Alexia's shoulders drooped a little, a hint of apology in her expression. "Right, she's his legal assistant," Alexia corrected herself, her tone softening.

Florence noticed the subtle distinction and wondered if it was a point of pride for Melissa, the difference between a secretary who answered phones and took dictation, and a legal assistant who handled more complex tasks and required specialized training. Melissa's emphasis on the title seemed to suggest that she was more than just administrative support staff, but rather an integral part of the legal team. "Don't ask me for any favors because I am swamped and Xander doesn't like to share," Melissa added, her eyes narrowing slightly as if she'd overheard the whispered conversation, her gaze flashing with a fierce intensity that made Florence take a step back.

Florence turned back to Melissa with a courteous smile still plastered on her face.

"Thank you for clarifying your role, Melissa," Florence replied coolly. "I think I'll be in good hands with Alexia here, so I won't be needing to tap into your expertise anytime soon."

Alexia's eyes widened in surprise, her face lighting up with a mixture of shock and delight. She pushed her glasses up the bridge of her nose, her fingers trembling slightly as she struggled to contain her grin. Florence winked at Alexia, who suppressed a smile, while Melissa's face darkened in a huff.

They walked away from Melissa's desk, and Alexia leaned in close. "Be careful around her, Florence," she whispered. "There's something...off about her."

Florence raised an eyebrow, intrigued by the warning. "What do you mean?" she whispered back, but Alexia just glanced nervously at Melissa's desk and shook her head.

"And here we have Ryan," Alexia smiled, gesturing to a tall, handsome young attorney.

"Florence, meet Ryan, our expert in white-collar crimes."

Ryan extended a genial hand, his brown eyes bright with intelligence."Nice to meet you, Florence."

"Ryan's genius lies in unraveling complex financial trails aka white-collar crimes," Alexia explained.

Ryan chuckled. "In homicide, you follow the bloodstains. In white-collar crime, you track the digital breadcrumbs."

Alexia nodded sarcastically, "Right. He's relentless in pursuit of justice."

Ryan's smirk hinted at a dry sense of humor, and Florence found herself smiling in response.Finally, Alexia stopped outside a door with Florence's nameplate.

"This is where you'll be working," Alexia said, opening the

door to reveal a spacious office with a stunning view of the city of Tampa.

Florence's eyes widened. "Wow, this is incredible."

Alexia smiled wistfully. "Yeah, it's one of the best views in the office. Xander must think you're very valuable.My desk will be right outside your office." Alexia pointed to a small black desk perpendicular to her glass door.

As Florence steps outside her office to observe Alexia's desk, she noticed a stack of LSAT prep study materials lying flat on the desk's corner."You're studying for the LSAT?"

Alexia sighed. "Trying to. But I just can't seem to score high enough to get into law school."

"Don't give up, Alexia. You're already doing great work in the legal profession. The LSAT is just one hurdle."

Alexia's expression softened."Thanks, Florence. That means a lot coming from you."

As Alexia left to attend her daily tasks, Florence took a moment to absorb her new surroundings. She felt a surge of determination to make a positive impact in this office.Her trained eyes scanned the office with precision. Being detail-oriented was crucial in the legal field, where a single overlooked fact could make all the difference in a case. She made a mental note to pay attention to every detail, no matter how small it might seem. A defendant's clothing, for instance, might be a crucial piece of evidence – a torn thread, a unique accessory, or even the brand of their shoes could help link them to a crime scene. Similarly, the make and model of their car could provide valuable clues. Florence's mind was already racing with possibilities as she took in her new environment.

Since no one had yet assigned her a task, she decided to

decorate her new office. Heading down to her car, Florence retrieves a small box of her personal items before heading back to her office and setting up her workspace with a few photos and mementos. The sound of footsteps approaching interrupted her, and she looked up to see Xander standing in her doorway.

"Good morning, Florence," he says, his deep voice warm and inviting. "Welcome to the team. I must say, I'm thrilled to have you on board."

Florence's gaze met his, noting the strong features and piercing dark eyes."Thank you, Mr. Reyes," she replied, her smile gracious. "I'm excited to be here."

"Please, call me Xander. We're a friendly team here."

Florence's eyes lingered on his tailored suit, noticing the subtle stitching and luxurious fabric."Is that Armani?"

Xander chuckled, "Guilty as charged. I have to say, I'm impressed. Not many people can spot an Armani suit from across the room."

Florence smiled. "I have an eye for fashion, I guess."

Xander's expression turns serious."I just wanted to let you know that we had a big win in court today. We put away a murderer, and the jury voted unanimously for him to receive the death penalty. There's nothing more satisfying than that."

Florence's eyebrows arched in interest."Congratulations."

Xander's expression turns introspective, his voice softening."You know, my sister Marguerite died because of her boyfriend's actions. Every case I work on, I see her face. Every victory is solace, reminding me that justice can be served."

Feeling a wave of empathy, Florence nodded. "I'm so sorry, Xander. Losing someone to violence is unbearable."

Xander's gaze locked onto hers, his eyes burning with

determination. "That's why I do what I do, Florence. And I'm glad to have you alongside me in this fight." Xander's gaze drifted to the photo on her desk. "Your family?"

Florence nodded, a hint of melancholy crossing her face. "My boyfriend, Kevin, and my parents." Her voice was barely above a whisper. "My… my parents were killed in a car accident about a year ago. The worst part of it all was that I didn't get a chance to say goodbye, much less pay for a proper funeral."

Xander's eyes filled with compassion. "Losing a loved one is never easy, especially when it is unexpected."

Florence offered an awkward smile tinged with sadness. "Thank you. It's still tough, but I'm finding my way again. Kevin's been my rock, supporting me through everything."

Xander nodded . "You're strong, Florence and I can see that. Well, I'll let you get started on your cases. There's much work to be done."

As Xander walked out of her office, Florence's gaze lingered on the doorway, his charismatic presence still palpable. She shook her head, impressed by his confidence and expertise. She aspired to emulate his dedication to justice, his passion and his precision in her own career, and she hoped to one day match Xander's skill and conviction.

* * *

Later that evening, Florence met Kevin at Bella Vita, a quaint Italian restaurant where they had shared their first date. She couldn't help but feel a rush of excitement and nostalgia as she walked in, remembering the laughter and conversation they had shared on that special night.

"Congratulations on your first day, beautiful!" Kevin said,

presenting her with a bouquet of white roses.

Florence's heart swelled as she placed her hand on his cheek. "You always know how to make me smile." She gently touched the petals, admiring their beauty. "I love white roses. Their thorns may be hidden, but they're always ready to defend themselves. A clever mechanism, don't you think?"

Kevin smiled. "You always see beyond the surface. That's one of the things I love about you."

The hostess, dressed in elegant attire, greeted them with a warm smile. "Buona sera, welcome to Bella Vita! Right this way, please." She led them through the cozy restaurant to their table, where a crisp white linen cloth was adorned with delicate rose petals. "Your table for tonight," she said, gesturing to the beautifully set table. "Giorgio will be your waiter this evening. Giorgio, please take care of our lovely couple."

Their waiter greeted them with a warm smile. "Buona sera, I'm Giorgio, your waiter tonight. Can I start you off with some drinks?"Florence and Kevin perused the menu, while Giorgio recommended a few of their specialty cocktails. After some deliberation, Florence ordered a glass of Pinot Grigio, while Kevin opted for a Merlot. Giorgio nodded, his eyes sparkling with enthusiasm. "Excellent choices! I'll bring those right out."

While they waited for their drinks to arrive, Giorgio took their food orders. Florence opted for the spaghetti Bolognese, and Kevin chose the chicken parmesan. Giorgio nodded, his pen moving swiftly across his notepad. "Fantastic choices! Our spaghetti Bolognese is made with ground beef and pork, simmered in a rich tomato sauce. And our chicken parmesan is breaded to perfection and served with a side of garlic mashed potatoes."

Their drinks arrived, and they sipped their wine, enjoying the soft piano music playing in the background. As they savored their meal, Florence asked about her boyfriend's day, and Kevin shared stories of his investigative journalism work at the Tampa Bay Sun-Times.

"I've been digging deep into a potential corruption case," he said, his eyes gleaming with excitement. "You're going to say I'm sticking my nose in places it doesn't belong, but I won't back down. The public deserves to know the truth."

Florence's concern flickered. "Just be careful, Kevin. You're not exactly known for subtlety."

Kevin chuckled. "But that's what gets me the best stories, babe! I've got sources hinting at a mysterious organization called Los Maliciosos."

Florence's eyes widened. Her knowledge of Spanish came from her Latina roots, and she often found herself drawing on it in her daily life. "Los Maliciosos? That means 'the malicious ones' in Spanish."

"You're right. And they have been linked to several high-profile crimes. Reporters and news casters are saying they have a leader who calls himself El Cazador."

Florence's brow furrowed. "El Cazador? That means 'the hunter.'"

Kevin nodded. "Exactly." He opened his mouth as if to add something, but just then, Giorgio came by to refill their drinks. "Everything okay here?" he asked, his friendly smile a welcome interruption.

Kevin's eyes darted up, and for a moment, he seemed nervous. "Yes, everything's great, thanks," he said, forcing a smile.

Giorgio nodded and refilled their glasses before moving on. As they finished their meal, Kevin nodded to the piano player, and the music transitioned to 'A Thousand Years' from the movie *Twilight*. The soft melody filled the restaurant, and Florence felt a pang of nostalgia She had told Kevin that this would be the perfect wedding song, and they had danced to it together on their first date in this very restaurant.

As the music swelled, Kevin reached into his pocket and pulled out a small box. "Florence, from the day I met you, I knew you were the one for me," he said, opening the box to reveal a stunning white gold pear-shaped ring, encrusted with diamonds and a glowing red ruby in its center. "This ring holds a special significance," Kevin continued, his voice trembling with emotion. "The band itself has been passed down through my family for generations. The ruby I added today is said to possess ancient, protective powers. I want you to have it, to keep you safe from harm."

Florence's curiosity was piqued. "Where did you get this ruby from?"

Kevin's eyes locked into hers, his gaze intense. "I acquired it from Los Maliciosos. They didn't deserve to wield its power. I know they can't have it, and you are the only one I would trust with it." "Florence," Kevin's voice softens as he gets down on one knee, "will you marry me? Be my partner, not just in life, but in our fight against Los Maliciosos. With this ring's power, you'll be protected, and together, we can bring justice to Tampa."

"Yes! Absolutely yes!"

Tears of joy stream down her face as she wrapped her arms around his neck and leaned in closer to him to give him a kiss.

As Kevin slid the ring onto Florence's finger, an electric

surge coursed through her body. A sudden rush of energy flooded her senses, and she felt the veil between the physical and spiritual realms lift. Her mind expanded, and she was bombarded with thoughts and images from those around her.

She heard the waiter's silent congratulations, the elderly couple's warm wishes as they thought, *"Ah, look, they're engaged now,"* and the gentle hum of the piano music took on a new, supernatural quality.

Florence's gaze drifted past Kevin's shoulder, catching sight of her reflection in the large mirror behind the piano. Her eyes widened in shock as she saw her own face; her pupils had turned a deep, fiery red. Kevin's lips brushed against hers, his kiss tender yet passionate. Florence felt the energy coursing through her, a mix of exhilaration and wonder. She was aware of everything around her, the thoughts, the emotions, the very fabric of reality seemed to be unfolding before her. The ring's power was awakening a part of her she never knew existed, and she felt herself becoming something more.

"Forever, Florence. We'll face whatever comes next, together."

As Kevin bent down to kiss Florence again, the ruby glinted on Florence's finger, a symbol of their love and Kevin's determination to protect her.

3

Chapter Three: The Ruby's Dark Conception

(One Week Before)

Kevin Vega stormed into Alejandro Reyes' office, his notebook and camera clutched tightly.

They'd first met in NYU, both were majoring in journalism, but Alejandro had consistently competed with Kevin, often stealing his ideas and presenting them as his own. Alejandro's aggressive approach earned him top grades, while Kevin's meticulous research went unnoticed. Their professor praised Alejandro's "initiative", leaving Kevin frustrated.

Kevin had grown accustomed to Alejandro's competitive nature, seeing it as a double-edged sword that fueled their best work while also testing the boundaries of their friendship. Alejandro's competitive nature was rooted in his childhood as a middle child, where he often struggled for attention from his parents, and Kevin understood this about him. Despite this understanding, Kevin sometimes felt betrayed by Alejandro's tendency to take credit for his ideas. Nonetheless, their shared passion for uncovering the truth and mutual drive to succeed had allowed their friendship to endure.

Their paths diverged sharply after college, with both landing jobs at the same newspaper, the Tampa Bay Sun-Times. However, the tragic loss of Alejandro's sister Daisy to suicide had profoundly affected their relationship. Kevin's memories of Daisy lingered, and the note she left him before her passing—a heartfelt plea for him to watch over Alejandro, who had always felt unloved by his parents— weighed heavily on his conscience. Though Alejandro blamed Kevin and what was left of their friendship had crumbled under the weight of guilt and grief, Kevin still couldn't bring himself to sever ties completely. Being around Alejandro kept Daisy's memory alive, and he felt a sense of obligation to honor her request, even as his working relationship with her brother became increasingly strained. Now, as Alejandro's subordinate, Kevin seethed under his condescending leadership, a dynamic that was a far cry from their once-enduring friendship.

"You're late, Kevin," Alejandro said curtly. "Why were you late?"

Kevin ignored the rude tone. "I had something I had to pick up this morning. I promise, it was urgent."

As he spoke, he slid his hand into his pocket, ensuring the small box containing Florence's engagement ring was still safely tucked away. He hadn't wanted to leave it out of his sight, and the rush back to the office had made him nervous it might have fallen out. Satisfied it was still there, he focused on Alejandro's expectant gaze.

"Now that I'm here, I want to discuss something just as urgent with you. There is a story of a lifetime brewing, Alejandro, and we need to cover it right away! Los Maliciosos, who have been running the streets of Tampa, are involved in black magic. It's true, and I have proof," Kevin urged.

Alejandro's expression turned cold. He had seen the news reports about Los Maliciosos and their alleged involvement in witchcraft; the rose gold tarot cards left at recent crime scenes were a disturbing signature.

"Black magic? You expect me to believe that?" he asked, his tone dripping with doubt. "As your editor, I order you to drop that idea, Kevin. We can't afford to stir up trouble. This isn't the type of attention our newspaper needs."

Kevin's frustration boiled over. "You're silencing the truth? What kind of a journalist are you?"

"A practical one." Alejandro's voice rose, his tone dripping with superiority. "I won't risk our reputation or staff safety for made-up nonsense. Now, go and focus on something easier like sports, the weather, or the upcoming city council elections."

"How dare you minimize my creative talents?" Kevin shouted, slamming his fist on Alejandro's desk.

"I thought you'd be excited for this opportunity," Alejandro said calmly, sliding a manila folder toward Kevin.

Kevin snatched the folder and opened it. "You want me to interview Jameis Winston, the new quarterback of the Tampa Bay Buccaneers?" he exclaimed. "Look, Alejandro, thank you for this, but we need to focus on—"

Alejandro raises his hand. "I don't want to hear any more about Los Maliciosos. You may see yourself out."

Kevin marched out of Alejandro's office, hardened with determination. He knew he had to expose Los Maliciosos, despite Alejandro's opposition.

* * *

The moon cast a silver glow over Kevin's bedroom, illuminating the sparse yet cozy space. The walls were adorned with framed photographs of sunsets and Manhattan's cityscapes, their colors muted in the dim light. A faint scent of old books and worn leather lingered in the air, a reminder of Kevin's love for reading and history. Florence lay beside him, her chest rising and falling with each peaceful breath. Kevin lay in bed, his mind racing as he stared at the ceiling, unable to shake off the memories of the night before.

He had met Jorge Rivera, a member of Los Maliciosos, in an abandoned alley. His investigation had started a month ago, when Jorge had showed up at the Tampa Bay Sun-Times office, desperate to talk to someone about Los Maliciosos. Jorge had been a member of the gang but he wanted out, and he was willing to become an informant in exchange for his freedom to leave for Colombia, where his wife was about to give birth to their baby. Kevin had agreed to meet him in the alley, and now, as he lay in bed, he recalled the details of their conversation.

The alley was a dimly lit, narrow passageway between two crumbling buildings. The smell of garbage and decay had filled the air, and the steaming humidity made the atmosphere feel heavy and oppressive. A sleek black cat had watched from the shadows, its eyes gleaming in the darkness like two green lanterns. As Kevin approached Jorge, he'd felt the cat's gaze upon them, and his mind wandered back to a conversation he'd had with Florence, who'd told him about Bastet, the ancient Egyptian goddess who'd protected women's secrets, guarded homes and families from evil spirits, and kept malevolent entities at bay. Kevin remembered Florence's words: *Bastet's power is said to ward off the whispers of the dead, and keep the shadows from creeping into the light.*

He'd wondered if this cat was a fitting namesake, or if it was just a coincidence. The cat's ears had perked up, and it had emitted a low, warning meow, which seemed to echo through the alley like a summons. The sound sent a shiver down Kevin's spine. This cat was no ordinary feline; its eyes seemed to hold a malevolent intelligence, and its meow seemed to carry a dark intent. As the cat's gaze locked onto Kevin, he felt another chill wrack his body. It was as if the cat was warning someone—or something—that a stranger lurked in the shadows. He knew he had to be careful; Los Maliciosos wouldn't hesitate to take him down if they discovered his true intentions. The thought sent a surge of adrenaline through his veins.

Jorge had arrived shortly afterward, visibly nervous despite his attempts to stay calm. Sweat dripped from Jorge's eyebrows, and his hands trembled as he clasped them together.

"I need to know more about El Cazador's plans," Kevin said, his voice low and serious.

Jorge's gaze darted around the alley, his eyes wide with fear. Kevin pressed the man for more information, mentioning that he'd heard whispers about a ruby. Rumors of this powerful gemstone had been circulating on the streets, and he'd been investigating its connection to Los Maliciosos. Jorge's nervous demeanor only confirmed his suspicions.

"Tell me about La Piedra Roja," Kevin pressed, his voice low and urgent.

The man's gaze darted back and forth, his pupils dilating as fear took hold. "This could get me killed," he whispered, his voice barely audible over the distant hum of a car engine. "I just want out of Los Maliciosos and back to Colombia, to be with my family."

His words trailed off, and he swallowed hard, his Adam's apple bobbing in his throat. Kevin grabbed a fistful of Jorge's shirt, the fabric bunching up in his fist.

"I can get you on the next flight to Colombia," he promised, his tone firm but measured. "But you need to tell me about this ruby. Every detail."

Jorge's eyes welled up with tears, and he nodded frantically. "There's a ritual tonight," he stammered, his voice trembling. "They'll imbue a ruby with dark energies, and Los Maliciosos believes it will grant El Cazador supernatural powers from the underworld."

Kevin let go, pressing play on the recording device in his pocket. "Go on," he instructed, his voice calm and steady. "What's the ritual about?"

Jorge's gaze darted around the alley, his eyes flashing with fear as he leaned in close."They'll invoke ancient powers, sacrificing innocence for darkness. El Cazador wants to be the most powerful gang leader this city has ever seen. And... and he speaks with his dead sister." Jorge's voice dropped to a whisper. "He gets information on people's whereabouts from her. That's why he knows who to trust and who to eliminate."

Kevin's mind worked overtime as Jorge spoke about the ruby's supernatural energies and El Cazador's plans. He couldn't help but think that El Cazador was no match for the kind of power that lay within the ruby, if what he'd heard was true. But he knew someone who might be, someone with a deep understanding of the mystical and the unknown: his girlfriend, Florence. She had a way of sensing things that others didn't, a trait that ran deep in her family's bloodline. Kevin remembered Florence telling him about her 17th century ancestors, who'd been accused of witchcraft in Salem, and how one of them, a great-grandmother seven generations back, had lost her life to the hysteria. Florence had always spoken about her heritage with a mix of pride and wariness, and Kevin had seen glimpses of her inherited clairvoyance in the way she sometimes knew things before they happened. He couldn't shake off the feeling that she might be the only one who could protect the ruby from falling into the wrong hands. Given Florence's gifts, Kevin wondered if there might be a way to harness her abilities to counter the ruby's power. The pieces seemed to be shifting into place, and a nagging sense of familiarity ticked in the back of his mind. He'd heard whispers of ancient symbols, etched into stone or metal, that held the power to contain darkness. A fleeting image of intricate lines and geometric patterns flashed through his mind, but he couldn't quite grasp it.

While Jorge spoke, Kevin's expression grew more intense, his jaw clenched in determination. When Jorge finished speaking, Kevin nodded curtly. "I'll get you out of here," he promised. "You're going to be okay." He pulled out his phone and dialed a number, his eyes never leaving Jorge's face. "I've booked you a room at the Holiday Inn," he said, as a black sedan pulled up beside them. "This driver will take you anywhere you want to go, and tomorrow morning, you'll be on the next flight to Colombia."

Jorge's face lit up with hope as he opened the car door. "Oh, thank you, señor...thank you," he said, his voice filled with gratitude. "I want to start fresh and be with my family. My wife is about to have our first child, a baby girl. We're thinking of naming her Flor."

Kevin smiled, a warmth spreading through his chest as he thought of Florence. "That's a beautiful name," he said, his voice sincere.

As Jorge settled into the car, Kevin leaned in through the open window. "One last question. Where will the ritual be held tonight?"

Jorge's gaze faltered, and he glanced around nervously before answering in a low tone, "The abandoned warehouse on Broadway. That's the meeting spot for Los Maliciosos."

Kevin nodded, his determination growing. "I'll keep in touch," he promised, as he closed the door to the black sedan.

He walked a few blocks, and before he knew it, he was on Broadway. The black cat from the alley followed him, leaping from rooftop to rooftop with an eerie agility. The cat's meows echoed through the night air, a haunting melody that seemed to signal the approach of something ominous. As Kevin walked, the cat's meows grew louder, and he could sense its eyes fixed on him like a guardian. To his left, Kevin saw a group of men dressed in black leather jackets walking towards the abandoned warehouse.

Without hesitation, Kevin tailed the men in black jackets, his journalist's instincts screaming that this was the break he'd been waiting for, but at what cost?

What if I don't make it out of this? he wondered. *Will I ever see Florence again? Will she be safe?* His heart pounded in his chest like a drum, his palms grew sweaty with every step, and he felt a thrill of anticipation mixed with a creeping sense of dread.*If I get out of this alive, I'll ask her to marry me. She's the one, the love of my life.*

Kevin sneaked inside the warehouse, camera at the ready.

The smell of burning sage wafted through the air, mingling with the mildewy scent of old crates and boxes. Ahead, he could hear a faint chanting. Every step creaked beneath his feet, and he froze, his heart pounding in his chest, as a faint meowing echoed through the darkness. Kevin held his breath, but the meowing stopped, and the chanting grew louder, drawing him deeper into the warehouse. He edged forward, his senses on high alert, as the muttering voices guided him toward the back corner. Peeking through the door, he saw a group of Los Maliciosos gathered around a glowing red ruby, their eyes closed in rapt attention. The chanting echoed through the space, and Kevin's journalist's instincts screamed that this was the break he'd been waiting for. Capturing this on tape would be proof of the paranormal realm, making his story believable, turning myth into reality. This footage would cement his reputation as a top journalist.

Door ajar, his gaze swept across the meeting room, studying each figure in the dimly lit space.The flickering candles cast eerie shadows on the walls, like dark spirits trying to claw their way out of the underworld.

One of Los Maliciosos stepped forward, his voice low and gravelly, "El Cazador will be pleased with the power of the ruby."

Kevin's eyes narrowed when he realized that El Cazador wasn't among the group. The lack of guards and his absence suggested a level of confidence, or perhaps a calculated risk. And yet, their only guardian seemed to be the black kitty cat, which sat motionless, staring directly at Kevin with an unblinking gaze. Its eyes glowed like emeralds in the dark, piercing through the shadows with an unnerving intensity. The cat's stillness was almost more unsettling than the ritual itself, as if it was watching Kevin's every move, waiting for him to make a wrong step.

Members of Los Maliciosos began to shift, their movements hesitant, as if drawn to some unseen force. Some members exchanged nervous glances, while others leaned in, their eyes fixed on the ruby with an unnerving intensity. Gradually, they formed a circle around the gemstone, their hands extending to clasp one another. The group's leader stepped forward, his eyes gleaming with an intensity that made some of the others shift uncomfortably.

A faint whisper seemed to carry on the wind. "Victor, dux foederis..." The sound echoed through the air like a haunting reverberation.

The words sent shivers down the spines of the group members. Their skin prickled with goosebumps, and they trembled as if the very air vibrated with malevolent energy. Some trembled, their hearts racing with anticipation, while others seemed transfixed, their eyes frozen on Victor. Victor's gaze swept across the circle, his eyes narrowing in annoyance as he noticed the hesitation in some of the members.

His voice was low and menacing as he spoke, "Do you not feel it? The power is building... we must join our voices to unlock its true potential."He paused, his eyes glinting with expectation. "Let us not falter now." His voice dropped to a whisper, but the urgency was unmistakable."Carissimi spiritus, inter nos move et appare. Te recipimus mentibus et cordibus apertis.'"

The group's voices joined in, some louder than others, as Victor's gaze bore into those who seemed reluctant to participate. The chanting grew louder and more intense, the words echoing off the walls as the group's energy built to a fever pitch.Kevin's finger trembled as he pressed the record button on his camera, capturing the surreal scene unfolding before him. The group's whispers seemed to seep into his bones, their words dripping with malice.

"Victor, why don't we steal the ruby for ourselves and become rich and powerful," one member suggested, their tone laced with avarice.

"What an arrogant man El Cazador is. I can't stand working for him," another member spat, their resentment simmering just below the surface.

Victor's eyes flashed with fury, his voice low and menacing. "Shhh, you fools," he hissed, his words cutting through the group's murmurs like a knife. "Don't you know he will find out and have us all slaughtered? Would you like to see him unleash his wrath upon us? You dare question El Cazador's authority? You all do as you're told, or you will suffer the consequences. If you fail, El Cazador will hunt you like prey and rip your life from your very soul. And he will slaughter your family without hesitation, their screams echoing in your mind long after they're gone."

The group fell silent, their faces pale and frightened, as if the weight of working for El Cazador had finally dawned on them. The chanting continued, louder and more frantic this time, their voices invoking dark energies that seemed to writhe and twist in the air like living things.

"Carissimi spiritus, inter nos move et appare. Te recipimus mentibus et cordibus apertis." The words seemed to take on a life of their own, echoing off the walls as the group's fervor reached a fever pitch. "CARISSIMI SPIRITUS, INTER NOS MOVE ET APPARE. TE RECIPIMUS MENTIBUS ET CORDIBUS APERTIS!"

The room plunged into darkness, the only sound the creaking of old wooden beams and the distant rumble of thunder. Kevin's heart raced as he strained to see what was happening. Then, like specters from the underworld, spirits began to materialize around the room. Their ethereal forms seemed to seep from the very walls themselves, their presence making the air feel heavy and oppressive.

"INTRA RUBINUM...INTRA RUBINUM... INTRA RUBINUM," the group chanted, their voices rising to a cacophonous crescendo. A bolt of lightning flashed down from the heavens, illuminating the room in a brilliant flash of light. The ruby pulsed with an otherworldly energy. The spirits let out a blood-curdling scream as they began to enter the ruby, their forms dissolving into its crimson depths like mist in the sun. The room fell silent, the only sound being the heavy breathing of the group members. Only darkness remained.

"That was creepy," one of them exclaimed.

The warehouse's dim lighting seemed to amplify every sound, every movement. Kevin's nerves were stretched taut, his senses on high alert, observing the group from a distance. The black cat had been still the entire time, its eyes fixed on Kevin with an unnerving intensity. Finally, it moved, its green eyes glowing like embers in the night, and its meowing grew louder, more insistent. Kevin's grip on his camera faltered, and it slipped from his hands, crashing to the ground with a loud report that echoed through the space like a gunshot. The members exchanged nervous glances, their eyes darting towards the shadows.

"*¿Quién está ahí?*" one of them whispered, his voice trembling slightly. "Who's there?"

Another member grabbed his flashlight and turned it on,

casting a beam of light across the warehouse. *"Busquemos,"* he said, his voice firm. "Let's search."

Kevin grabbed the cat, but it was having none of it. The cat's claws swiped wildly, scratching through Kevin's arms as he wrestled to hold it tight. The cat's meows turned into ear-piercing shrieks as Kevin struggled to maintain his grip. His arms stung and he could feel warm blood trickling down his fingers. When the group momentarily hesitated, their flashlights wavering as they conferred with each other, Kevin spotted his chance. The distraction was all he needed. With a swift motion, he tossed the cat towards the flashlights, distracting the group. The cat landed with a thud, its fur standing on end as it arched its back.

"¡Maldita sea!" one of the members cursed, shining his flashlight towards the cat, which was now darting across the floor with a menacing hiss.

The cat's meows grew louder, more insistent, as it weaved in and out of the flashlight beams.

"¡Cuidado!" one of the members warned, trying to catch the cat. "Be careful!"

Kevin's eyes darted around the room, his heart racing with fear. He had to get out of here before they realized he'd seen everything. A treasure chest in the corner caught his eye, its alabaster surface gleaming faintly in the flashlight beams. It was hidden under an intricately carved, ornate wooden desk. His gaze landed on the ceiling vent above the desk, and without hesitation, he sprinted towards it.Heart pounding in his chest, Kevin climbed up onto the desk and pushed open the vent cover. He hoisted himself up into the narrow space just as the group turned their attention back to the area. From his hiding spot, Kevin watched as the group searched the room, their flashlights casting eerie shadows on the walls. The cat stood in the center of the room, its eyes fixed on the vent, meowing loudly. The group's frustration grew, and they began to search more aggressively.

Los Maliciosos' frustration boiled over as the cat's meows grew louder.

"*Cállate, gato maldito,*" one of them snarled, kicking at the cat with a scuffed boot. "Shut up, stupid cat! What's it even guarding?"

"Nothing, just a bunch of old crates and junk," another member chimed in.

Victor shot them a warning glance, but his eyes were equally filled with disdain for El Cazador's cat. As they gave up searching, Los Maliciosos began to murmur among themselves, their voices hushed but urgent.

"Let's go before El Cazador gets here," one member urged.

"What about the ruby? Let's bring it with us," another suggested.

The cat, sensing their departure, darted between their legs, its tail twitching ominously. Victor tried to step around it, but the cat tugged on his pant leg, its claws digging into the fabric. With a swift kick, Victor sent the cat flying across the room, its furious hisses echoing off the walls.

"You fool! How dare you even think to step from El Cazador's plan!" Victor's voice rose above the others, his tone sharp with reprimand. "Don't touch the ruby, it can burn right through you if you do. Leave it there. El Cazador will be coming soon, and he wants to be alone with the prepared ruby."

An uneasy silence fell over Los Maliciosos as they slowly made their way towards the exit. The darkness seemed to swallow them whole. Kevin remained hidden, holding his breath, and watched as they disappeared one by one into the night. When Los Maliciosos' footsteps faded into the distance, Kevin crawled out of the vent and snuck into their meeting room, dodging the spider webs that collected by the door. He entered the room, stopping for a moment to admire the beauty of the red ruby and its mystical red glow that sat on an altar.

Que pedazo de roca tan impresionante, Kevin thought to himself, his eyes fixed on the ruby. *This ruby is stunning.*

He carefully wrapped the glowing red ruby in a black satin napkin, fearing what would happen if he touched it. Los Maliciosos' conversation still echoed in his mind: *Whoever gets this ruby will gain mystical powers from the underworld.*

Their leader can't get his hands on this, Kevin thought.

Just as he was about to leave, the cat appeared again, its eyes fixed intently on Kevin like glowing orbs in the dark. The cat's fur stood on end as it jumped onto the table, positioning itself between Kevin and the altar where the ruby lay. A black satin napkin lay on the table next to the altar, untouched by the cat's swishing tail. Kevin took a step back, surprised by the cat's abrupt movement.

"You're a feisty one, aren't you?" Kevin said, trying to edge around the animal.

The cat swiped at him, its claws outstretched like razor-sharp talons. Kevin dodged just in time, but the cat's persistence was unnerving. *This creature is more than just a guardian of this place,* he thought. *It's a sentinel, a watcher, a protector of secrets.* Kevin knew he had to get rid of the cat if he wanted to escape. He carefully backed away, trying not to make any sudden movements that would provoke the cat further. As he reached the edge of the room, the cat followed, its eyes never leaving Kevin's face. Kevin spotted a small ventilation grate on the wall, partially hidden by crates and shadows. The grate was old and rusted, with a narrow opening that led to a dimly lit crawl space. Before he could move, the cat darted towards the grate and squeezed through the opening, disappearing into the darkness. Startled, Kevin watched as the cat emerged on the other side, running towards a car that had just pulled up. The cat darted towards the vehicle with an air of urgency, as if trying to alert the occupants to an intruder. As the driver stepped out and opened the door, the cat ran around to the other side, rubbing against the leg of the person emerging from the vehicle. Kevin's eyes widened as he recognized the driver—Captain Ramone from the Hillsborough police department, a man he had interviewed before and knew to be corrupt.

"Here we are, señor Cazador," the driver said, opening the door.

Kevin's eyes widened further as he realized who the cat was greeting. Kevin pressed the record button on his camera, capturing video footage of El Cazador. He continued filming as El Cazador greeted the cat, his voice low and soothing. Kevin fought a wave of panic, quickly grabbing the black satin napkin and wrapping the ruby up in it to protect himself from the heat. With the ruby safely in hand, he knew he had to get out of there fast. With his device still recording, Kevin carefully made his way towards the ventilation grate, trying not to draw attention to himself. He squeezed through the narrow opening, finding himself in a cramped and dusty crawl space. The air was thick with the smell of mold and decay, and cobwebs clung to his face as he crawled through the darkness and emerged in the alleyway.

Sprinting through the sweltering Tampa streets, the humid air clung to his skin like a damp shroud, and sweat dripped down his face, stinging his eyes. His heart pounded in his chest like a jackhammer, and the rush of adrenaline still coursed through his veins, electrifying every nerve. He felt alive, vibrant, and ready to take on the world.

I made it out alive, he thought, a triumphant smile spreading across his face. *And now, I get to spend the rest of my life with the woman I love.*

Florence's face flashed in his mind, her bright smile and sparkling eyes igniting a surge of determination and desire. He remembered the way she smelled, her perfume a delicate blend of jasmine and other exotic flowers He wanted to make the most of this moment, to build a life with her that was filled with laughter, adventure, and love. At any moment, El Cazador—the Hunter—would be unleashed, and Kevin knew he'd be hunted down for stealing the ruby, but for now, he pushed the thought aside, focusing on the promise of a new beginning.

The sign of Ricardo Morales Jewelers came into view, a beacon of hope in the midst of his mental chaos. Kevin burst through the door, out of breath, and slammed into the counter. The store's interior was a treasure trove of sparkling jewels, with glass cases curving around the room like a crescent moon. Diamond bracelets and rings glimmered on velvet pedestals, casting a kaleidoscope of colors across the floor. The air was filled with the sweet, heady scent of polished gemstones and a hint of vanilla. Ricardo looked up from the diamond he was inspecting, his eyes narrowing slightly at Kevin's disheveled appearance.

"I need... I need your help with an engagement ring," Kevin

said, his chest heaving with exertion. Sweat dripped down his face, and his eyes burned with determination.

"Who's the lucky lady?" Ricardo asked, his voice calm and soothing, a gentle contrast to Kevin's urgency.

"She's the love of my life. My girlfriend, Flor," Kevin replied, his eyes fixed on the ruby wrapped in the black satin napkin. He pulled out a worn leather box, opening it to reveal his grandmother's engagement ring, the diamond sparkling in its familiar setting.

"I want to replace the diamond with this ruby," Kevin said, his voice filled with emotion. "It's a family heirloom, and I want it to be perfect for her."

When Kevin unwrapped the ruby, it pulsed with the same inner light as before, its deep red glow illuminating the surrounding diamonds like a burning ember. Whispers seemed to emanate from the stone, soft murmurs of "Expecto dominam meam" – the ruby itself seemed to be stirring, eager to find its way to its rightful owner.

Ricardo's eyes widened in surprise, taking in the ruby's radiance."Wow, this is a stunning rock," Ricardo breathed, his eyes fixed on the ruby. "In all my thirty years in the jewelry business, I have never seen anything quite like it."

He was mesmerized by the deep red glow, his gaze lingering on the jewelry.

"Just, please don't touch the ruby itself," Kevin instructed, his voice low and urgent. "Wear gloves for your own safety. It's…precious."

Ricardo nodded, his hands moving instinctively to don a pair of gloves. Kevin watched as the old jeweler carefully examined the ruby."I'll remove the diamond and set the ruby in its place," Ricardo said. "Now, let's talk about the cut. What kind of shape would you like the ruby to be?"

"Cut?" Kevin looked puzzled for a moment. "Um, what do you mean?"

Ricardo smiled, understanding Kevin's lack of knowledge with rings."The cut refers to the shape and proportions of the stone. Let me show you some options."He handed over a pamphlet showing different settings of cuts for rings."This is a princess cut...quite popular, and this is round, halo, and pear..."

Kevin's eyes scanned the pages, his mind racing with possibilities."Pear," he replied confidently. "My girl would love a pear-shaped engagement ring."As Ricardo nodded, Kevin pointed to a sample picture on the counter."And I'd like diamonds to be encrusted around the ruby, like this," he said, his eyes shining with excitement.

Ricardo's eyes lit up as he examined the picture."Ah, a pavé setting. That's a beautiful idea. We can definitely work with that."

Kevin nodded, a smile spreading across his face."I want it to be stunning. Can you make that happen?"

Ricardo nodded, his confidence reassuring."A beautiful stone for a beautiful soul. I'll craft something stunning."

"I need it as soon as possible," Kevin added, his voice laced with urgency.

Ricardo's smile deepened, his eyes sparkling with a knowing glint. He seemed to interpret Kevin's urgency as eagerness to marry the love of his life.

"How can I get in the way of love?" Ricardo said, his voice filled with warmth. "I'll work on it all night, and you'll be able to pick it up tomorrow morning. I'll make sure it's perfect."

Kevin reached out and shook Ricardo's hand, a firm gesture

of gratitude."Thank you, Ricardo. I appreciate it."

Ricardo's smile broadened as he shook Kevin's hand firmly."I'll get started right away."

The memory of Ricardo's handshake lingered in Kevin's mind as he lay in bed, his thoughts racing. He tossed and turned, careful not to disturb Florence, who had turned to her side, snoring slightly in a deep sleep. His mind was consumed by the thought of El Cazador's men finding him, or worse, finding Florence. A chill ran down his spine as he thought about it. His gaze drifted to the nightstand beside him. He opened the drawer, and a soft glow emanated from within. The pear-shaped ruby sparkled, its deep red color pulsing with an inner light. His heart swelled with emotion as he gazed at the ring. He looked over at Florence, her face serene in sleep. "You're going to love this ring," he whispered to himself, his voice barely audible. He thought about the mystical powers it would awaken in her, the way it would amplify her clairvoyant abilities. At first, she might feel burdened by the weight of this responsibility, but he knew her strength and determination would prevail. She would be its greatest caretaker, and her abilities would far exceed anything she had ever imagined. Kevin's thoughts turned to her ancestors, particularly her great great great grandmother, who had been executed in the Salem witch trials. He smiled, thinking about how Florence's family's legacy would live on through her, and through him, as they built a life together. The ruby would be a symbol of their love, and a reminder of the incredible gifts that lay ahead. He smiled, feeling a sense of peace wash over him. The ruby would be perfect on Florence's finger, a key to unlocking her true potential.

* * *

Unbeknownst to Kevin, the night he stole the ruby, El Cazador's rage ignited like a wildfire. El Cazador stood alone in the dimly lit warehouse, the only sound the soft meowing of the black cat with piercing green eyes that seemed to watch his every move. The cat's gaze was fixed on him, as if sensing the turmoil that was about to begin. El Cazador reached down to pet her, whispering her name softly, "Gatita."

The air was thick with tension, heavy with the scent of old crates and dust, as El Cazador's eyes landed on the altar, now empty and bare. The ruby, once the centerpiece, was gone.

"NOOOOO!" El Cazador's scream echoed through the warehouse, his voice like thunder. The sound seemed to shake the very foundations of the building. He flipped the table, sending candles and stones crashing to the ground. The scent of melting wax and dust filled the air as the candles shattered. Gatita, startled by the outburst, darted to the side, her eyes fixed on El Cazador. The warehouse reverberated with his fury as he cursed the thief, his words hanging in the air like a challenge. The door creaked open. Captain Ramone, who had driven El Cazador to the warehouse, stepped inside. His eyes widened as he took in the scene before him - the overturned table, the shattered candles, and El Cazador's face twisted in rage.

"*Señor?*" Captain Ramone ventured, his voice cautious. "What happened?"

"Call Victor," El Cazador barked, his eyes blazing with anger. "Get every member of Los Maliciosos here now. I want to know who is responsible for this theft."

Captain Ramone nodded hastily, pulling out his phone to

44

dial Victor's number. Within minutes, the warehouse was filled with the members of Los Maliciosos, all summoned to face El Cazador's wrath. They stood before him, their eyes cast downward.

"Where is my ruby?" El Cazador yelled, his anger palpable. The room fell silent, the only sound the creaking of old wooden crates. El Cazador's face turned red with rage as he repeated himself, throwing a chair at them. "WHERE IS MY RUBY!" The chair shattered against the wall, sending splinters flying.

Victor, the leader of the group, finally broke the silence. "Señor, we don't know what happened. No one was in here. We even searched the warehouse."

Gatita, agitated by Victor's incompetence, began to meow loudly. Her eyes seemed to bore into him, as if trying to reveal the truth.

El Cazador's face twisted in fury. "Incompetence!" he shouted, his voice echoing through the warehouse. "You're telling me that no one saw or heard anything? You're all useless! I can't get good help these days!"

He scanned the room, his gaze fell upon an empty space where Jorge usually stood. "Where is Jorge?" El Cazador demanded, his voice cold and menacing.

Raul, Jorge's cousin, stepped forward, his voice trembling. "I… I think he might be with his wife, señor. She's having a baby."

El Cazador's eyes narrowed. "Find him," he growled. "I want to know what he knows about this theft."

The members nodded hastily, dispersing to carry out El Cazador's orders while Captain Ramone stood in place waiting for his next order.

"I want to be alone," El Cazador growled, his voice low and menacing. Captain Ramone hesitated for a moment before nodding and exiting the warehouse, closing the door behind him.

When the warehouse fell silent, El Cazador pressed a button near the wall, revealing a secret room to his candlelit chambers to commune with his deceased sister. At the center of his chambers stood an altar, which held pictures of his sister encircled by stones and gems from all over the world. Gatita followed him into the secret room, rubbing against his leg. A faint mist began to coalesce, and from within its swirling tendrils, a figure slowly took form. The mist dissipated, revealing his dead sister Daisy's ethereal presence. Her blue-gray glow illuminated the space, casting an otherworldly light on the room. She wore a flowing nightgown, her presence both soothing and unsettling. Daisy, though dead, was stuck in the spirit realm, bound by rules that governed the human experience. She was not always able to reveal information to the human realm, for it was crucial that humans experience life and learn from their own struggles. But the ruby, a stone of immense power, would change everything for El Cazador, making him all powerful and knowing, able to communicate with anything that breaths.

"Calm yourself, mi hermano," Daisy said, her voice like a gentle breeze.

"Who dares steal from me, Daisy?" El Cazador asked, his rage barely contained.

Gatita meowed softly, as if responding to his question. In a silent exchange, Gatita telepathically reveals information to Daisy. Daisy's ethereal voice replied, "Kevin... Vega... journalist... danger to our cause."

El Cazador's face twisted in fury."Show him to me."

An image of Kevin and Florence embracing at the front door of their apartment appeared in a mirror set at the corner of his chambers. El Cazador's face contorted into a maniacal grin, and he erupted into sick laughter.

"Ah, Kevin," he said, his voice dripping with malice. "I've been waiting for this moment for so long. The story of a lifetime is finally coming together, and it's going to be served up in the most exquisite, agonizing way possible."

4

Chapter Four: The Ruby's Dark Awakening

Bella Vita's twinkling lights faded into the background as Kevin's lips brushed against Florence's, their passion igniting in the dimly lit car. The humid Tampa air clung to their skin, heavy with the scent of ozone and wet earth, hinting at an impending storm. His mouth claimed hers, tongues entwining, as the ruby in the engagement ring, adorned with mystical powers, gleamed on her finger, casting a subtle red glow. Soft music drifted from the radio, but their kiss was the only melody that mattered.

Kevin's lips trailed down Florence's neck, his warm breath sending shivers down her spine. His tongue danced, slowly licking her skin, arousing her. Florence let out a moan as her hands wrapped around his head, deepening the kiss. The sounds of the night swirled around them, crickets chirping, distant thunder rumbling, a sensual, primal accompaniment to their passion. She rubbed against him, her body swaying to an unspoken rhythm. Kevin's arousal grew, his hands exploring her curves. The air thickened with tension.

Florence's moans filled the car, her voice barely above a whisper.

Kevin's thoughts echoed in Florence's mind: *"I'm in love with you Flor, I want you to be mine...forever."*

Her voice trembled as she responded to his thoughts aloud, "I love you too, Kevin," she breathed, caressing his face, her fingers tracing the lines of his jaw. "And I'll be yours forever."

The words hung in the air, and for a moment, time seemed to stand still. Kevin's eyes widened with the realization that Florence's clairvoyant abilities were growing stronger.

Before he could comment on it, Florence suddenly pulled back, her expression confused."Do you hear those voices?" she asked, confusion etched on her face.

Kevin listened intently, but the only sounds were the crickets chirping and thunder rumbling in the distance. "No, my love. What's wrong?"

Florence's brow furrowed as she stared out of the car window. "I could've sworn I heard… Never mind."

When she turned back, Kevin gasped. Florence's eyes glowed with an ethereal red hue, burning with an other-worldly intensity.

"Look," he whispered, handing her a make-up mirror from her purse.

Florence gasped at her reflection. Her eyes were glowing red."What's happening to me?"

"The ruby in your engagement ring, Flor. I believe it's awakening your clairvoyant abilities."

The scent of white roses Kevin had brought her earlier filled the car, their sweet fragrance a stark contrast to the darkness unfolding outside. Florence's eyes still held that ethereal glow as she turned to Kevin, her voice soft as silk. "What does this ruby mean for me, Kevin? You remember what I told you about my family's… gifts, don't you?"

Kevin's smile grew wider as he took her hand, his fingers intertwining with hers."Yes, my love. Your family's history is rich with clairvoyant abilities. Your great grandmother from the 17th century, was a real witch known for her prophecies and visions, wasn't she?"

"Yes!" Florence nodded, a hint of excitement in her voice."She was a powerful seer and witch, but was executed during the Salem witch trials after local farmers accused her of casting spells that brought about the mysterious deaths of their livestock, claiming her dark magic had brought about their misfortune. But our family's gifts didn't start there. We have ancestors from ancient Egypt, where they would weave magic spells from the Book of the Dead. My grandmother used to tell me stories about our lineage, how we'd inherited the ability to see beyond the veil."

Florence's eyes glazed over, and she felt herself being pulled into a vision. She saw ancient Egyptian walls adorned with golden hieroglyphs, the air thick with the sweet, resinous scent of frankincense and myrrh, heavy with mysticism. She saw a woman who looked just like her, dressed in traditional Egyptian garb, standing before an altar. The woman's eyes locked onto Florence's, and a sudden sense of déjà vu washed over her, as if she'd lived this moment before. In the vision, Florence saw the woman, a lector priestess, performing a spiritual ritual. She was reciting spells from the Book of the Dead, invoking the power of Heka to guide the deceased through the afterlife. The priestess's hands moved deftly, placing amulets and shabti figurines in a intricately carved coffin. Canopic jars sat nearby, their lids shaped like the heads of protective gods. Florence watched, mesmerized, as the priestess called upon the gods to ensure the deceased person's safe passage to the realm of Osiris. The priestess's voice was hypnotic, her words weaving a spell of protection and magic. Florence felt the power of Heka coursing through her veins, a force that permeated all aspects of existence. The vision faded, and Florence found herself back in the car, Kevin's hand still holding hers. She took a deep breath, her mind reeling with the images she'd seen.

"I see why I'm drawn to Egyptian history, Kevin," she murmured, her face aglow with wonder. "It's not just the magic and mysticism, but the reverence for life and death. They believed in an afterlife, where the heart was weighed against the feather of truth, symbolizing the ultimate test of one's morality and integrity. If the heart was lighter than the feather, symbolizing a life lived in balance and harmony, the soul would be granted eternal life in the Field of Reeds. But if the heart was heavier, consumed by the darkness of one's own deeds, it would be devoured by Ammit, the monster that awaited the unworthy. There's a profound justice in that. The universe itself demands balance and truth."

A gentle smile spread across his face as his thumb continued to caress her hand, his voice low and soothing. "You're a true descendant of the pharaohs, Florence. Strong, intelligent, and gifted. And now, with this ruby, your abilities will only grow stronger."

Florence's eyes locked onto the ring, the red glow pulsating in sync with her heartbeat."What can I expect from this ruby, Kevin? What kind of abilities will I have?"

"From what I've uncovered about El Cazador's work, I think the ruby might amplify your gifts. My informant told me that

El Cazador can communicate with his dead sister...and she gives him insight into things he wouldn't know otherwise. If that's true, with this ruby, you might be able to tap into even more profound knowledge and see further than ever before."

The ruby's glow continued to pulse with a hypnotic intensity as it whispered to her in Latin, "Electa mea es, domina mea" - *you are my chosen one, my master.*

A shiver ran down Florence's spine as she felt the weight of the ruby's words. She was the master, the one destined to wield its power. If Tutankhamun, the boy king of Egypt, could ascend to the throne at nine years old and leave his mark on history, she could certainly claim her place as the ruby's master. A sense of pride and purpose swelled within her, and she felt the ancient bond between her and the ruby stir to life. The secrets of the Egyptian priestesses, the guardians of the sacred gemstones, began to unfurl in her mind like a papyrus scroll. She recalled the whispers of Isis, the goddess of magic and fertility, and the ruby's power seemed to resonate with the ancient deity's.

Accipio donum tuum, Florence thought. *I accept your gift.* She smiled, recognizing herself in the priestess she'd seen in her vision, a sense of inherited power and magic stirring within her. Power coursed through her veins, and she took a deep breath, the scent of the white roses filling her lungs, as she smiled at Kevin. Just as she opened her mouth to thank him again, she heard the strange noise a second time.

Florence's eyes darted around, her expression alarmed.

"There it is again! You don't hear that?" she urged.Kevin shook his head.The soft yellow lights from Bella Vita cast a gentle ambiance, but the darkness beyond seemed to amplify the terror in Florence's eyes as she listened to the screams."A...

a man…is screaming for help," Florence said, her voice hesitant, as if doubting her own ears.Her eyes flashed with a fierce light, like embers igniting, as she turned to him.

"There's no one screaming, Florence," he said, his brow furrowed in concern. Her eyes, once a fiery glow, now faded to a hazy red, drifting aimlessly as if lost in another world. "I'm seeing…an abandoned suitcase," she said slowly. "Someone who never made it home." Fear for their safety spiked through him, his mind racing with worst-case scenarios. He gritted his teeth, his palm growing sweaty on the steering wheel. "Let's go home," he said finally, his voice low and urgent.

The key turned smoothly in the ignition under Kevin's hand, and his face tensed with worry as the engine purred to life. The soft hum of the car filled the silence as they sat there, the only sound the gentle whir of the air conditioner and the soft tick of the dashboard lights.

"Wait a little longer," Florence said, her voice husky with emotion as she placed a gentle hand on his, halting his movement towards the gearshift. Her fingers wrapped around his wrist like a tender restraint, her eyes locked onto his, shining with love and adoration, as if the ring on her finger and their promise to each other were the only thing that mattered in the world. "I want to freeze time and savor the sparkle of our love, and this ring, for just a little while longer."

A tender smile spread across his face, his eyes filled with love and adoration for the woman beside him, and for a moment, he drifted off into the boundless possibilities of their future together, his heart overflowing with hopes and dreams that he couldn't wait to share with her.

Florence felt a sudden invasion of Kevin's thoughts, like a gentle breeze carrying the whispers of his heart. She saw

53

glimpses of a future he envisioned: exchanging vows on their wedding day, surrounded by the sweet scent of red roses and the soft glow of candlelight; holding their newborn child in her arms, feeling the warmth of her skin and the gentle rhythm of her heartbeat; taking photos of their daughter's first day of kindergarten, with the smell of fresh pencils and paper wafting through the air; celebrating Christmas together, surrounded by the aroma of sugar cookies and the twinkling lights of the tree; growing old together on a porch, sipping lemonade and reading books, as they watched their daughter pull up in her car, with the sound of laughter and chatter filling the air as their grandchildren spilled out, eager to spend their summer break with them. The visions were warm and golden, filled with the promise of a life shared. But as the images faded, Florence's mind began to receive its own visions, like a disjointed echo of Kevin's thoughts. She saw herself standing alone, her eyes fixed on a weathered gravestone beneath a rain-soaked sky. The air was heavy with mist, and droplets fell like tears from the branches of a nearby tree. The gravestone read "Kevin Vega" in worn letters, and Florence felt a chill run down her spine. The rain pounded against her skin, and she shivered, feeling the weight of a future without Kevin. The radio crackled to life, jolting her back to reality.

"Breaking news: A member of Los Maliciosos, Jorge Rivera was just found dead moments ago, apparently killed by one of his own. The victim was en route to the airport when the attack occurred. A rose gold death tarot card depicting The Hanged Man was discovered in his front pocket, bearing a message of some kind."

Kevin's face darkened. Florence felt a shiver run down her spine as Kevin's guilty thoughts flooded her mind: *"This is all my fault... I pushed Jorge for information, knowing the risks. He never made it to Columbia safely. I broke my promise to him. Now his daughter will be raised without a father. This is all my fault, just like it's my fault Daisy took her life because I broke her heart when I told her I was in love with someone else. Alejandro was right, I should have been honest with his sister sooner."*

Florence's unease gave way to frustration as Kevin's thoughts continued to assault her mind. She felt like an unwilling participant in his inner turmoil, forced to witness his self-blame over Jorge's death, and the painful memories of his ex-girlfriend Daisy. The weight of his emotions threatened to consume her.

"Kevin, stop talking to yourself," Florence ordered, her voice laced with desperation. "I can hear your thoughts… and I… I don't want to hear them. I don't know how to shut it off."

Kevin's eyes met hers, filled with a deep sadness, as if he realized he'd been dumping his burdens on her without meaning to.

Without warning, gunshots echoed through the night. Kevin's head jerked up, his eyes locked on something outside."Get down!" he yelled.

Florence's heart raced as she squeezed herself under the passenger seat.Members of Los Maliciosos sprinted toward their car, their shouts filling the air.

"Let's kill him for forcing us to kill one of our own!" Raul shouted.

"No, we were instructed not to," Victor countered. "El Cazador's orders. He wants him brought to him alive. But we can still teach him a lesson."

"Make sure he gets the Ten of Cups… in reverse," Raul sneered. "It signifies challenges in love, betrayal, and separa-

55

tion and El Cazador told us he's got a pretty little girlfriend. This lesson will teach him to reassess his priorities.

"No, you imbecile. He wants us to bring Kevin to him alive. We leave a divination card, nothing else," Victor shot back.

A wiry figure barely clearing five feet, snarled, "We'll make him wish he was dead."

Another hulking man in his thirties with broad shoulders, chimed in, "We'll beat him good, so bad he'll eat from a straw for the rest of his life!"

The group erupted into menacing laughter.Florence's eyes widened as she heard their taunts from inside their car.

"Kevin, they know who you are! I can hear what they're saying!" Florence screamed.

Kevin's eyes locked onto hers, filled with fear, but also a deep acceptance. He knew if his life ended tonight, Florence would be okay. With her newfound abilities, she'd become the hero he always knew she was.

They slowly emerged from their cramped positions, Florence unfolding from under the glove compartment and Kevin straightening up from beneath the steering wheel. Kevin leaned in, his lips quivering, and pressed a gentle, desperate kiss to her lips.

"*Soon, my love...*" Kevin thought, ensuring Florence heard, "*...you'll move on, find love again, and have the family we always dreamed of. You'll shine brighter than ever.*"

"Don't think that!" Florence pleaded. "We're going to make it out of this mess."

5

Chapter Five: Black Rose

The sound of gunfire still echoed in their ears. Florence's eyes locked onto Kevin's, and without a word, their hands reached out for each other, intertwining fingers as they took in the scene unfolding before them.

Raul's figure materialized out of the darkness, his eyes blazing with anger as he strode toward the driver's side door. He held a police baton, and with a swift and brutal motion, he smashed the driver's side window. Glass shattered into a thousand shards, raining down on the seats and floor. The sound was deafening, and Kevin and Florence recoiled from the sudden attack.

Florence clutched her engagement ring, the deep red ruby glowing softly in the faint moonlight. Kevin's warning echoed in her mind: *Don't let them get hold of your engagement ring.* Florence immediately took off her engagement ring, losing access to any potential powers, and slipped it into a hidden compartment of her coat pocket.

"*¡Vas a sentir el dolor pronto!* You're going to feel the pain soon!" Raul spat, his voice dripping with venom. "You stole two things from us, and now you will pay the price."

Raul reached in and yanked open the door, grabbing Kevin and pulling him out of his car by his shirt, then slammed him into the vehicle. Sweat formed at Kevin's temples as he gasped, feeling his heart race in terror. The streetlights cast long shadows across the deserted street, making Raul's face seem even more menacing.

"I don't want any trouble," Kevin said, trying to keep his voice calm. "You've got the wrong guy."

Los Maliciosos erupted in laughter."Trouble has found you, *borsa de mierda*," Raul replied, smiling menacingly. "Hand over the ruby, and your pretty little girlfriend won't get hurt."

"I don't know what you're talking about," Kevin said.

A chilling grin spread across another member's face as he approached the passenger side of Kevin's Audi, making eye contact with Florence. "Look, he does have a pretty little thing in the car. I'm sure we can get her to talk."

The man hauled Florence forcefully out of the car, pulling her arms behind her back. She immediately regretted taking off her ring as she felt defenseless to fight back.

Kevin's protectiveness flared. "You leave her alone," he yelled.

Raul immediately punched Kevin in the stomach. Kevin's knees buckled and he gasped for air as Raul forced him to stay on his feet."You're going to regret ever crossing El Cazador," Raul snarled, his face twisted in rage.

Victor's voice cut through the tension, his eyes fixed on Kevin with a calculating gaze. "Raul, remember El Cazador's orders. We need to bring him alive.Search them for the ruby."

Raul, Victor, and the other members began to frisk Florence and Kevin, their hands rough as they searched for the ruby.

Kevin, weak to stand up, allowed them to search him. Florence subtly ensured the ring remained secure in its hidden compartment, her heart racing as they began to frisk her with perverted pleasure.

"It's not on them," one of the members complained.

"Busquen en el carro" - search their car! Victor instructed. "If it's not on them, they must have hidden it somewhere."

They descended upon Kevin's Audi, ransacking the interior. The sound of shattering glass and tearing fabric filled the air as they threw Kevin's belongings and some white roses onto the pavement. Without warning, Raul swung another punch at Kevin's stomach, sending him crashing to the ground. Kevin let out a loud moan as his knees crashed into the pavement.

"Compliments of El Cazador," Raul sneered as he looked up at the other members, signaling for them to stop their search and join in on the fun. "Let's beat the shit out of him," he howled.

At that order, all the members rushed toward Kevin and began to stomp on him like a cockroach. Florence struggled against her captors, feeling helpless at the sight. "Leave him alone!" she screamed.

Los Maliciosos' brutality intensified, kicking and punching Kevin on the paved road. Blood oozed from his mouth, his face swelling. Florence began to fight back, tugging against her captor's grip.

"Ahhh, *maldita sea!*"he yelped as Florence's foot stomped down hard on his instep, a precise pressure point strike that sent him stumbling. The grip on her arms loosened, and she felt a rush of freedom as she broke loose from her captor's grasp with an aikido roll. With a swift motion, she spun around, landing a precise roundhouse kick to the face of the man who had held her, followed by a sharp elbow strike that sent him stumbling back. Finally free, Florence rushed to Kevin's defense, unleashing a flurry of swift jabs and kicks, her movements a testament to her martial arts training.

"Leave him alone!" she screamed, her voice hoarse with rage.

Victor ran toward Florence, yanking her by the hair and pulling her close to him, locking her in place. "Where do you think you're going, you feisty little cat? You need to watch this."

Florence winced at the sight, paralyzed to stop it.

Raul loomed over Kevin, vengeance burning in his eyes. "My cousin Jorge didn't want to talk, but you made him. He was supposed to have a baby girl, but we had to end his life because of you." In that moment, Raul pulled a gun that was holstered onto his belt and lifted it toward the heavens, the steel barrel glinted in the moonlight.

"Raul, wait," Victor called. "El Cazador's orders were clear. We need to keep him alive."

Raul's eyes flashed with defiance, but Victor's firm tone gave him pause. For a moment, it seemed like Raul might relent. But then, his face twisted in a snarl. "This isn't about El Cazador, this is about my family."

Victor's expression remained calm, but his eyes narrowed. "Raul, don't—"

Raul's hand moved swiftly, the gun pointed straight at Kevin's heart as he pulled the trigger. Kevin's body jerked as the bullet pierced his body. Blood immediately poured from his chest. Florence screamed, her voice echoing off the pavement.Kevin groaned, pressing his hands desperately against the wound.

The stormy sky unleashed its fury, torrential rain pounding against the pavement, releasing the sweet, primal scent of petrichor, which mingled with the metallic tang of blood.

"No!" Victor shouted, suddenly uneasy. "*Que hiciste?*" - What have you done? El Cazador will have our heads for this, you fool!"

Victor's face darkened as he began to notice people walking out of Bella Vita, noticing the commotion, their faces pale and frightened. One of them pulled out a phone and dialed 911, their voice shaking as they reported the shooting. At the sight of people, Florence felt herself being released, and patrons started to surround her, their faces filled with concern.

Victor's voice rose above the din. "Everyone, get back!" he shouted as he pulled out his own gun toward the crowd. He shot a warning bullet into the air to control the crowd, who immediately yelled and cowered in fear. The crowd was growing, and the sound of sirens could be heard in the distance.

"What's going on here!" one of the restaurant employees shouted.

"It's time to get out of here, Victor!" one of the members of Los Maliciosos urged.

"*Vamanos,*" - let's go, Victor instructed as they all began to run away.

Walking toward Raul, Victor checked his shoulder in anger, bumping him off balance. "You bastard," he snarled at Raul, who only huffed, his expression twisted in defiance. "Leave the message you wanted, then," Victor said, handing Raul a rose gold tarot card from his pocket. "At least his death will muddy the waters."

Kevin struggled to stand, his vision blurring.

61

"You think you're above death, Vega?" Raul sneered as he turned toward him. With one swift motion, he slapped Kevin with the heel of his gun, knocking him down on the wet pavement. Kevin had no strength left to get up. Florence, in tears, turned away as he smacked him, unable to see the pain that her beloved was enduring. *"Vete pal carajo!"* - go to hell, Raul spat, tossing the rose-gold Ten of Cups tarot card onto Kevin's chest as it landed in reverse.

The tarot card landed on Kevin's blood-soaked shirt, its edging absorbing the crimson liquid. Kevin gazed at the card, his eyes welling up as Raul fled the scene, his footsteps faded away with the thunder. The image depicted a joyful family, three children playing ring around the rosy, their parents waving at the sky beneath a vibrant rainbow. "The future... our future," Kevin whispered, his voice cracking. "We were supposed to build a life together, have children, grow old."

Florence rushed to Kevin's side as the police sirens began to fill the rainy night sky. "Oh God, oh God!"

"Where's the ring?" Kevin whispered, his voice weak.

Florence's fingers instinctively went to the hidden compartment in her coat pocket. "I have it here." She slipped the ring back onto her left ring finger, and the ruby immediately pulsed brighter, its red glow intensifying as her mystical powers surged.

"Never take it off... It will protect you from them. You can fight them," Kevin said, struggling for air. "They probably don't know I gave it to you."

"Don't speak," Florence instructed. "You must save your energy." A shiver ran down her spine as she began hearing his thoughts. *I love you so much and I will miss you.* Florence fell down to her knees, kissing Kevin's lips. "Shhh, don't think like that. I'm right here. Stay with me, please…don't leave me. You're all I have in this world," Florence sobbed.

Seeing that Kevin was losing too much blood, she looked for something on the pavement to stop the bleeding. She glanced under the car and saw one of the white roses that Kevin had surprised her with earlier that evening, congratulating her on her new job, lying vibrantly on the ground. Desperate, she grabbed the rose to apply pressure to Kevin's wound. As her fingers touched the white petals, they transformed before her eyes into solid black, radiating an ethereal glow.

Kevin looked up at the black rose, then smiled back at Florence before his spirit finally drifted away.

6

Chapter Six: Bumbling Justice

The police car screeched to a halt, its lights bathing the scene in a stark, pulsing glow. Sergeant Lopez gripped the steering wheel tightly, his eyes fixed on the chaos unfolding before him, while Detective Martin sat rigidly in the passenger seat, his gaze scanning the area with equal intensity. A cacophony of sirens pierced the air, while sweet charcoal smoke with a hint of sulfur wafted through the car's windows, a pungent reminder of the violence that had unfolded here. Detective Martin's eyes widened in horror as he took in the lifeless body on the ground, a dark stain spreading from beneath it like a macabre shadow. A young woman, likely in her early twenties, knelt beside the body, holding the man's hand and sobbing uncontrollably. Her anguished cries echoed above the sirens, a heartbreaking counterpoint to the chaos surrounding them.

Sergeant Lopez picked up the handheld transceiver in his vehicle and spoke over the police radio, his voice accompanied by static and crackling. "Dispatch, this is Sergeant Lopez. We've got a possible homicide in front of Bella Vista restaurant on Sunrise Street. Requesting paramedics. We also have a group of men running from the scene heading north toward Main Street, requesting backup."

The radio crackled in response, the dispatcher's voice laced with static. "Sergeant Lopez, witnesses report the killer threw a rose gold tarot card at the victim. This could be another link to El Cazador, similar to the previous cases."

Before Lopez could respond, Captain Ramone's voice cut in over the radio, his tone detached. "Lopez, don't pursue those men. Attend to the victim and secure the area."

Lopez glanced over at Detective Martin, his eyes fixed on the scene unfolding before them. "But, Señor—" Lopez started to say, but Captain Ramone cut him off.

"Do as you're told, Lopez. Secure the scene and do not pursue those men."

Lopez's gaze followed the retreating figures, their dark clothing and swift movements catching his attention. "Roger that, Captain. We're on it."

The radio crackled again, Captain Ramone's voice steady. "And Lopez, we've had a report of a ruby stolen a few days ago. Given the circumstances, it's likely this case is connected. We can expect more violence until it's recovered. If you find any connection, contact me directly."

Lopez's eyes narrowed as he replied, "Understood, Captain."

He exchanged a look with Martin, who raised an eyebrow. "A stolen ruby? What's the connection to witchcraft?" Martin asked, his voice low.

"If I knew how a ruby was relevant to witchcraft, I'd have it by now," Lopez said.

Martin's eyes lit up. "So you know its whereabouts?"

Lopez's face contorted in a mixture of amusement and

exasperation. "I meant if I had the ruby, this case would already be resolved, stupid." Let's stop wasting time and attend to the victim, shall we?"

With a practiced air of routine, they both emerged from the vehicle in tandem, like a well-rehearsed dance duo, the doors creaking softly in perfect harmony. Lopez's trained eyes took in the scene before them, while Martin's gaze was fixed on the victim. They both quickly surveyed the area, taking note of the surrounding details. Paramedics arrived soon after, rushing to attend the victim.

Sergeant Lopez directed the growing crowd of onlookers from Bella Vista back behind the police tape, which was being set up by additional officers who had arrived at the scene. "Move back, please," he said firmly. "We need to secure the area."

Some onlookers grumbled, their voices laced with fear and concern. "Is the victim okay?" someone asked. "Is he dead?"

"What's going on in this city?" another cried.

"This is the work of El Cazador, isn't it?" A woman nearby trembled her eyes wide with terror.

Lopez's expression was compassionate. "We'll get answers for you, I promise. We're doing everything we can to figure out what happened. For now, please stay behind the tape and let us do our job." Lopez's gaze fell on an officer approaching with a roll of yellow barricade tape, its bright color muted by the rain. The polyethylene tape crinkled as he unrolled it, the bold black letters "CRIME SCENE" standing out starkly. Lopez nodded curtly. "Secure the area, and let's get the tape up," he instructed.

The officer nodded and began to string the tape between the restaurant and the victim's car, the yellow ribbon fluttering in the rain-soaked wind as he secured it with a metallic click. The paramedics were already at work, the young woman still clinging to the victim's hand.The paramedics worked around her, their faces somber as they assessed the situation. Lopez caught a glimpse of the woman's anguished face, his compassion rising. The sound of sirens grew louder as more police cars arrived, their strobing lights added to the sense of urgency and disorder.

Customers from Bella Vista spilled out onto the sidewalk, their faces pale and pinched with worry as they gathered behind the police tape. Some whispered to each other, their voices barely audible, yet laced with fear."Did you see them?"

"Those were members of Los Maliciosos," one replied, eyes darting nervously around the scene.

"I saw on the news that their leader is called El Cazador," another murmured.

"Poor young woman," said an elderly patron, her eyes welling up with tears.

"I heard they just got engaged tonight," a waiter added, and the crowd's murmurs turned to sympathetic sighs and sorrowful glances.

Others snapped photos or videos with their phones, but their attention was drawn to the grieving woman, their faces softening with pity. Sergeant Lopez, his broad face creased with concern and his dark mustache drooping slightly, approached the woman with a gentle stride. His deep-set eyes, warm and kind, locked onto hers. Detective Martin, a slender man, stood beside him, his eyes filled with compassion.

"Ma'am, we need to ask you some questions about what happened here tonight," Lopez said. "May I have your name?"

Florence looked up, her eyes glowing strangely red in the

dim light. "My name is Florence Avila and this... this... this is my boyfriend Kevin Vega," she stammered.

Lopez nodded gently. "Florence, you will need to step away from Kevin now, as we must begin our investigation." He guided Florence to the side, nodding to his team to come over and begin their investigative work.

Detective Martin took over the questioning. "Ma'am, we're investigating this homicide, and we need your help understanding the circumstances. Kevin may have been a witness to something relevant to our case. Can you tell us more about him and your relationship? Have you noticed anything unusual about his behavior recently? Has he told you anything?"

Lopez's gaze remained steady on Florence, but his thoughts wandered. *I wonder if she knows anything about the stolen ruby?*

Martin's thoughts drifted in a similar direction. *I don't get why there would be something as serious as murder over a single ruby.*

Florence caught their thoughts, her expression guarded as she weighed their good intentions against her own doubts. She subtly moved her thumb, adjusting the pear-shaped ruby on her finger to face her palm, hiding it from their view.Her face saddened as memories flooded her mind of the night Kevin had left their apartment, drawn away by a sudden husky whisper in the air. *"Amor... vincit... omnia... nocte... sequenti,"* she recalled, the words echoing in her mind. A shiver ran down her spine, but she chose to keep this detail to herself. In her heart, Florence trusted Kevin, believing his late-night absences were for his investigative journalism.

"My boyfriend's name was Kevin Vega," she began. "We were celebrating my new job at the District Attorney's office." She kept her response measured, deciding to withhold information about Kevin's marriage proposal and the engagement ring he gave her. Given the ring held the stolen ruby, she wasn't willing to take any chances with revealing too much.

Sergeant Lopez's expression turned thoughtful. "I see," he said, his voice neutral. "I heard murmurs from the crowd that you and Mr. Vega were celebrating a rather special occasion tonight. They mentioned something about a proposal?"

Florence's eyes flashed with a hint of defensiveness. "Yes, we did discuss marriage," she said coolly, "but I don't need to tell you more about my personal life."

Seeming to sense the tension, Lopez shifted gears, his tone becoming more conversational as he steered the conversation towards her professional life.

"You mentioned you started working for the District Attorney's Office. Are you working for District Attorney Xander Reyes?" Florence confirmed with a nod. Lopez nodded enthusiastically. "I know Xander! Poor guy, it was just a few years ago when his sister died. I was called to the scene and had to break the news to him. He took her death so hard and has never been the same after her passing."

Martin frowned, confused. "What does that have to do with this homicide?"

Lopez glared at Martin for challenging his remarks. "I'm just making conversation, *estúpido*." Sergeant Lopez pulled out a pencil and notepad. "We need to get a statement from you."

Florence's eyes welled up with tears as she began to relive the final moments she had with Kevin.

"We were eating at Bella Vista, celebrating my new job," she said, her voice trembling. "Kevin had shared with me that he was assigned to do a news story on the new quarterback for the Tampa Bay Bucs and was excited to be interviewing the quarterback."

Detective Martin's eyes lit up. "Oh yes! You think the Bucs will finally win the Super Bowl with this new starting quarterback? They haven't won a Super Bowl since '03."

A small smile played on Florence's lips as she saw a vivid vision of a Bucs jersey materialize before her eyes. The number 12 stood out in bold, with "BRADY" emblazoned above it in proud letters. She envisioned Raymond James Stadium, its electric atmosphere pulsing with the cheers of Tampa Bay fans clad in red and pewter. The pirate ship in the north end zone rocked back and forth, its cannons firing imaginary shots as the Buccaneers took the field. The roar of the crowd was deafening, with chants of "Go Bucs!" and "Tom Terrific!" echoing through the stadium. Fireworks exploded in the sky, their vibrant colors illuminating the night. The crackle and boom of the fireworks added to the euphoria of the moment. The voice of the announcer boomed in her mind, a thunderous baritone that sent shivers down her spine: "And here it is, folks, a historic moment in football history! The Tampa Bay Buccaneers are the first team in NFL history to play and win a Super Bowl in their home stadium. What an exciting time for Tampa Bay fans!" The crowd erupted in cheers, their voices hoarse from shouting in triumph.

Florence's eyes snapped back into focus, and she looked directly at Martin and Lopez with an excited grin. "They'll win the Super Bowl when Tom Brady gets traded to the Bucs," she replied, her eyes gleaming with pride.

Martin and Lopez erupted in laughter at the thought of the Patriots quarterback leaving them to play for the Tampa Bay

Bucs. "That'll be the day," Lopez replied, his belly jiggling with laughter.

For a moment, Florence forgot the tragedy unfolding before her. She looked past Sergeant Lopez and Detective Martin, her gaze drifting to the paramedics, who were carefully placing Kevin into a body bag. The sound of the zipper closing echoed through the air, and Florence's heart sank as she saw Kevin's lifeless body being taken away. The smell of disinfectant and the faint scent of Kevin's cologne wafted through the air, making her stomach churn.

Sergeant Lopez offered a gentle pat on her shoulder before continuing. "Can you tell us what you remember happening this evening?" he asked, his pencil poised over his notepad.

Florence's voice trembled as she began to recount the events leading up to the shooting. Lopez listened intently, his eyes never leaving hers. Martin stood beside him, his expression somber. "I recall members of Los Maliciosos calling the shooter, Raul. Raul told Kevin that he was out for vengeance and blamed him for the members of Los Maliciosos having to kill his cousin Jorge, the member who was killed on his way to the airport today. Kevin and I heard the news over the radio just before Los Maliciosos surrounded our car."

Lopez's mind began to wander, connecting the dots between this case and the one he'd responded to earlier that evening. A rose gold tarot card, the Hanged Man, had been found in Jorge's front shirt pocket, tucked away alongside his passport and ripped-up plane ticket to Columbia. The image of the card lingered in his mind—a man hanging upside down from a tree branch, his face serene, his hands bound behind his back. Was Jorge supposed to represent the man in the card? Was it a symbol of torture, death, or something else entirely?

He couldn't shake the feeling that the card held a key to understanding the case, but he was lost in a sea of unfamiliar symbolism. Witchcraft, tarot cards, vengeance... it was all so far outside his realm of expertise. He glanced at Martin, who looked just as lost. *Where do we even start with this?* The thought echoed in his mind as his pencil scratched across the notepad, jotting down the names. *Raul, Los Maliciosos, vengeance, the Hanged Man...* The pieces swirled in his head, but he couldn't quite fit them together. Sergeant Lopez's pencil scratched across the notepad as sweat formed above his brows as he worried he might forget important details if he didn't write everything down fast enough.

The silence was palpable. Florence's piercing eyes were fixed on him. She sensed he was a good man beneath the badge, one who genuinely wanted to unravel the tangled threads of the case. Her intuition told her that she could trust him, that he would listen without judgment.

"The Hanged Man," she said softly, her voice breaking the silence. "In this context, it might suggest that Jorge's death was a form of sacrifice, a twisted offering to some dark purpose." Her eyes locked onto his. "Or perhaps the killer was trying to send a message, to signal that Jorge's actions were seen as a betrayal, and his punishment was to be suspended, figuratively and literally, between life and death."

He took a step back, his eyes widening in amazement. "How do you know about the Hanged Man?" he asked, his voice barely above a whisper. It was as if she had plucked the thoughts right out of his mind.

Her gaze never wavered, her expression calm. "I heard it on the news broadcast over the radio," she said, her voice gentle. "They mentioned finding a tarot card on Jorge's body."

Lopez's mind reeled as he scribbled down some notes. *Hanged Man: possibly means Jorge betrayed El Cazador and/or Los Maliciosos.* He looked up at her, a mixture of amazement and gratitude on his face. "You've given me a new lead, a new perspective," he said, his voice filled with appreciation. "I don't know what I would have done without your insight."

The crunch of tires on gravel signaled Captain Ramone's arrival, a sound Lopez knew all too well. Ramone emerged from the vehicle, a striking man in his forties with dirty blonde hair and a goatee that lent him a handsome air, though the meanness in his eyes detracted from his looks. His gaze scanned the area, settling on Lopez and Martin, who was interviewing Florence. Walking toward them, another detective handed him a Ziploc bag of a rose gold tarot card of the ten of cups. The corners were coated with Kevin's blood. The card glinted in the light, and the image of a happy family under a rainbow seemed almost jarring against the somber backdrop of the crime scene.

"This was found in reverse on the victim's body," Detective Figueroa informed Ramone as he took the bag from him. "It's been confirmed that this is the work of El Cazador. It's the ten of cups and it matches the same rose gold tarot deck used in other crimes."

Ramone nodded at the detective. "Not the card that was supposed to be left tonight. Good work in recovering this. Who else have you disclosed this to?"

"Just to the people who need to know this and are...forgetful, Captain," he said, winking at the discretion.

"Keep it that way. Let's not let this information get out to the press this time."

"*Si señor,*" Detective Figueroa said with a sly smile.

Captain Ramone approached Lopez and Martin, intent on distracting them from the investigation. He had worked with them before and knew their limitations. Leaving them with the tarot card would likely lead to confusion and delays, buying El Cazador more time to further their goals. With a Ziploc bag containing the rose gold Ten of Cups tarot card in hand, he pretended to present significant evidence. Captain Ramone's ultimate goal was to become Commissioner, a position he believed was within reach if he maintained his alliance with El Cazador. However, Florence sensed his true intentions and became immediately defensive, realizing that Captain Ramone's actions were motivated by self-interest and potentially more sinister allegiances.

"Lopez, I need you to take a look at this," he said, his voice low. Lopez took the bag, his fingers brushing against Captain Ramone's. "This is the tarot card of the ten of cups," Ramone continued. "It's is a positive message of fulfillment and completeness. Try to figure out why they threw it on Kevin…maybe there was a marriage proposal."

Florence realized that Captain Ramone had purposely left out that it was placed on Kevin in reverse which meant the opposite meaning from the one he'd just given. She pursed her lips as she contemplated when would be a good time to reveal that important detail to Lopez; she couldn't contradict Ramone directly or he'd be suspicious.

Sergeant Lopez's clumsiness almost got the better of him, and he nearly dropped it. Captain Ramone's eyes narrowed, and an embarrassed Lopez quickly handed the bag over to Martin, who fumbled with it, his fingers struggling to get a grip. Ramone rolled his eyes, muttering under his breath as he walked away.

Florence glared at his retreating back. Interrupting her gaze, Sergeant Lopez stammered, "Does this card belong to Kevin?" He held up the bag for her to see.

Florence's eyes widened, and tears streamed down her face as she stared at the rose gold tarot card with Kevin's stained blood visible on the plastic bag. The happy family underneath the rainbow seems like a distant dream now. "No... the person who shot him threw it on him," she whispered. "And it was purposely placed on Kevin in reverse which in tarot means a disruption of emotional fulfillment and harmony," she added.

Lopez's eyes widened as he quickly jotted down this important detail, finally understanding that the disruption may have meant more than just taking Kevin's life. "Thank you for explaining that. I didn't know that tarot cards could have different meanings when placed in reverse."

"That's helpful for us to know for future investigations," Martin added.

Florence nodded. "Yes, the orientation of the card can significantly alter its interpretation. Keeping that in mind might help you better understand the motivations behind these crimes."

Lopez and Martin exchanged nods, grateful for the insight and impressed by the complexity of the cryptic messages left with the victims. *But who are these messages intended for?"* Lopez wondered. *Not the dead, surely.* "We'll do our best to investigate this incident, ma'am," he said, his voice gentle.

Florence's patience was wearing thin. "Can I go home now? I need to contact Kevin's parents before they hear about his death on the news."

Lopez nodded sympathetically. "Of course. We'll be in touch." He handed her a business card. "If you remember anything Kevin might have been working on that could be related to the case, please don't hesitate to call us."

"Hey, you have a business card?" Martin chimed in. "I want one too!"

Florence smiled at the duo's banter, sensing the good-natured dynamic between them. As she walked away, she overheard Lopez teasing, "Don't worry, I'll give you one with 'Clumsy Sidekick' printed on it!"

7

Chapter Seven: The Ruby's Gift

Florence stepped into the home she'd once shared with Kevin, the sound of ocean waves crashing against the shore, a bitter reminder of the emptiness she felt inside. The smell of saltwater and seaweed that had once brought her peace now left behind the stench of loneliness.

She walked through the familiar spaces, her eyes lingering on memories etched in every corner. The soft creak of the floorboards beneath her feet seemed to echo with Kevin's laughter. In the bedroom, Kevin's neatly folded clothes still sat atop the dresser, as if waiting for him to put them back in their designated drawers. The smell of Chanel Bleu lingered in their shared closet, transporting her back to nights when Kevin would spritz himself before taking her out. Florence's heart ached as she sniffed at the familiar scent, now a poignant reminder of his absence. The cologne's woody aromatic fragrance with its fresh, clean sensual scent filled her senses, making her feel like she was suffocating under the weight of her grief.

She wandered into the living room, where the sofa held

memories of countless nights spent watching movies together, laughing and snuggling under blankets. The worn cushions seemed to sag under the weight of her memories. The kitchen's usual warmth was gone, replaced by an unsettling quiet, the pots and pans idle, awaiting the return of the chef who brought them to life.

Tears welled up in Florence's eyes as she recalled the joys they had shared in this very apartment. Her mind replayed the memories of their time together, and the pain of losing him felt like a physical blow. She made her way to the phone, her hands shaking as she dialed Kevin's parents' number, each digit pressed weighing heavily on her fingers.

She heard Sandra's excited voice on the other end, followed by Kevin Sr.'s warm tone. "Hello?" they said in unison, evidently expecting good news.

Florence could sense their anticipation, their thoughts filled with joy and expectation. *Kevin must have popped the question today,* Sandra thought, her mind racing with excitement as she envisioned wedding bells and family gatherings.

We're finally going to be grandparents, Kevin Sr. thought, as she envisioned a smile spreading across his face.

"You both need to sit down," Florence whispered. "I…"

Her words trailed off, and suddenly, she felt an intense connection to the ruby on her finger. The weight of her grief and the pain of delivering devastating news to Kevin's parents seemed to unlock a deep well of power within the ruby, granting its master a gift she never could have imagined. The force lifted her off the floor with a surge of electrifying energy that coursed through her body like a potent elixir, the ruby's deep hue radiating a celestial glow. The jewel appeared almost alive, illuminating her surroundings with an intense, fiery light that symbolized love, passion, and power, reminiscent of its revered status as the "King of Gems". Florence's eyes widened in shock, her body weightless. The rush of adrenaline was intoxicating, and she felt invincible, like nothing could stop her.

"I can fly," she thought, her mind racing with wonder and terror as she soared upwards, narrowly avoiding the ceiling fan.

Excitement coursed through Florence, but panic quickly took hold as she struggled to control her newfound ability. She flailed her arms wildly, careening off the walls as she desperately tried to steady herself. The phone slipped from her hand, landing on the floor with a soft thud.

On the other end of the line, Sandra's voice grew concerned. "Hello? Hello? What's going on?"

Kevin Sr.'s voice joined in, "Florence, is everything okay?"

Florence could hear the TV clearly in Kevin's parents' home, a news anchor's somber voice filled the airwaves, about to deliver the news of Kevin's murder before she could break it to his parents. Her heart sank as she struggled to get back on the ground and grab the phone to warn them to turn off the television. She knew she should be the one to deliver the devastating news to Kevin's parents. The weight of her task settled back onto her shoulders, and her excitement about flying gave way to terrible dread.

She put her hands toward the ground as if she was diving into a pool full of water, her body awkwardly angled as she tried to reach the phone. Her face hurtled towards the floor, her feet dangling wildly in the air, as she stretched out her arms and fingers to grab the phone. But it was too late.

"Breaking news," the news caster reported. "Tragedy has

struck once again in the Tampa Bay community. Kevin Vega, a beloved journalist with the Tampa Bay Sun-Times, has been found murdered. Witnesses describe the scene, and some are pointing to El Cazador and his gang, Los Maliciosos. Here we have the editor in chief of Tampa Bay Sun-Times Alejandro…"

Florence's world came crashing down around her as she heard his parents sobs over the other end of the receiver, the anguished wails piercing her eardrums like a cold, harsh wind. She felt her body give out, her flying ability abandoning her, and she crashed to the floor, her face hitting the ground with a soft impact, the sound of her own despairing moans mingling with the distant sobs. The weight of her own disappointment was enough to ground her, and with it, the ruby's gift.

8

Chapter Eight: Blood Oath

El Cazador's secret room was shrouded in darkness, illuminated solely by flickering candles. The walls were crafted from black tourmaline, the dark, glossy surfaces reflecting the guttering flames like a still, mysterious pool. As a natural shield against negative energies, the black tourmaline walls enclosed El Cazador in a protective cocoon, filtering out malevolent forces and amplifying his own dark powers. Shadows danced across his face as he communed with his sister's spirit, Daisy. Her presence calmed his turbulent mind, but tonight's message ignited a firestorm.

"Raul disobeyed your orders, *hermano*," Daisy warned, her ethereal voice laced with urgency. "He murdered Kevin."

The words hung in the air like a death sentence.El Cazador's eyes blazed with fury. He slammed his fists on his desk, sending papers and pens scattering.

"*¡Maldito!*" he growled, his voice echoing off the walls.

The room trembled with his rage. His mind raced as he envisioned Raul's betrayal. He had specifically instructed the gang to bring Kevin to him alive, to confront him alone. Raul's disobedience was a direct challenge to his authority, and if left unchecked, it would undermine the discipline and respect he demanded from his members. With trembling hands, El Cazador dialed Victor's number.

"I need you to gather Los Maliciosos," he ordered. "Everyone. I want them in front of the warehouse now."

Victor's voice was hesitant on the other end. "*S-sí, jefe.* I'll get them there."

El Cazador's voice was low and menacing. "See that you do. I want no excuses. No delays. You understand me?"

Victor's reply was swift. "Yes, *jefe.* I'll make sure they're there."

The call ended, and the minutes ticked by with a morbid slowness, as if each passing second counted down to a final, fatal hour. Finally, the gang congregated outside the warehouse, their faces tense with anticipation. In front of the warehouse, Los Maliciosos remaining nine members stood in a line, their faces illuminated by the faint moonlight. Raul, Hector, and Victor stood alongside Angel, Jose, Roberto, Mateo, and David, a diverse group of men ranging in age and experience. At one end, Alex, the youngest at just 18, looked around with a mix of excitement and nerves while David, a seasoned member in his mid-30s, stood resolute on the other end, his expression unreadable.

Gatita's low, menacing hiss echoed through the night air, her piercing green eyes seeming to receive some unseen command, as she held them at the curb with an unyielding gaze. The warehouse's dimly lit exterior loomed behind her, a stage for the impending reckoning that would seal Raul's own betrayal.

The men gathered nervously in front of the warehouse, their faces etched with anxiety. Raul paced, his eyes darting nervously, sensing impending doom. The night air was heavy with foreboding. Suddenly, Daisy's ghostly form materialized before him, wearing a tattered nightgown. Los Maliciosos froze in shock, their bodies paralyzed by fear. Goosebumps rose on their skin, their hair standing on end. They had heard the rumors of El Cazador's conversations with his dead sister, but to see her materialize right before them was a different story altogether. The fear was palpable, the air electric with terror.

"Run," Daisy taunted to the members of Los Maliciosos, her voice cold and menacing. Her spectral hands grasped Raul's shoulders, holding him in place with an unyielding grip.

The words seemed to hang in the air like a challenge, as the neighboring apartment complex across the street seemed to loom closer, their windows like empty eyes staring back. From the shadows of these windows, a trio of restless spirit guides drifted towards the warehouse, their ghostly forms drawn to the dark energy unfolding before them like moths to a flame.

The air was thick with the scent of decay and neglect, and the spirit guides' ethereal forms seemed to ripple with distaste, as if drawn to the darkness despite their gentle natures. There was Abuelo, a gentle elderly spirit with wispy white hair and spectacles perched on the end of his nose, who kept a loving eye on his granddaughter, a woman who still grieved his passing with a depth that seemed to echo through the decades. He had been guiding her through her darkest moments, offering what comfort he could as she navigated the complex emotions of grief. Alongside Abuelo stood Rose, a young woman who shone with a soft, otherworldly light. Her kind face was framed by a simple coif that covered her hair, and she wore a modest shift beneath a worn waistcoat. Faint, rope-like marks on her wrists seemed to whisper stories of their own. With a gentle gaze, she watched over her great-granddaughter, whose sensitive nature and inner sight seemed to be awakening, and she guided her through the mysteries of the unseen world. With her free hand, Rose gently grasped Emily's ethereal fingers, the little girl's sorrowful expression a poignant contrast to her vibrant 1950s-style polka-dot dress, her curly brown hair tied up in pigtails, and a faint bruise visible on her right arm. Emily's eyes seemed to hold a world of pain, and yet she radiated a quiet strength as she guided her older sister, who had lived a full life but now dwelled alone in her apartment across the abandoned warehouse, forgotten by her family and in need of gentle guidance and companionship.

"This is wrong," Abuelo whispered, his voice like a soft breeze that carried the scent of old books and dusty attics.

"She's playing with fire, but we cannot intervene," Rose reminded him, her voice barely audible.

"The living must make their own choices." Emily nodded, her eyes wide with concern. "But it's not right. She's hurting someone."

The spirits exchanged worried glances, their ethereal forms undulating with disapproval. Her creepy laughter echoed through the night air, sending a telepathic shiver toward the watching spirits. Her dark energy seemed to clash with their peaceful essence, prompting a stern vigilance from the spirit guides. Abuelo's eyes narrowed, and with a subtle flick of his wrist, he sent energy toward a nearby streetlight. The light had been dark for years, but now it pulsed with a faint, otherworldly energy like a malevolent heartbeat. The flickering light cast eerie shadows on the ground, making it seem like the very spirits of the dead were dancing in the darkness. Raul's eyes darted toward the now flickering light, his face contorted in terror as he realized he was trapped.

Abuelo's telepathic whisper crackled with urgency, her name etched in the shared consciousness of the spirit realm. "Daisy, you're going too far." Fear and warning warred for dominance in his voice, but his words fell on deaf ears.

Consumed by her own malevolent desires, Daisy seemed to embody the darkness that closed in around them all. Her gaze slowly shifted towards the spirit guides, her head twitching with an unnatural, jerky motion. The spirit guides felt a chill run down their ethereal spines as her eyes locked onto them.

The members of Los Maliciosos, watching from the shadows, gasped in terror as the spirit guides' forms became visible to them for the first time.

Victor's eyes went wide, his mouth hanging open in shock. "*¡Dios mío!*" he breathed, his voice barely audible.

Beside him, Alex stumbled backward, his face pale and sweaty. "What's going on?" he whispered, his eyes darting wildly between the spirit guides.

Hector's face twisted in a mixture of fear and fascination, his eyes fixed on Rose's shimmering form. "*Están aquí,*" he muttered, his voice trembling. "They're really here."

The others seemed frozen in place, their faces reflecting their terror as they gazed upon the spirit guides.

Daisy's hand rose, her fingers splayed like claws, and a pulsing force shot towards the spirit guides. Rose raised her own hand, and a shimmering barrier of light appeared, deflecting the energy. The force rebounded, amplified, and crashed back towards Daisy and the members of Los Maliciosos, sending them all tumbling to the ground. Daisy struggled to get back to her feet, her eyes blazing with annoyance and frustration. She seemed to be having trouble maintaining her hold on Raul, who stood frozen in fear, his eyes wide with terror. Daisy reached out telepathically to Gatita, warning her of the spirit guides' presence. *Gatita, the spirits are here. Take care of them.*

The cat darted into the street, her eyes glowing with an otherworldly intensity. The spirit guides backed away, their eyes fixed on the cat's powerful form.

"Stay back," Rose warned Abuelo and Emily, her voice firm but controlled. "This feline is an ancient guardian. We don't want to provoke her."

The spirit guides hesitated, watching Gatita with a mixture of concern and wariness. Daisy's frustration turned to a malevolent snarl as she dug her ethereal fingers deeper into Raul's shoulders, struggling to pin him down despite her own stumbling form."Now, *hermano*," she hissed telepathically to El Cazador, her voice a cold whisper in his mind.

Headlights pierced the darkness, illuminating the desperate scene. The roar of El Cazador's engine growled to life, its exhaust pipes snarling as he floored it. The tires shrieked in protest, their rubber squealing as they struggled to grip the pavement. The car surged forward, a bullet of steel and glass hurtling towards Raul's frozen form.

The members of Los Maliciosos scattered, their panicked voices rising in a frantic chorus. "Move!" "Get out of the way!" "LOOK OUT!"

But their cries were born of cowardice, not courage, as they desperately tried to distance themselves from the horror unfolding before them. The car struck Raul with a sickening crunch, sending his body flying. The vehicle reversed, its tires screeching, and drove forward again, striking Raul a second time as Daisy's laughter grew louder.

Raul's spirit began to leave his body, the agony of being hit twice with a car melting away, replaced by a gentle, painless sensation. His essence began to untether from the battered flesh, freed from the mortal suffering that had defined his final moments.Abuelo, Rose, and Emily floated towards his lifeless form, their ethereal bodies radiating a warm, comforting presence. They surrounded Raul's body, their gentle faces filled with compassion. The two spirit guides who had been assigned to Raul's human journey stood beside him now, their ethereal forms radiating a warm, comforting light. They had been with him every step of the way, guiding him through life's challenges and triumphs, though he had never been aware of their presence. Raul's spirit gazed at them curiously, memories stirring of his childhood imaginary friends. He had often talked to them in his mind, sharing his deepest secrets and fears. Now, their faces seemed familiar, yet shrouded in a soft, ethereal glow. The spirit guides formed a gentle circle around Raul's spirit, their ethereal forms radiating a warm, comforting light as they waited for a family member of Raul to arrive and escort him into the spirit realm. Suddenly, a brilliant beam of light shot forth, and Jorge's spirit emerged, his eyes filled with love and concern. He stood before Raul, offering a reassuring smile and an outstretched hand. Raul's spirit reached out, and Jorge's hand enveloped his, providing guidance and comfort. A brilliant white light enveloped Raul as he accepted Jorge's hand, filling him with peace and tranquility. A symphony of heavenly music filled the air, a chorus of pure joy and celebration that seemed to come from beyond the stars. With his spirit fully emerged, Raul gazed down at his lifeless form below, a sense of detachment washing over him.

"What's going on?" Raul's spirit asked, his voice calm and accepting, already understanding that he had transitioned.

Jorge's spirit smiled softly."You've passed on, *primo.* I'm here to guide you through this transition. Now, you'll meet the Master of the Universe, and review the choices you made in life. You'll reflect on your actions, and the impact they had on others." Jorge's eyes held a deep wisdom, as he added, "You'll have the opportunity to learn from your experiences, and find peace."

The heavenly music swelled, and the white light grew brighter, as Raul's spirit began his journey towards the afterlife.

Meanwhile, back in the mortal realm, silence gripped the scene, the stunned survivors frozen in a tableau of horror, their eyes fixed on the lifeless form that lay motionless on the ground.El Cazador emerged from the shadows, clad in black. His rose gold tarot card glinted in the moonlight - the Five of Cups seemed to mock Raul's lifeless form.

"Este es el precio de la traición… this is the price of betrayal" he spat, his voice venomous. "My actions demonstrate what will happen if you defy me."

Daisy drifted beside El Cazador, her smile unsettling as she reveled in the knowledge that mortals feared death, yet had no concept of the afterlife.

El Cazador's thoughts drifted to Daisy's tragic fate. Memories of their childhood flashed through his mind. He recalled their laughter, tears, and whispered secrets. After her death, the Divine Master had appointed Daisy as one of his spirit guides, meant to offer guidance and protection from beyond; yet El Cazador's all-consuming grief had driven him to master the darkest corners of witchcraft, ultimately allowing him to summon her essence into the mortal realm, where she stood before him now, a testament to his unyielding obsession.

Fear crept over Victor like a cold mist, seeping into his bones as he beheld El Cazador's unwavering devotion to his ghostly sister. He trembled at the thought of his own fate if he ever chose to defy his leader. "We won't betray you, El Cazador," he whispered proclaiming his allegiance.

The warehouse's outer walls seemed to whisper tales of bloodshed and loyalty. Los Maliciosos shivered, sensing the weight of El Cazador's legacy. They exchanged fearful glances as their leader's gaze swept the group, his eyes burning with intensity.

Daisy's spirit lingered, her malevolent presence suffocating the group. Her eyes blazed with an unnatural light, and her voice was a low, menacing whisper. "You should have obeyed," she hissed, the words dripping with malice.

The group stood frozen, their faces pale and sweaty, as they avoided eye contact with her. They seemed to shrink away from her, their bodies tense with fear, as if expecting her to unleash some new horror upon them. El Cazador's anger hung in the air like a challenge, but even his bravado seemed to falter in the face of Daisy's unholy power.

"*¿Entendido?*... Understood?" El Cazador demanded, his voice echoing through the night.

Los Maliciosos nodded frantically, their fear for their lives palpable, acknowledging that disobedience would not be tolerated.

"Good. Now, where is the ruby?" El Cazador demanded.

Victor trembled. "We didn't find it. Kevin didn't have it on him."

Daisy's ghostly form materialized beside Victor, her eyes blazing with an unnatural light. "That's because you didn't look hard enough," she screeched, her voice dripping with menace. "You were too busy failing as leader, too distracted by your own ineptitude. You couldn't even maintain control over the nine men sworn to follow El Cazador. Jorge betrayed us, and Raul disobeyed, costing us Kevin's life. And still, the ruby remains lost. You forgot your duty, your purpose. Your failure is staggering. You have accomplished nothing so far!"

With supernatural strength, Daisy lifted Victor off the ground, his feet flailing wildly as he let out a terrified yelp. She hurled him over El Cazador's parked car, the sound of his body sailing through the air like a rag doll, followed by a loud, metallic crunch as he crashed onto the hood. The impact sent a shockwave through the vehicle, and the windshield spiderwebbed outwards from the point of impact. Victor's groan was a low, pained rumble, his body motionless except for the slow slide down the hood, leaving a smear of blood on the glass.

"Find the ruby! FIND IT NOW!" El Cazador snarled, his eyes blazing with a fierce, savage intensity that made the shadows around him seem to twist and writhe.

Victor scrambled off the car, his movements stiff and awkward as he limped back to the group, his breath coming in ragged gasps.

"*Si, señor,*" the men chorused, their voices trembling with fear, the words tumbling out in a panicked rush.

El Cazador's eyes narrowed, his gaze piercing the darkness like a cold blade. "*Recuerden, lealtad es la vida. Traición es muerte...* Remember loyalty is life. Betrayal is death." His voice was low and menacing, the words dripping with a deadly sincerity. He paused, surveying his loyal followers with a calculating gaze, his eyes lingering on each face before moving on. "Jorge and Raul's fates serve as a reminder. YOU ARE ALL EXPENDABLE!" he shouted, his voice echoing off the warehouse walls, the sound waves seeming to vibrate with menace.

The men of Los Maliciosos dispersed, backing away into the shadows, but their eyes lingered on Daisy, their gazes flicking back to her ghostly form with a mixture of fear and fascination. With that, Daisy's form began to fade, but not before a low, menacing chuckle escaped her lips. She turned and floated towards the warehouse, her body bathed in a sickly gray-blue glow, as if the very light around her was being drained of color. Abuelo, Rose, and Emily watched from the apartment complex, keeping their distance from her dark energy. Upon reaching the front door of the warehouse, Daisy walked through it, her ghostly form passing seamlessly through the wood as if it were made of mist. The sound of her laughter lingered, growing fainter until it was nothing more than a distant, mocking whisper.

El Cazador got into his car, the engine roaring to life as he drove off into the darkness, the tires screeching on the pavement. The night swallowed his figure whole, the darkness closing in like a shroud. The only sound that remained was the faint, mournful mewling of Gatita, a small, pitiful cry that seemed to echo with the sound of betrayal.

* * *

El Cazador stepped out of his sleek black car, the garage door closing behind him with a soft hum. He entered his mansion, surrounded by opulent crystals and chandeliers refracting light into miniature rainbows. The grandeur contrasted sharply with the emptiness within; the warm embrace of a lover and laughter of children were conspicuously absent.

He approached the secret room through a second entrance concealed behind a bookshelf. The door slid open, revealing a dimly lit space filled with artifacts and relics.

"Daisy," El Cazador called out, his voice low and husky. "Those incompetent fools didn't get the ruby from Kevin."

Daisy's ghostly form materializes beside the antique mirror. Her eyes fixed on El Cazador. "Kevin had the ruby," she whispered. "I know he did."

"Where is it now?" El Cazador demanded.

Daisy's eyes glazed over as she meditated, her connection to the spiritual realm allowing her to sense the ruby's power. However, the specifics of its location and the extent of its abilities remained shrouded in mystery, hidden from her by the veil of the unknown. The only vision revealed to Daisy was a pear shaped engagement ring encrusted with diamonds and the ruby in its center.

"It… it looks like he placed the ruby into a ring. An engagement ring. The ruby itself has already claimed its master, but the remnants are still out there, waiting for their own. Since they've been cut into smaller pieces, their power will be less than the whole ruby's, but still significant. I can sense their magic, but I don't know where they are located. The only vision I'm seeing is a black leather briefcase."

El Cazador's eyes narrowed. "Show me."

Daisy's ethereal fingers touched the mirror. The glass rippled, revealing Ricardo Morales Jewelers on Main Street, a few blocks away from the warehouse. El Cazador grinned for a moment, thinking of his next move. Ricardo was a well loved member of the community and most importantly the father of Alex, the youngest member of Los Maliciosos. His grin lingered as he watched Ricardo carefully place the ruby into the engagement ring. His thoughts turned to Alex, and a pang of interest sparked within him. He could see himself taking Ricardo's place in Alex's life, guiding him, shaping him. The idea of Alex, soon to be fatherless, tugged at a part of him he'd long thought dormant. El Cazador's gaze never wavered from the mirror as he mused, "I wonder how Alex will fare without his *padre* to guide him. Perhaps I'll be the one to show him the way."

Daisy's voice cut through his reverie, her tone dripping with malice. "You would be a great father figure to Alex. We need that ruby, and Ricardo knows too much. It must be done for the better good of this city."

El Cazador's lips curled into a snarl, a begrudging respect flickering in his eyes. "Clever little fella, wasn't he?" he said, his voice dripping with sarcasm. "Kevin, I mean."

Daisy's ghostly form seemed to ripple with agitation as she hissed, "I never liked engagement rings. I always felt like they symbolize women becoming a man's property."

El Cazador's laughter was low and mocking. "You feel that way because you never got the chance to be proposed to, *hermana*. Don't be bitter. You didn't miss much."

With a smirk spreading across his face, El Cazador dialed Victor's number.

"Victor, we need to cut Ricardo Morales' life short tonight. He has the ruby and he knows too much of its power. The ruby will be inside a diamond ring. Bring it to me and any remnants of it! Oh, and one more thing: I want you to look for a black leather briefcase. Tell the men to check every location that's professionally significant to our targets. Leave no leads unexplored. Find that briefcase as well, and bring it to me directly."

Victor's hesitant voice echoed through the speaker. "*Señor,* isn't Ricardo—"

El Cazador's tone turned glacial. "No questions, Victor. Get it done. Now."

Victor's reply was immediate. "*Sí, señor.*"

"Oh, and Victor, make sure your men are in line. I won't tolerate any mistakes. Just imagine what will happen if you disappoint me again."

Victor's voice was laced with a mix of understanding and fear. "*Sí, señor.* I'll take care of it personally."

Victor stepped into the dimly lit alley in front of their warehouse, flanked by the imposing figures of Los Maliciosos.

"Alright, listen up," Victor said, his voice firm and commanding. The group of Los Maliciosos quiet down, their eyes fixed on him. "We have a job to do. We need to retrieve the ruby. Ricardo's jewelry shop by our warehouse has it, or at least remnants of it. He also wants us to find a black leather briefcase. Search everywhere, especially where our targets work." Victor's gaze swept across the group, his eyes lingering on each face. "This is a priority for El Cazador, and I expect everyone to follow orders without question."

The group nodded, their faces set with determination. They began their walk towards the jewelry shop, the silence between them thick with anticipation. Alex's eyes widened in stunned silence, his mind racing with the realization that his father was their next target.

"Time for another killing, Victor," Hector said, his voice laced with a mix of excitement and unease.

"I'm still spooked about Daisy," David chimed in.

"I'm telling you, she's not right," Mateo added. "I've never seen anything like it."

Victor's expression darkened. "*Silencio!*" he barked.

"Let me make one thing clear: none of you will defy my orders or El Cazador's. If you do, I'll personally take care of you. You're all clear on that, right?" Victor's gaze lands on Alex, and his tone softens slightly. "Alex, you can go home. This doesn't involve you."

Alex's eyes filled with tears as he nodded mutely, his face pale, too scared to speak up, to say anything that might draw attention to himself. Victor's words are a reprieve, but Alex knew he was only being spared for now. He turned and walked away, the thought of his father's store being targeted making his stomach twist into knots. Yet he felt a wave of relief wash over him, knowing he was spared from the having to see everything play out.

For months, Alex had been entangled in Los Maliciosos' web, drawn in by the promise of power and wealth that seemed like a lifeline compared to the suffocating expectations of his father's jewelry store. As he walked, he remembered countless fights with his father, the frustration and anger that simmered beneath the surface as he was expected to take over the business and care for his mother and baby sister. His father had envisioned a future for him, one that Alex had no desire to follow. But El Cazador, with his commanding presence and aura of authority, had captivated him. The way he wielded power, bending men to his will, had been intoxicating. Alex had wanted to be like him, to have that kind of control and respect.

Now, though, he felt trapped. The money was good, but it always came with a price. He knew that leaving Los Maliciosos wasn't an option, not after seeing what had happened to Jorge and Raul. The thought sent a chill down his spine. He should warn his father, apologize for the way he had acted, for the pain he might have caused, but he didn't dare go against El Cazador. He feared for his father's life, and for the future his little sister would face without a dad.Alex turned down an alleyway, his eyes fixed on the ground as he struggled to process the horror of what was about to unfold. He turned on his phone and began dialing the jewelry shop, his fingers trembling as he punched in the numbers. Suddenly, a force like the wind blew his phone from his hands, sending it crashing into a brick wall. The screen shattered, the pieces scattering across the ground. Alex's head jerked up, and he saw Daisy standing before him, her presence seeming to draw the very light out of the air. Her skin was deathly pale, her eyes sunken and dark. The grey and blue hues of her aura seemed to swirl around her like a mist, casting an eerie glow on the surrounding buildings.

Her voice was barely audible, yet it sent shivers down Alex's spine as she whispered, "*Noli monere patrem, aut tota familia tua patietur,*" the Latin words hanging in the air like a curse. "Do not warn your father, or your entire family will suffer."

Alex felt a cold dread creeping over him, as if death itself was looming over him, its icy breath on the back of his neck. He didn't wait to hear more. He turned and ran home, his heart pounding in his chest, trapped in a nightmare from which he could never wake up.

The remaining members of Los Maliciosos followed Victor as they approached the front of Ricardo Morales' jewelry store.

"Surround the building," Victor demanded, his voice low and menacing.

Seeing them approach, Ricardo rushed to lock the door, but Victor's foot stopped him from closing it fully. "Sorry, *señores*, but we're closed!" Ricardo said, his voice trembling.

Victor smirked, shoving him against the door. "Don't worry. We're not here to browse." He pushed the door open, letting the other members of Los Maliciosos enter the store. Victor flashed a photo of the glowing red ruby in Ricardo's face. "Recognize this, Ricardo? Where is it?" Victor demanded, his voice forceful.

Ricardo's eyes widen as he recognized the ruby's mystical glow. "I've never seen that before," he lied.

Daisy's spirit materializes before him, her presence chilling. "LIAR!" she shrieks, her eyes boring into Ricardo's soul.

Ricardo trembled, frozen in place. Daisy's gaze seems to open up his mind, and she hears his thoughts: *That's the ruby...the one with the strange mystical power.* Ricardo's eyes darted around the store, taking in the imposing figures of Los Maliciosos. "I don't know what you're talking about," he stammered.

Roberto stepped forward, his voice cold. "If you value your life, you'll tell us."

Victor grabbed Ricardo by the shirt, but Ricardo pushed Victor off and fled towards the back entrance of his store. Daisy sealed the door shut, and Roberto and Mateo grabbed Ricardo, restraining him. Daisy's ethereal force shattered the glass displays, the sound of breaking glass filling the air.

"Tell me where it is," the ghostly apparition snarled. "This is your last chance."

"I swear, I don't know!"

Daisy's fingers curled around the jeweler's throat, lifting him off the ground. "You're lying!" she yelled, hurling him across the store.

"Okay!" Ricardo staggered to his feet, panting. "I made it into an engagement ring! I gave it to one of my customers... someone by the name of Kevin. He brought it to me and asked me to add it to an engagement ring so he could propose to his girlfriend."

"Where are the remaining pieces of the stone?" Daisy demanded.

The jeweler looked baffled. "I... I don't know. What I cut just... just vanished."

Daisy's expression turns thoughtful. *He's lying. I still can feel all of the ruby's energy.* She turned to Los Maliciosos. "He can't live knowing the secret of the red ruby. Finish him up, boys."

Los Maliciosos pummeled Ricardo, each taking a swing at him until he was left lifeless on the floor. Victor stared down at Ricardo, his expression unreadable. "He knew too much," he whispered, retrieving The High Priestess Tarot card from his pocket. "This symbolizes his silence." With chilling precision, Victor slipped the card into Ricardo's mouth, sealing his lips forever. "Our secrets will now die with him."

The members of Los Maliciosos nodded, understanding the grim message. Mateo's voice cut through the silence, "Look at all these pretty jewels," he said, his hands reaching for the front glass display. "Let's take them for ourselves."

Victor's response was swift and merciless. "NO!" he barked, slamming the hilt of his gun into Mateo's fingers. The sound of breaking bones is unmistakable. Mateo's scream echoed through the store as he cradled his injured hand. "We were never instructed to steal any jewels other than the ruby. *Entendido?*"

Mateo's eyes flashed with fear as he nodded frantically, realizing Victor's leniency had given way to ruthless authority.

Victor's gaze was icy, his voice unyielding. "We'll search this entire place until we find the ruby. Every display, every case, every inch of this store. Don't bother me if you find a simple ruby; if it's not glowing and you disturb me by calling me over, you'll get punched in the face."

* * *

Daisy's ethereal form materialized before El Cazador in the secret room, her eyes blazing with fury.

"*Hermano*, the men are searching for the ruby now. We'll have it soon. But I'm worried that it was cut and crafted into an engagement ring because it means the ruby lost some of its power. Ricardo claims the excess vanished, but that's a lie. I can still sense its full power."

El Cazador's grip tightened. "Show me."

Daisy's spectral fingers grazed the antique mirror, and the glass rippled, revealing Kevin's passionate proposal. Florence's tears glistened as she accepted the ruby ring. El Cazador's eyes narrowed as he stared at the ruby, now smaller and beautifully shaped as a pear stone. His face twisted in rage as he recognized Kevin's fiancée. "He deliberately stole my ruby to give its mystical power to her."

Daisy's voice dripped with venom. "Florence now holds the key to unimaginable power."

El Cazador's jaw clenched. "Florence, brilliant and beautiful... With this power, she's unstoppable. We have to find those missing pieces. Where are they?"

Daisy touched the mirror again, and it filled with darkness. "I cannot confirm their whereabouts," she replied. "This is not something I can show you." Her gaze bore into his soul. "What will we do, *hermano*?"

El Cazador's voice was cold and calculated. "She'll join us, willingly or not. Defiance will bring devastating consequences. And we must find those missing pieces… before it's too late."

He produced a rose-gold tarot card from his pocket—the Ten of Swords—and held it up. The flickering candlelight danced across its surface, illuminating the haunting image of a man pierced by ten swords, his face twisted in a silent scream. "This card foretells Florence's doom," El Cazador hissed. "Impending destruction, inescapable fate. Florence's defiance will seal her own destiny."

9

Chapter Nine: Decoding the Evidence

The early morning sun cast a golden glow over the ravaged jewelry store. Shattered glass sparkled like diamonds on the floor. Empty display cases stood like hollow eyes.

Sergeant Lopez and Detective Martin surveyed the chaos while Captain Ramone briefed them. "Victim's ID confirms Ricardo Morales, jewelry store owner. Detective Figueroa ID'd him from his fingerprints and personal effects, despite the condition of his face. Looks like Maliciosos' handiwork."

Lopez nodded grimly. "Their calling card?"

Captain Ramone handed Lopez a Ziploc bag containing the High Priestess tarot card. The rose gold card depicted a serene figure shrouded in a hooded cloak, her hands clasped in prayer. The moon glowed behind her, casting an ethereal light. Lopez's gaze lingered on the card, his eyes tracing the intricate details of the High Priestess's face. As he studied the card, his expression deepened into a mixture of fascination and confusion. He looked up at Captain Ramone, his eyes narrowing slightly. Martin's brow furrowed. "What do you think it means, Sarge?" Lopez's incredulity grew, his face a

101

map of unanswered questions. "Captain, can you give us some guidance on deciphering these tarot cards? We could use some insight."

Annoyed, Captain Ramone decided to nudge them in the right direction. "I can't do your job for you." Lopez and Martin exchanged hopeless glances as he continued. "Los Maliciosos are using Tarot cards, gentlemen. Each has unique meanings depending on orientation. You both need to study up. We need these messages decoded." He yanked a tarot card guidebook from his backpack and jabbed Lopez's belly with it. "Get to work."

Captain Ramone departed, leaving Sergeant Lopez and Detective Martin to unravel the cryptic clue. Lopez winced, handing the book over to Martin. "You're on tarot card duty, Detective."

Martin protested, "But, Sarge - "

Lopez silenced him with a glance. "Captain's orders."

Martin opened the book, scanning its pages. "Let's see... the High Priestess represents intuition, secrets, mystery and... silence. She indicates secrets kept hidden."

Lopez raised an eyebrow. "Secrets kept hidden, huh?"

Martin looked up. "Los Maliciosos were trying to silence Morales, I guess. But silence him about what? What did Morales know that was worth killing him for?"

Lopez's expression turned contemplative. "That's what we need to find out, Detective."

The store's devastation surrounded them - shattered glass, overturned displays and the silence of a crime scene. Lopez's gaze wandered to the victim's family photos, scattered on the floor. Martin whispered, "Sarge, what's Los Maliciosos' game?" Lopez's gaze lingered on the High Priestess. "I wish I knew, Detective."

Among the scattered papers, Lopez spotted a crumpled inventory sheet. He picked it up, smoothing out the wrinkles. "Martin, take a look at this." The inventory listed transactions for the past two weeks. Lopez's eyes scanned the page, his finger tracing the entries. "Look! Kevin Vega was the last customer, and it looks like he purchased alterations to an engagement ring."

Martin leaned in, his eyes narrowing. "What's this say?" He pointed to a smudged word.

Lopez peered closely, his brow furrowed. "I think it says 'ruby'. The pencil mark's been erased, but I'm certain that's what it says."

Martin's eyes widened. "And what's this entry before Kevin Vega?"

Lopez's finger slid up the page. "Maria Rodriguez. It says 'bracelet for quinceañera - regular customer will receive a discount'. Let's walk and do some questioning."

The sergeant tucked the inventory into his pocket, and they left the store, walking down the quiet streets of Tampa, the morning sun casting long shadows behind them. They nodded to the occasional passerby, their eyes scanning the area for potential witnesses. The smell of freshly brewed coffee wafted from a nearby cafe, drawing them in. They pushed open the door, and the bell above it rang out, announcing their arrival. Inside, the cafe was warm and cozy, the delicious aroma of baked goods filling the air. Lopez and Martin took a booth in the back, ordering two cups of coffee as they surveyed the patrons. Maria Rodriguez sat alone at a table, nursing a cup of coffee.

Lopez's expression changed to one of recognition. "That's

Maria Rodriguez, isn't it?" he whispered to Martin. "The one who's always calling about Los Maliciosos' activity on Broadway?"

Martin nodded, his eyes following Lopez's gaze.

Maria was a small, frail woman with silver hair and a kind face, but her eyes seemed to hold a deep sadness. She sat hunched over her black coffee cup, her spoon twirling absently in the liquid, her face seeming to belong to a bygone era; a time of innocence and simplicity. Her eyes, though red-rimmed, held a deep sadness that seemed to belong to a different lifetime.

Lopez approached her, his badge visible on his belt. "Ms. Rodriguez? I'm Sergeant Lopez, Tampa PD. I believe you may have heard about the incident at Morales' jewelry store?"

Maria looked up, her eyes clouding over. "Oh, yes... I heard it on the radio this morning. Poor Ricardo. What can I do to help?"

Lopez nodded sympathetically. "We'd like to ask you a few questions, if you don't mind."

"Oh, yes, of course. I'm so sorry, I'm just a bit... distracted." She smiled weakly. "My family doesn't visit me much anymore. It's like I've been forgotten." Her voice trailed off, and she gazed into her coffee cup. "But I did have the strangest dream last night. It was almost like my little sister Emily visited me. She was wearing that old polka dot dress she loved so much, and her hair was in pigtails, just like when we were kids." A faint smile played on her lips. "She told me to get some coffee. I know it sounds silly, but I woke up feeling like I had to come here today."

"That must have been a nice surprise," Lopez said gently. "Speaking of nice things, I understand you purchased a bracelet from Morales' jewelry store recently? Can you tell me more about that?"

Maria's eyes lit up. "Oh, yes! My granddaughter's quinceañera is coming up, and I wanted to get her a special gift. Morales' store has always been my go-to place for jewelry."

Martin pulled out his notebook, jotting down some notes. Maria's expression turned somber. "Ricardo was a good man," she said, her voice trembling. "He didn't deserve to die like that. Just like my sister Emily didn't deserve what happened to her." Her voice trailed off, and a hint of pain flickered across her face.

Lopez's expression softened, and he leaned forward. "Since you were a regular customer, do you recall if Morales had any issues or problems with anyone?"

Maria hesitated, her eyes darting between Lopez and Martin. "He mentioned some issues with suppliers… and something about his son."

Martin's ears perked up and he exchanged a curious glance with Lopez. "His son?" Martin asked, his voice low and even, inviting Maria to elaborate.

Maria nodded, her voice barely above a whisper. "Alex Morales. He's been acting strange lately. I've recently seen him on Broadway, associating with those Maliciosos hoodlums. I think he might be one of them."

Lopez and Martin exchanged a stunned glance, their faces reflecting their shock. Both men knew Alex; they had met him many times, playing basketball on the streets with Ricardo. Their bond was the kind that inspired envy—a father-son relationship that everyone in town admired and aspired to. It was hard to imagine Alex being involved with a gang as terrible as Los Maliciosos.

105

"Thank you, Maria," Lopez said. "If you can think of anything else, please give us a call." He handed her his contact card.

Maria took it, her eyes still red-rimmed. Lopez and Martin stood up to leave, and Maria's gaze drifted to the window. A delicate blue butterfly fluttered past the glass just then, its wings shimmering in the sunlight. Maria's eyes widened, and a soft smile spread across her face as she whispered, "Hi, Emily." A look of peace settled over her features, and she added, barely audible, "I'm glad you're okay, *hermanita*. Mom would be proud of you. Tell her... tell her the bruises don't hurt anymore."

The butterfly vanished from sight, leaving Maria with a sense of calm. With a nod, Maria returned her attention to Lopez and Martin, who were now standing by the door, unaware of the quiet moment she had just shared with her sister. Lopez and Martin walked out of the cafe in silence, their minds reeling with this new information. They returned to the precinct, determined to unravel the High Priestess' secret and piece together the truth about Alex's involvement with Los Maliciosos.

At his desk, Lopez stared at the tarot card, his mind racing. What secrets had Morales uncovered by Los Maliciosos? And what did it have to do with his son?

Martin approached, a stack of files in hand. "Sarge, I found something. Morales' son, Alex, has a record: petty theft, vandalism."

Lopez's eyes narrowed. "Bring him in."

Detective Martin radioed dispatch. "Unit 12, pick up Alex Morales at 345 Elm Street and bring him in."

Half an hour had passed before officers Fernandez and Patel

arrived with Alex Morales, an 18-year-old with an unsettling calm expression.Lopez and Martin exchanged a knowing glance.

"Have a seat, Alex," Lopez instructed.

The boy complied, his expression unchanging.

Martin opened a folder. "So, Alex, we're investigating your father's murder."

Alex's voice was flat. "I don't know anything."

"So, you're saying you don't know anything about your father's murder?" Lopez's voice was firm but controlled as he leaned forward.

Martin's gaze locked onto Alex's face, searching for any sign of deception. "Maria Rodriguez thinks differently. She believes you're involved with Los Maliciosos."

Alex's expression remained impassive, but his jaw clenched. "I don't know anything," he repeated.

Lopez leaned back in his chair. "Can you tell us where you were last night between 9 and 11 pm?"

"I was at home, studying."

Martin raised an eyebrow. "Alone?"

"Yeah, alone."

Martin scribbled some notes on his pad. "Maria Rodriguez also mentioned seeing you with Los Maliciosos in front of her apartment. Care to explain that?"

Alex shifted uncomfortably in his seat. "I don't know what that old lady is talking about."

Lopez's tone turned stern. "Alex, withholding information or assisting in your father's murder carries severe penalties. You could spend the rest of your life in prison. Take it from me I know the District Attorney very well in this county, and he will not budge."

Alex's mask of calmness began to slip. His mind flashed back to the text message he'd received from El Cazador earlier this morning: *Your father was weak, m'hijo. He couldn't protect you, couldn't provide for you. But I can. I'll be the father you need—strong, fierce, and unyielding. You'll learn to obey me, to fear me, and to love me. I'll show you what it means to be a true man.*

The words had crawled under his skin, fueling the resentment he already held toward El Cazador. The gang leader's manipulation and control had already felt suffocating, and now his father's death had brought it all to a head. Alex's thoughts turned to Lopez and Martin, and for a fleeting moment, he considered revealing the truth about El Cazador's involvement. The weight of his secrets threatened to spill out, but he bit back the urge, his anger and bitterness simmering just below the surface. The camera in the corner of the interrogation room captured the tension in Alex's body, but his face remained impassive, hiding the turmoil brewing inside. "Sorry I can't help you."

Lopez stood. "We'll take a break. Detective Martin, let's discuss our next move."

They exited, leaving Alex alone, and the room grew eerily silent. Daisy's presence seeped into the space, her awareness piercing Alex's thoughts. She sensed the turmoil brewing within him, the temptation to betray El Cazador and reveal his identity to Lopez and Martin. Daisy's eyes locked onto Alex, her gaze cold and calculating. With a subtle gesture, she summoned her energy. The camera in the corner of the room lurched to life, its lens whirring as it swung 180 degrees. It came to a jerky stop, its gaze fixed on a dusty corner of the wall, where cobwebs clung to the faded paint. The image on the screen froze, a stark contrast to the tension in the room.

Daisy glided towards the glass mirror in the investigation room, where Alex's reflection stared back. Alex's eyes met hers, his face pale with fear.

"I-I won't say anything," he stammered, his voice shaking.

Daisy's smile grew wider, her eyes glinting with amusement. With a crimson-tipped finger, she drew the Grim Reaper symbol from the Death tarot card. Blood poured from the markings, cascading down the mirror like crimson tears. Alex's eyes widened, fear flickering beneath his stoic facade.

"El Cazador watches," Daisy whispered. "Silence shields you. Betray him, and silence will be your eternal companion… just like your father." Her laughter echoed through the room, an evil, menacing sound.

The door swung open, and Sergeant Lopez and Detective Martin re-entered the investigation room. Daisy vanished, leaving Alex alone and shaken by her presence and the bloody symbol on the mirror.

"Sergeant!" Detective Martin shouted. "Look at the mirror!"

The Grim Reaper symbol glared back, its outline scrawled in crimson, blood dripping steadily from the figure's scythe, forming a small, growing pool on the floor.

Lopez's eyes widened. "What the…?"

Martin flipped through his tarot guidebook. "It's the Death card symbol, indicating something's coming to an end."

Lopez's gaze locked onto Alex. "But where did this come from? Did you cut yourself?"

Alex stood frozen. "May I leave now? I want to grieve my father's death."

"Okay, Alex. You're free to go for now," Lopez said gently. "But we have more questions for you tomorrow morning."

"Be here at 9:00 a.m. sharp," Martin added.

As the sun dipped below the horizon, casting the city in darkness, Lopez and Martin knew they were just beginning to scratch the surface of Los Maliciosos' sinister game.

10

Chapter Ten: The Briefcase

Florence walked towards her office, her eyes drifting to the city view outside the window. The sun cast a golden glow over the towering skyscrapers, but the scenery no longer impressed her. Her eyes felt dry, her heart heavy with grief. It had been a week since Kevin's murder and she was back at work, trying to distract herself from the pain that threatened to consume her. A brief, icy glance from Melissa was the only acknowledgment of her presence as she passed by. She pushed open the door to her office and was taken aback by the disarray. Files were scattered everywhere, papers spilling out of folders like autumn leaves. The photos on her desk were slightly askew, as if they had been knocked or moved. She frowned, trying to make sense of the mess.

"Who was in my office?" Florence asked, her frustration evident, as Alexia walked in handing her a steaming cup of coffee. The aroma wafted up, a comforting familiarity in the midst of chaos.

"It wasn't like this on Friday," Alexia said, her eyes wide in surprise. "But Xander did mention to me this morning that he was looking for the Gonzalez file."

"The Gonzalez file?" Florence's confusion deepened. "I don't recall having a Gonzalez on my caseload." She looked around her office again, trying to piece together what had happened.

As if he'd heard his name mentioned, Xander strode into the office. "Good morning, Florence. I see you're back in the office. Sorry about the mess I left. I was looking for the Gonzalez file. I needed to review it before Marcos Gonzalez's arraignment this morning."

"You were looking for the Gonzalez file... in my office?" Florence's left eyebrow rose in skepticism.

A smooth expression met her question. "Yes, I must have misplaced it. I'm assigning you to this case. It's a domestic violence case, and I'd like you to interview the victim, Brenda, Marcos Gonzalez's girlfriend." He turned to Alexia. "Can you add a meeting to our calendars to discuss the case further?"

A nod from Alexia confirmed the request. "I'll schedule it for the last appointment of the day. I'm already meeting with Ryan later this afternoon, so it works out perfectly."

"Hey, want to grab lunch before your meeting with Ryan?" Florence asked her assistant. "I could meet you at the cafe across the street from Tampa Bay Sun-Times. Just the two of us."

Alexia smiled. "Sure, I'd love that. Let me go and add that to our calendars and block out our times." With that, she stepped out of Florence's office. A few moments later, Florence's calendar pinged, displaying the lunch date they had just scheduled.

The sudden shift in attention brought Florence's focus back to Xander, still standing in her office. "How are you doing,

Florence?" Xander asked.

Florence's gaze softened slightly, and she looked away, trying to compose herself. "I'm... managing."

Xander's expression turned sympathetic. "You're part of our office family, Florence. We're here for you. If there's anything you need, don't hesitate to reach out. I know it's not easy to be back at work so soon after... everything." He paused, allowing Florence to collect herself before continuing. "When you're ready, let's get you up to speed on your new cases." He handed her a sheet of paper. "Here are a list of the cases that have been added to your caseload. Marco Gonzalez's domestic violence case is one of them."

Florence scanned the list, her eyes widening slightly as she saw the cases. At the bottom of the list, she saw "Kevin Vega" with a note that read: "Supporting role only—Ryan Mora lead investigator."

"What's this note about?" Florence asked, her brow furrowed. "I thought Ryan only worked on white-collar crimes."

"His expertise will be useful to this case," Xander said confidently. "In fact, I'd like you to join him on an interview he is having today with Kevin's editor, Alejandro. You'll provide support, but let's keep your involvement behind the scenes for now."

"Let's get him in the office now to discuss how we're going to proceed," Xander suggested. "Alexia," he called, "can you buzz Ryan and get him over here?" Alexia looked up from her screen, then reached out and pressed the intercom button to Ryan's phone line.

In a few moments, the sound of footsteps echoed outside the office door, and Ryan appeared in the doorway.

"Ryan, I just briefed Florence on being a supportive role on her boyfriend's homicide case," Xander explained. "She will be joining you today for your meeting with Alejandro at the Tampa Bay Sun-Times."

Florence caught Ryan's skeptical thoughts about her fragile state, his doubts evident in his expression. As her eyes glowed with an otherworldly red light, Ryan's gaze locked onto hers, his stare piercing and unblinking. Florence felt a flicker of discomfort at the intensity of his gaze, knowing her eyes betrayed her true nature. "I can handle this case," she said firmly, her tone cutting off Ryan's unspoken doubts.

"I never said you couldn't. I am just surprised that—"

"Save it," Florence cut him off, fighting back tears. "This is something I can handle."

Xander nodded in agreement. "I'll let you two get started on this case. I have to get back to court this afternoon." He excused himself from Florence's office.

"Alexia," Florence instructed. "Can you get Alejandro on the line and confirm our appointment with him today?"

"Yes," Alexia replied, leaning forward in her chair. Alexia dialed the number to Tampa Bay Sun-Times. "Hello, Alejandro? This is Alexia from the Hillsborough District Attorney's office. We're confirming our meeting time for today... Yes, 1:00 PM still works for us. Florence and Ryan have some questions they would like to ask you about Kevin Vega."

Alexia paused, listening to Alejandro's response. She looked up at Florence. "Alejandro is mentioning something about some personal items of Kevin that he'd like you to pick up." She offered the phone to Florence, who took it.

Unexpectedly, Florence heard Alejandro's thoughts. *That son of a bitch got what was coming to him.*

Florence's brow furrowed. "I beg your pardon?"

Alejandro cleared his throat. "I didn't say anything yet."

Florence gripped the phone tighter, making the palms of her hands sweaty. "You mentioned to my paralegal that you have some personal items of Kevin that you'd like me to retrieve?"

"Yes, if you don't mind. Though if you happen to find his briefcase or know its whereabouts, would you mind setting it aside for me? He had been working on some stories about Los Maliciosos that I'd still like to see published."

Perhaps the missing pieces of the ruby are in that briefcase, Alejandro thought.

A sense of unease crept over Florence as a vivid image flashed in her mind; a hunter stalking through the forest, eyes glowing with an otherworldly intensity, his companion a majestic wolf with eyes that glowed just as brightly. The wolf's gaze met hers, and for a moment, Florence felt a jolt of primal fear. "Of course, I'll keep an eye out for it. See you this afternoon."

She ended the call abruptly, hanging up on Alejandro without a proper goodbye. Taking a deep breath, Florence composed herself before turning to Ryan. His eyes widened in surprise at the sudden disconnect.

"Have a seat," she instructed Ryan, pointing to an empty chair in front of her desk.

Ryan sat down, pulling out his yellow legal pad and pen to begin jotting down notes. "I've been briefed on the homicide and Xander asked me to investigate Kevin's stories, particularly the one he was working on recently about Los Maliciosos and El Cazador," he said, his eyes scanning the pad.

A flicker of surprise crossed Florence's face as her fingers brushed against the ruby engagement ring. She fidgeted with the ring, her nervousness evident. "You're looking into the

115

journal notes from his investigative work?" she asked, trying to keep her tone neutral.

Ryan nodded, his gaze still on his notes. "From what I've gathered, Kevin had met with one of the members, Jorge, who gave him information about a mystical ruby supposedly holding supernatural powers from the underworld. It is rumored that he had stolen it from them."

Florence's eyes narrowed, her grip on the armrest of her chair tightening. "What makes you think he stole the ruby?" she asked, her voice laced with skepticism.

Ryan's smile faltered for a moment. "Let's just say we have our reasons to believe that's what happened." He glanced back down at his pad, his pen poised over the paper as he continued to jot down notes. "If you know anything, it would be helpful if you could share it with me. I'll find out eventually, anyway. It's just a matter of time."Florence rolled her eyes, unimpressed by his boast. When she made no answer, Ryan glanced at the clock behind Florence's desk. "We should get going. We don't want to be late for our meeting with Alejandro."

Florence stood up, her hands trembling slightly as she smoothed out her clothes. "Let's go."

Ryan stood up, his movements fluid and confident. "I'll drive," he said, his eyes never leaving hers.

Florence followed him out of her office, her heart racing with anticipation.

* * *

The Tampa Bay Sun-Times building looms before her, its sleek glass facade glinting in the sunlight. Palm trees swayed gently in the breeze, their leaves rustling softly. Kevin always loved palm trees, which was why he moved to Florida from New York.

As Florence gazed out at the palm trees, their slender trunks rising like sentinels against the Tampa skyline, a memory washes over her. She was transported back to a sunny afternoon, strolling through the Tampa waterfront alongside Kevin. His bright brown eyes sparkled with excitement as he turned to her, his smile radiant.

"It's like living in summertime every day," he said, his voice filled with wonder. Florence's heart had skipped a beat as she gazed into his eyes, deeply in love with this man who brought so much joy into her life.

"You know," Kevin's eyes crinkled at the corners as he continued, "palm trees were introduced to Florida by the Spaniards back in the 16th century. They brought their own species, like the Paurotis palm and the Royal palm, which eventually thrived here."

Florence giggled, captivated by Kevin's irrepressible enthusiasm. "How do you know all these random facts?" she teased, her eyes never leaving his.

The memory faded, leaving Florence standing outside the Tampa Bay Sun-Times building, the palm trees surrounding her a bittersweet reminder of happier times. Ryan fell into step behind her as she approached the entrance, his eyes scanning the surroundings with quiet intensity. She took a deep breath, steeling herself to face the task ahead: collecting Kevin's belongings from his office. With Ryan at her back, she pushed through the revolving doors and into the building.

When the elevator arrived, Florence stepped in, barely noticing the elevator music playing in the background. Ryan followed her inside, his presence a quiet calm in the small space. When the elevator doors slide open, Florence steps out into the hallway of the thirteenth floor, her gaze drawn to a dark brown wayfinding sign that maps out the labyrinthine office complex, arrows pointing the way to various suites.

"Down the hall and to the right," Ryan said with quiet confidence, navigating the hall without bothering to glance at the signage.

The overhead lights flickered erratically with an out-of-sync rhythm, a stark testament to the building's neglected maintenance. Florence proceeded down the hall, her gaze drawn to the art paintings hanging on both ends, their dusty golden frames still elegant enough to be an accompaniment to the paintings. Together they turned right, the doors to the Tampa Bay Sun-Times office looming large ahead. Ryan reached out to open the door, his gesture gallant as he stepped aside. "After you."

The newsroom buzzed with activity. Florence scanned the room, taking in the rows of cubicles, the journalists hammering away at their keyboards, some shouting across the room. "We're going to blow this story wide open!" one man called.

Others pumped their fists in triumph, their faces alight with excitement. The atmosphere is electric, filled with the thrill of the chase and the promise of a big scoop.Alejandro strode towards them, a warm smile on his face. "Florence, my deepest condolences. I can only imagine how difficult this must be for you." His voice was low and soothing, and he offered his hand in a gesture of sympathy. Florence took it, feeling a brief squeeze of comfort. Alejandro then turned to Ryan, his smile broadening. "Ryan, great to finally put a face to the name. I've heard a lot about your work."

He extended his hand, and Ryan shook it firmly, his handshake confident. "Likewise, Alejandro. It's a pleasure to meet you."

"I'd like to discuss your interview with me further," Alejandro added. "Shall we step into my office? Florence, I've left empty boxes at Kevin's desk for you to gather his personal belongings. Take all the time you need."

The sound of murmured conversations and rustling papers filled the air as coworkers glanced over, their faces somber. Ryan followed Alejandro to his office, the soft hum of the air conditioning and the murmur of their voices fading into the background as Florence walks over to Kevin's desk. The familiar scent of his cologne lingered on the chair, transporting her back to tender memories of their time together.

She recalled walking up behind Kevin on his 30th birthday, just a year ago. Her hands covered his eyes, and she'd whispered, "Guess who?"

Her breath had tickled his ear, and he'd turned around, his face alight with a radiant smile and had swept her into his arms, spinning her around the office. Coworkers' whooping and applause had filled the air, mingling with the sound of ringing phones and rustling papers. His lips had brushed against hers, sending goosebumps rippling across her skin.

The memory faded, leaving Florence standing alone at Kevin's desk. Biting back tears, she began filling the empty boxes with Kevin's personal items: pictures of his parents, their faces warm and loving. Florence's hands moved with deliberate care, each item she packed stirring a memory, but her mind was elsewhere. Her gaze darted across the desk,

119

searching for something that had been nagging at her since she'd started clearing Kevin's belongings. A sense of unease settled in as she noticed a faint disturbance in the usual order of Kevin's workspace. Her eyes locked onto a hidden compartment beneath the desk, and her heart quickened. With a sense of trepidation, she reached in and pulled out the worn leather briefcase, wedged tightly into the narrow space. The one place Kevin would have hidden something precious—or something he wanted to keep hidden. A heavy feeling settled in her chest as she wondered what secrets it might hold, and whether El Cazador was indeed searching for this very same thing.

Crouched under Kevin's desk, Florence was acutely aware of the journalists' curious glances, their whispers carried on the air like a gentle breeze.

"What's she doing under there?" one of them murmured, eyes fixed on her as she methodically gathered Kevin's belongings.

Another journalist leaned in, voice barely audible, "She'd be perfect for our team, meticulous like a detective ensuring every detail is accounted for."

Florence tucked Kevin's camera, flash drives, and recording device into an empty box, carefully concealing the worn leather briefcase beneath them. The metal surface felt cool and impassive beneath her fingers. With her task complete, she stood up, her arm brushing against the mouse, jolting it into action. The computer screen flickered to life, casting an eerie glow over the dimly lit space. Suddenly, the shadows seemed to deepen, as if the very darkness itself was listening, waiting to see what secrets the computer might yield.

The air was thick with curiosity, whispers floating through

the room like wisps of smoke. Nearby journalists leaned in, their thoughts drifting toward her like murmurs in a crowded hallway.

What's she doing? one wondered, eyes fixed on her movements.

Is she legally allowed to look through Kevin's computer as part of the investigation? another journalist speculated.

Her gaze drifted toward the journalist who had wondered about the legality of her search, and their eyes met briefly. She nodded, a hint of a smile playing on her lips. The journalist smiled back, her expression a mix of intrigue and approval. With the brief exchange, she refocused on the task at hand, her fingers poised over the keyboard as the computer screen cast an expectant glow.

"Hmm, no password, Kevin?" she murmured, a hint of surprise in her voice. She paused for a moment, then began to type, the keyboard clicking softly under her fingers. She navigated through his files, her eyes scanning the screen with a mix of curiosity and guilt. One file catches her eye: "Engagement Announcement." Her heart skipped a beat. "He knew I was going to say yes," she muttered as her eyes well up with tears again.

The announcement was beautifully written, with a photo of the two of them together. One sentence in particular stood out to her: *From the moment I met you, Florence, I knew that you were the sunshine that would brighten every day of my life.* Florence's eyes lingered on the words, her mind reeling with memories of their time together. A wave of grief washed over her, followed by a surge of anger and determination. She continued to scroll through Kevin's files until a headline caught her eye: *TOP SECRET: Los Maliciosos.* Her curiosity piqued, Florence read the article, her eyes skimming the screen with growing interest. *El Cazador, the leader of Los Maliciosos, is a mysterious figure shrouded in secrecy. He's known to communicate with his dead sister, named Daisy. His sister is said to guide his actions and decisions. El Cazador also uses rose gold tarot cards to send messages to his victims, often leaving them at the crime scenes. The card seems to be a twisted signature, a calling card that strikes into the hearts of those who dare to oppose him.* Florence's skin crawled as she read on. A dark, grainy photo accompanied the article, but Florence couldn't make out any defining features.

The memory of the tarot card left on Kevin's body flashed back—the Ten of Cups in reverse, its symbolism now ominously clear. Goosebumps prickled on her skin as she grasped the card's significance.

Alejandro opened the door to his office, letting Ryan out. "Thanks for your time, Ryan," he said. Florence looked up, and a familiar image flashed before her eyes—a hunter running through the forest, a wolf racing alongside him, their eyes glowing in the darkness. The wolf's eyes locked onto hers, and her ruby engagement ring began to glow with an intense, fiery light, as if sensing her rising emotions.

11

Chapter Eleven: Elevated Truth

The hum of office equipment and faint scent of fresh coffee filled the air near Kevin's cubicle, where three boxes stacked beside it held the remnants of his life's work. The sound of footsteps echoed through the office, growing louder as Alejandro and Ryan approached Florence, their shoes clicking against the floor in a deliberate cadence that seemed to match the pounding of her heart.

Suspicion clouded her mind, her eyes fixed on Alejandro with an unnerving intensity as the vision of the hunter and wolf continued to haunt her, their glowing gazes still seared into her memory like a branding iron, leaving her skin to prickle with unease. Ryan's gentle smile, warm and reassuring, highlighted a sharp divergence from Alejandro's intense gaze, which seemed to bore into her very soul.

"Hey, need any help with those boxes?" Ryan asked.

Alejandro's gaze, however, took a different path, his eyes drifting to Florence's left hand with an almost imperceptible intensity, lingering on the band of her engagement ring, which was artfully hidden from view by her clever positioning of the ring, the ruby facing inward, a habit she'd developed since her encounter with Los Maliciosos.

"No, thank you. I've got it."

Alejandro's gaze snapped back to the boxes. "What's in there?"

Ryan intervened, his calm and collected tone a steady counterbalance to Alejandro's growing agitation. "Alejandro, remember our discussion about the search warrant? We have Judge Garcia's signature on the document, and we'll proceed with collecting and processing the evidence by the book."

Alejandro's face darkened, his thoughts boiling over like a curse in her mind. *Maldita sea! Los Maliciosos never targeted this office in time.*

Her eyes widened in stunned realization, the truth about Alejandro crashing into place like a puzzle finally complete, her deepest suspicions confirmed. Alejandro's scrutiny was almost tangible, his gaze piercing as his thoughts probed relentlessly about the ruby and the black leather briefcase. Her mental broadcast flickered and shifted, Alejandro's probing thoughts giving way to a disjointed stream of whispers and speculation from the nearby journalists. Snippets of conversation fragmented across her mind like static on a radio dial:

That's Kevin's girlfriend... I heard she got engaged to him the night he was murdered.

Alejandro's still resents Kevin for dumping his sister, another voice chimed in.

Wasn't Kevin a total player? I heard at one point he juggled three girlfriends at once, a third journalist chimed in.

The cacophony of thoughts swirled around her, a maddening blur of sound that made her head spin. She pressed her temples, trying to tune out the chaos, but the journalists' chatter only grew louder, a relentless barrage of speculation and rumor. She gathered the boxes from Kevin's desk, her movements swift and controlled, but her voice strained as she battled to keep her emotions in check. "I'm ready for a break. Let's bring these back to the office."

Ryan stepped in, his eyes crinkling at the corners as he offered to help. For a moment, she hesitated, her hands tightening around the boxes, but calm demeanor reassured her, and she relented, allowing Ryan to take two of the boxes. Her grip remained firm, however, on the box containing Kevin's briefcase, a tangible connection to the task at hand.

"We'll stay in touch," Ryan said as they parted ways with Alejandro.

They walked out of the Tampa Bay Sun-Times office, bathed in the warm, golden light of a newsroom that pulsed with creativity and dedication. The hallway was a different world altogether - dimly lit, with flickering overhead lights that cast uneven, wavering patterns on the walls, which were adorned with post-impressionist masterpieces and Rococo paintings depicting the excesses of the aristocracy. Florence's gaze wandered over the vibrant colors and lush scenes, her eyes lingering on a particularly captivating piece: Jean-Honoré Fragonard's "The Swing". The young woman in the pastel pink dress, her skirts billowing in mid-air, seemed to embody a carefree spirit, unencumbered by the constraints of society. Florence couldn't help but admire the joyful abandon of the subject, her eyes drawn to the whimsical beauty of the painting. Yet, the dim lights seemed to drain the artwork of its usual vibrancy, the masterpieces lost in the shadows, their beauty unappreciated in this drab, forgotten space.

Ryan followed her gaze and nodded in appreciation. "Rococo paintings like these were all about capturing the essence of luxury and elegance in 18th-century Europe," he said, his eyes bright with enthusiasm.

"They represented the carefree, indulgent lifestyle of the aristocracy, didn't they?" Florence replied with a smile as memories of Kevin's fact-filled rants flooded back to her. "You know, Kevin would've loved to see this painting," she said, her smile growing wider. "He'd probably tell us about the symbolism behind every cherub and cloud."

Ryan chuckled, and Florence felt a spark of camaraderie with him. Together they turned toward the elevator, Florence awkwardly shifting the box in her arms to free up a hand to press the down button, her fingers fumbling slightly as she tried to balance the box. The elevator's arrival was announced by a soft ding, followed by the gentle whoosh of the doors sliding open.

An elderly woman, her hair silver and styled in a precise bob, stepped out with a quiet confidence, her thoughts a tangled web of nervous anticipation and preparation for her upcoming interview with Alejandro about the police reports she had bravely made on the whereabouts of Los Maliciosos.

Stay focused, Maria, you've got this... just talk about the facts... don't let him twist your words, Maria thought to herself, her inner voice firm but laced with a hint of vulnerability.

The woman's warm smile enveloped Florence and Ryan as she faced them, her expression a mix of nervousness and determination. "Excuse me, do you by chance know where the Tampa Bay Sun-Times is?" she asked, her words tumbling out. "I have an interview with the editor-in-chief today about a news story he's covering, and I'm running a bit behind schedule."

As Maria spoke, Florence's gaze wandered past her to a little girl standing beside her with an unnerving stillness, as if she had drifted out of the air itself. The child's pigtails and 1950s-style dress seemed almost incongruous with the unnatural calm that surrounded her. There was something unsettling about the girl, a sense that she wasn't quite... alive.

The little girl's gaze locked onto Florence's, and in an electrifying flash, a telepathic connection crackled to life. *My name is Emily, and this is my sister Maria Rodriguez, whom I'm watching over,* the child's voice echoed in Florence's mind. *Her life is in grave danger. She needs your help, Florence.*

Before Florence could process the words, Emily's form began to shimmer and lift, her tiny body floating effortlessly above the floor. Emily's ethereal fingers touched Florence's temples, and a torrent of visions and knowledge flooded her mind; the spirit realm, the role of spirit guides, and the mysteries of the afterlife.

Ryan's gaze flicked between Florence's pale face and Maria, a hint of concern etched on his features as he wondered what had unsettled her so profoundly. "Go down that hall and make a right," he said. "The Tampa Bay Sun-Times is just around the corner."

"Thank you so much," Maria said, her thoughts already racing ahead to the interview, mentally rehearsing her responses. *Alejandro will ask about Los Maliciosos... just stick to the facts... she* thought, nodding a distracted good day to Ryan and Florence.

The woman walked away, Emily gliding silently beside her. They moved down the hallway, lined with an eclectic mix of artwork, until Emily's tiny finger extended, delicately tilting Van Gogh's "Sorrowing Old Man" just a fraction off-center.

The painting shifted on its hook, its melancholy subject seeming to lean in, as if sharing a secret. Maria passed by, and the sudden movement caught her eye; she spun back to see the painting askew, and for a moment, she was frozen in surprise, wondering if she'd imagined it. The familiar contours of the artwork transported her back to her family's old living room, where this very same print had hung on the wall the night her parents took her sister's life. Tears pricked at the corners of her eyes as the memories came flooding back: the sound of her parents' rage, the helplessness, the final, brutal blow that ended Emily's life. A shudder ran through Maria's body. For a moment, she hesitated, her resolve wavering, before she steeled herself and continued on to her meeting with Alejandro. Emily's small form glanced back at Florence with an unnerving intensity before dissolving into thin air.

Florence's skin crawled with unease as she tried to process the bizarre encounter, her mind reeling with questions about the ghostly child and her cryptic warning about her sister.

"Shall we?" Ryan said, his hand sweeping out in a courteous gesture, inviting Florence to step into the now-empty elevator.

The doors slid shut, and Florence jolted, her nerves still frayed from the unsettling encounter with Emily. Ryan, sensing her tension, attempted to ease the atmosphere with small talk. "So, how are Kevin's parents doing?"

Florence's response was terse, her mind still reeling from the ghostly apparition. "They're devastated." Her eyes flashed with irritation, her gaze fixed on some distant point beyond Ryan's shoulder.

She clutched the box with desperate intensity, her eyes brimming with tears as the thought of Kevin's parents learning the truth about his fate seared her heart. Her eyes began to glow red, illuminated by the fiery power of the ruby.

The soft, lilting melody of the "Dance of the Little Swans" floated through the elevator's speakers, an incongruous accompaniment to Florence's turmoil. Her emotions surged, and the ruby erupted into life, its power bursting through her like a torrent of liquid fire. Her hands blazed with a fierce, red glow, the light spilling from her palms like molten lava. Her eyes flashed crimson red, and she shot upward, her body lifting off the ground with a jolt. The box tumbled from her grasp, crashing to the floor with a sickening crunch, Kevin's leather briefcase bursting free. Florence thrashed about, her limbs flailing wildly as she careened off the elevator walls, her awkward, stumbling movements an amusing counterpoint to the delicate music. She was a puppet on a string, out of control, her body bucking like a wild animal. She was mortified that Ryan was witnessing her secret, her face burning with humiliation, as his eyes widened with shock.

"No, no, no!" she screamed, her voice echoing off the metal walls.

Ryan's head jerked upward, his eyes locked on Florence with stunned amazement. "You… you have the stolen ruby, don't you?"

Ryan's accusation sparked a jolt of fear within her and the ruby's power, sensing her turmoil, abruptly withdrew its gift. Just as the music swelled to its final, dramatic notes, Florence plummeted to the floor with a resounding thud, her grand flying debut ending in a graceless splat; more pratfall than pirouette.

12

Chapter Twelve: A New Alliance

The humid wind whipped through their hair as they walked toward Ryan's car. Ryan juggled his keys in one hand, balancing two boxes and Kevin's briefcase on top with the other. He popped open the trunk, carefully depositing the boxes inside, and helped Florence add the third. Ryan's silence spoke volumes, and Florence's anxiety spiked as she wondered if she'd misjudged him. The palm trees surrounding the Tampa Bay Sun-Times building swayed gently, their leaves rustling softly in the breeze, a soothing serenade that contrasted sharply with the turmoil brewing inside her colleague.

"Ryan..." Florence faltered, her words tangled in uncertainty.

He looked up, his gaze piercing, as he opened the back seat of his car to deposit Kevin's briefcase. "You want to tell me your side of things?" he asked, his face a mask of stone, his eyes unreadable.

"It's not what you think," Florence said, her voice low and hesitant.

Ryan's raised eyebrow and outstretched palms invited her to continue, his silence a palpable challenge to explain herself.

"Kevin was going to do a story on Los Maliciosos," Florence said, her words spilling out in a rush. "Alejandro, his editor, shut it down before it ever saw the light of day. Something about not wanting to stir up trouble for the newsroom and compromise everyone's safety."

Ryan's eyes narrowing slightly as he listened, his expression a mixture of skepticism and curiosity, yet Florence could sense him leaning in, willing to believe.

"He had interviewed Jorge, one of the members. But they ended up killing him for revealing too much to Kevin," Florence continued, her voice steady despite the gravity of the topic. "Jorge wanted out, and he was willing to trade information about El Cazador for help escaping this country and returning to Colombia. Kevin told me that on the same night he met with Jorge he broke into Los Maliciosos' meeting place. He witnessed them performing a witchcraft ritual that was invoking spirits from the underworld and they were able to infuse a ruby with mystical powers and supernatural gifts. This ruby was intended for El Cazador." She extended her left hand, revealing the mystical glowing red ruby in the center of her engagement ring. "Kevin knew he couldn't have it and trusted me with it to be its guardian."

"Why you?" Ryan asked. His unspoken thoughts followed, a biting commentary that stung Florence like a slap: *You lack so much confidence in its gifts... it's almost comical.*

Florence's shoulders shrugged in a helpless gesture as she absently twisted her engagement ring, the red ruby flashing in Ryan's direction. "I don't know," she admitted. "Maybe it's because I come from a family with a history of clairvoyant abilities. One of my great-grandmothers was even accused of witchcraft during the Salem witch trials. She was burned at the stake."

Ryan's eyes narrowed further, his curiosity evidently piqued by Florence's revelation. "Clairvoyant? As in... you have family members who can read minds?"

Florence nodded "Yes, I can hear thoughts and interpret visions too. It's gotten stronger since I was given this ruby."

For a moment, Ryan's gaze lingered, and a wave of unease washed over him. "We need to bring the team in on this, and Xander," he said finally, his voice firm.

"No, please don't," Florence pleaded, her voice low and urgent. "No one can know. El Cazador would hunt down anyone with knowledge about this ruby. I was told he even speaks with his deceased sister – who knows what she can reveal to him?"

Ryan's jaw clenched as he contemplated their next steps. "In that case, let me keep Kevin's belongings at my place while you remain the ruby's guardian."

Florence started to object, but Ryan's thoughts reached her first: *I need to help Florence. She's been through too much and she can't fight El Cazador alone."*

"Fine," she agreed. "But please don't reveal anything yet to the team about anything you discover with the contents of Kevin's investigation until you review it with me first."

"Agreed," Ryan said with a smile as he opened the passenger car door for Florence.

"Sorry, I actually have a lunch date in a few minutes with Alexia," she said, a hint of amusement dancing in her voice.

"Oh?" Ryan's eyebrow arched in surprise. "Don't keep her too long, I have a meeting with her today about Los

Maliciosos," he reminded her. Florence flashed a quick smile before turning away, crossing the street toward the cafe.

Ryan took a deep breath, trying to shake off the unease that lingered within him, and settled into the scorching heat of his car. The sun's intense rays seemed to amplify the turmoil that gripped him. His thoughts drifted back to Florence, her determination to uncover the truth about El Cazador and Los Maliciosos burning bright in her eyes. He admired her tenacity, but it was that same fierce spirit that put her squarely in harm's way.

Ryan's gaze lingered on the Tampa Bay Sun-Times building before he pulled out his digital voice recorder. "Meeting with Alejandro," he began, his voice low and methodical. "Discussion of Los Maliciosos' and the alleged ties to El Cazador…" He paused, collecting his thoughts as he continued to speak into the recorder. "Alejandro stated that…"

Suddenly, Alejandro's voice echoed in his mind, and Ryan's words trailed off as he relived the meeting. He sat across from Alejandro in his brightly lit office, surrounded by Tampa Bay memorabilia—a vintage Rays poster of Evan Longoria diving in the air to catch a baseball hung alongside Buccaneers jerseys and Tampa Bay Lightning hockey gear, a testament to Alejandro's city pride. Behind Alejandro's desk, a framed picture of the Sunshine Skyway Bridge stood out, its bright yellow support cables glowing warmly in the sunlight, set against the stunning backdrop of the Tampa Bay's blue waters. Alejandro leaned back in his chair, a subtle smile playing on his lips, his eyes betraying a hint of evasiveness.

"How long had you known Kevin?" Ryan asked, pulling out his notebook and pen. Alejandro's fingers steepled together as he leaned back in his chair, his gaze drifting into the past.

"We met in college, NYU. We were roommates, actually. And we've been friends ever since."

Ryan's eyes widened in surprise. "You were roommates?

Alejandro nodded, a hint of nostalgia giving way to a somber tone. "Yeah, we've been through a lot together. We were always pushing each other, trying to one-up each other with our stories. We were the best of friends until something happened with my sister, Daisy."

"What happened?"

Alejandro's eyes dropped, his voice cracking with a deep-seated resentment. "Kevin dated my sister for three years, but he broke her heart. He told her he wasn't in love with her anymore, and that he had fallen hard for someone else... Florence, actually."

Ryan's gut twisted, a knot of empathy forming as he sensed the raw pain and bitter betrayal that still lingered in Alejandro."What happened after their breakup?"

Alejandro's eyes welled up with tears, his voice cracking as he spoke. "Daisy took her own life. She was devastated by Kevin's rejection... it destroyed her. And she didn't want to live anymore." Alejandro's face contorted in anguish as he suddenly leapt to his feet, his voice rising to a raw, anguished shout. "AND I BLAME KEVIN FOR PUSHING HER TO HER BREAKING POINT!" he thundered, his words echoing through the room.

Ryan's pen paused mid-sentence on his legal pad as he looked up, his expression a mix of shock and concern.Alejandro's intensity dissipated, and he let out a self-deprecating laugh as he smoothed out the wrinkles at the bottom of his shirt, his hands betraying a hint of agitation. He sank back into his chair, his expression sobering. "Things were never the same between us after that."

A deep sadness washed over Ryan, a sense of regret mingling with his empathy. He had been unaware of the depth of Kevin's past or the pain he had inflicted on Alejandro and his family. "I'm so sorry to hear about your sister's suicide, Alejandro." Ryan said. "I had no idea."

Alejandro nodded, his eyes still shining with unshed tears. "It's not something I like to talk about, but I wanted you to know the truth about Kevin and me."

Ryan nodded thoughtfully, his expression somber."I appreciate your honesty, Alejandro. It couldn't have been easy to share that with me. But I have to ask, did Kevin have any other close relationships or alliances that you're aware of, anyone he might have confided in about his investigations on Los Maliciosos?"

Alejandro smirked, eager to answer his question and exploit Kevin's double life. "He had another chick on the side. She's actually your boss's secretary."

"Xander's secretary? Melissa?" Ryan's eyes widened in surprise. He couldn't believe it. Kevin had been cheating on Florence with Melissa, and possibly Daisy as well.

"Do you think Florence knew about Melissa?" Ryan asked, his voice carefully neutral.

Alejandro shook his head. "No, I don't think so. If she did, I'm certain she wouldn't have given him the time of day. He was involved with Melissa even before he met Daisy. He always had this weird fixation with Melissa that never made sense to me."

Ryan's mind reeled, a maelstrom of emotions swirling inside him. A pang of anger towards Kevin mingled with a deep sadness for Florence, whose relationship might have been entirely built on lies. The thought churned in his stomach, making him feel queasy. Taking a deep breath, Ryan struggled to collect himself. "Can you tell me about the last story Kevin was working on?"

Alejandro's expression shifted, and he leaned forward, a hint of nervousness creeping into his voice. "Actually, I assigned Kevin to work on a story about the Tampa Bay Buccaneers. I wanted him to interview their new quarterback for a human-interest piece that would really resonate with our readers." A fleeting smile crossed his face. "I'm convinced Tampa's gonna take the Super Bowl this year."

Baffled, Ryan blinked. "That's the story he was working on?"

Alejandro nodded solemnly. "Yeah, I thought it'd be a great chance for him to showcase his skills."

Ryan's mind was racing, the discrepancy between the expected story and the actual assignment sparking a flurry of questions. "I could have sworn he was investigating a story on Los Maliciosos and El Cazador."

Alejandro's expression darkened, and he leaned back in his chair, a nervous flicker crossing his face. "Where did you hear that from?"

"Just answer the question."

Alejandro's voice rose, laced with indignation. "No, of course not. Why would I approve a story that would compromise the safety of this entire newsroom?He came to me to pitch it, of course, but I didn't want Kevin to pursue that story. I told him it was too dangerous, that it could put him and others at risk. But he wouldn't listen." Alejandro's gaze darted to his clock, the ticking seconds seemingly amplified by the tension in the room. Sweat began to bead above his brow as he shifted uncomfortably in his seat. "I don't mean to rush you out, Ryan, but I have an interview shortly with someone and she'll be here any minute. Is there anything else you need from me?" The abruptness of his gesture seemed to underscore his growing unease.

"Not at this time, but I will let you know if anything comes up."

His memory of the meeting with Alejandro began to fade in the background as Ryan pressed the stop button on his recording device, the click echoing softly in his car.

His gaze fell upon Kevin's sleek black leather briefcase, nestled securely in the backseat of his car. He reached for it, but his fingers stilled as he realized it was locked. A swift scan of his surroundings yielded a paperclip holding together a sheaf of court documents. With a surge of curiosity, Ryan unraveled the clip and set to work on picking the lock. Five minutes of precise manipulation later, the wafer lock yielded, and the briefcase creaked open. Inside, stacks of papers, photographs, and notes spilled out, revealing the tangible remnants of Kevin's final investigation.

The first few pages revealed cryptic notes on Los Maliciosos and El Cazador, but it was the photographs that seized his attention. Grainy images of an abandoned warehouse on Broadway depicted shadowy figures, their faces obscured, yet Ryan's instincts screamed that these were members of Los Maliciosos. The photos seemed to hint at something bigger, something hidden beneath the surface. The next photograph that made Ryan's heart skip a beat—an obscured snapshot of a man in a suit stepping out of a car, the image grainy and distorted, as if ripped from a surveillance video. Ryan's eyes narrowed as he studied the photo; though the man's face was indistinct, his tailored suit and confident demeanor spoke of wealth and power. The setting was unmistakable—the abandoned warehouse on Broadway—and Ryan's gut told him this man was El Cazador.

Ryan's thoughts turned to Kevin's cryptic notes, which he'd been poring over in search of a lead. One entry in particular sent a shiver down his spine: *El Cazador seeks guidance from his dead sister, and she reveals to him who will betray him...or rather, who his next victim will be.* The words resonated uncomfortably with the conversation he'd just had with Florence, and Ryan's mind began to piece together the disturbing connections.

His expression darkened as the true nature of El Cazador's relationship with his sister began to take shape.Kevin's hand-written notes revealed the sister's name: *Daisy.* A chill ran down Ryan's arms as he fixated on the implication—a dead woman, Daisy, allegedly feeding El Cazador intel that led him to his next victims. The thought sent a shiver through him, the coincidences between Alejandro and El Cazador suddenly taking on a sinister life of their own.

Ryan skimmed Kevin's notes, and the cryptic tarot messages left at the crime scenes emerged as a crucial part of the puzzle. The Eight of Swords, the Knight of Cups... each card seemed to whisper a hidden truth, a thread waiting to be pulled. Kevin's research suggested that El Cazador was using these tarot cards to convey a message. Ryan stepped out of his car and opened the trunk, searching through the boxes for any relevant materials. After a few moments of rifling, he spotted a flash drive. He grabbed it and jumped back into his car, plugging the drive into his laptop. As the files loaded, Ryan's eyes homed in on a suspicious folder labeled "Erebus". Ryan's heart beat faster as he realized this could be the break he needed.

He typed "Erebus" into his notes, his mind racing with connections. A college lecture on Greek mythology came flooding back—Erebus was the personification of darkness and shadow. The association sent a shiver down his spine; why would El Cazador choose this name?

A recent briefing flashed back to him—a new strain of malware dubbed "Erebus" was on the loose, a sophisticated program that allowed hackers to create "dark" networks, invisible to law enforcement. The connection was too coincidental to ignore; El Cazador might be using Erebus to stay one step ahead of the law, hiding his digital tracks in the shadows.

Ryan's gaze returned to the picture of El Cazador, and as he flipped it over, a Ziploc bag slipped onto his lap. It had been taped to the back of the photo, hidden from view. Inside the bag, fragments of red rubies glowed like embers, eerily similar to the ruby in Florence's engagement ring.A small post-it note on the Ziploc bag bore the same handwriting as before, the words "remnants of ruby" scrawled in a hasty script. Ryan's gaze lingered on the bag's contents, and a shiver ran down his spine as he felt an unsettling connection to the ruby fragments. They seemed to radiate a strange, almost palpable energy, as if the gemstones were imbued with a power that defied explanation.

Ryan stared at the fragments, feeling an inexplicable pull toward them.He was a prosecutor, not a superhero, but something about them told him he couldn't ignore this for long.He carefully placed the Ziploc bag back in the briefcase, his mind racing with questions. Why had Kevin decided to keep fragments of the ruby? And why had he made it into an engagement ring for Florence, knowing full well that he had been unfaithful to her?

Ryan started the car and pulled out of the parking lot, cold with the realization that he'd stumbled into something far more sinister than he'd ever imagined. *Xander doesn't need to be briefed on this just yet,* he thought. "I'm not sure what your game is, El Cazador, but I'm on to you."

He pulled up to the bus stop in front of the parking lot's exit, where Maria Rodriguez sat down on the weathered bench, fanning herself with a traditional Spanish abanico, its leather pieces sewn at the edges with lace and adorned with a drawing of the city of Madrid, a souvenir from a recent trip that had left her enchanted. She gazed wistfully at the fan, her thoughts drifting to the narrow streets and vibrant plazas she had walked through last Christmas, and the fleeting thought of starting anew in that storied city crossed her mind, a respite from the growing unease that had taken hold in Tampa. Maria's gaze remained steady, following the group of men walking towards her from across the parking lot, a flicker of wariness crossing her face. They were Latino, their faces chiseled, their eyes fixed on Maria with an unnerving interest, each wearing a black leather jacket with a scorpion emblem emblazoned on the back. The men approached the bus stop and sat down next to her, their movements eerily synchronized, their gazes lingering on her frail frame. Maria shifted uncomfortably on the bench, her eyes darting towards the approaching bus, a mix of relief and unease crossing her face as she adjusted her position, her unease growing as the eight men, muttering in hushed Spanish tones, closed in around her, their words unmistakable to her experienced ears; she knew the tone, the cadence, the warning signs, and she instinctively knew they were members of Los Maliciosos.

Meanwhile, Alejandro's gaze pierced down through his office window, his eyes scanning the scene below, monitoring Ryan's car and Maria's fragile form at the bus stop with another, his cellphone pressed to his ear as he whispered into the receiver, tracking their every move.

13

Chapter Thirteen: The Silent Partner

Florence's mind raced as she approached the cafe, the aroma of freshly roasted coffee beans enveloping her, mingling with the sweet scent of French vanilla and the savory smell of freshly baked bread. She slipped on her headphones and pressed play on her favorite playlist, letting the soothing jazz music wash over her.The noise of the city, the conversations between passersby, and the constant barrage of thoughts from those around her begin to fade into the background as the music took center stage. The melodies and harmonies created a shield, protecting her from the overwhelming cacophony of thoughts that threaten to consume her.Music might be the key to silencing the constant noise in her mind that has become stronger in the week she has been wearing the ruby, and she made a mental note to explore this newfound discovery further.

With a newfound sense of calm, Florence pushed open the door to the coffee shop and stepped inside. The cozy atmosphere surrounds her as she spotted Alexia already seated at a small table by the window, typing away on her laptop.

Florence waited in line to order, her excitement and nervousness about the meeting with Alexia simmering just below the surface. She mentally prepared to broach the topic of the Los Maliciosos investigation, eager to tap into Alexia's expertise and gain valuable insight. Though Florence would play only a supporting role in Kevin's homicide case, her determination to see justice served drove her to dig deeper, ensuring every detail of the incident is scrutinized. Alexia's perspective could be the key to unlocking crucial information.

With her order in hand—a freshly brewed coffee and a warm, flaky croissant—Florence joined Alexia at the table. Her paralegal was already savoring her lunch, the soft glow of her laptop screen illuminating her face. Florence smiled as she set down her coffee and pastry, ready to discuss the case with Alexia.

"Hey, thanks for meeting me here," Florence said, setting her order down on the small table.

"Of course, Florence. How are you? I'm happy to see you back in the office." She took a sip of her steaming chai, the warm spices of cinnamon and ginger rising up with the fragrant tea, complementing the coffee shop's rich aromas.

"I won't sugarcoat it," Florence said, her voice low and measured, as she glances around the coffee shop,scanning the crowded room to ensure no one is listening in. Satisfied that their conversation is private, she leaned in slightly. "This grief is taking me back to when my parents were killed in a car accident,a tragedy that felt eerily similar to this one, where I was powerless to stop it. There was nothing I could've done to save them." Tears welled up in her eyes, and her ruby engagement ring pulsed with an inner fire, casting a fiery glow on her fingers as her emotions intensified.

Alexia's face went rigid, her gaze locked onto Florence's as she stared, transfixed. "Your eyes! They're... glowing red!" she stammered, her voice trembling with a mix of fear and awe, the words barely escaping her lips.

Florence's expression faltered for a moment before she forced a fragile smile. "Just the aftermath of tears, I'm afraid," she said quickly. "I've been crying all day." Before Florence could weigh the risks of revealing her secrets, Alexia's thoughts flooded her mind, a jumble of self-doubt and determination. *I hope I'm good enough for her, that I can really make a difference in this case. I'm just a paralegal, barely scraping by... and that LSAT, ugh, I'm just not smart enough. What if I mess up? What if I'm not good enough to help her take down El Cazador and Los Maliciosos? I want to see her in court, putting those monsters away for life... but what if I'm the one who screws it up? What if I'm stuck in this role forever, always feeling like a fake, like I'm just pretending to be something I'm not?*

Florence reached out and gently clasped Alexia's hands in hers. "You are an intelligent and capable young woman, Alexia," she said, her voice filled with sincerity. "I need your sharp mind and expertise to help me take down El Cazador and Los Maliciosos. Your skills as a paralegal will be invaluable in this case."

Alexia's face lit up with a radiant smile, her eyes shining with gratitude. "It would be my privilege to help you," she said, her voice filled with conviction.

"So, what have you uncovered about this ruthless organization?"

Alexia settled back into her chair, cradling her cup of chai, and took a sip before launching into her report. Her half-eaten tartine, fragrant with the scent of turkey and tomatoes, sat on the plate, momentarily forgotten. "Los Maliciosos is a mysterious organization that's been linked to several high-profile homicides and crimes in Tampa," she began, her voice steady and professional. "They're known for leaving tarot cards at each crime scene. And the fact that they're using the name Los Maliciosos, which translates to 'the evil ones' in Spanish, implies they're embracing their dark nature."

"That makes sense," Florence said, her mind racing with the implications. "And El Cazador translates to 'the hunter'." She leaned in, her voice taking on a more intense tone. "I think we're dealing with a group that sees themselves as predators, stalking their prey with precision and calculation. It's a chilling thought, but it would explain the calculated brutality of their crimes."

"I think you're right. The tarot cards they leave behind are more than just a signature – they're a deliberate message." Alexia pulled out a folder filled with her research, handing Florence a series of photos depicting rose gold tarot cards found at various crime scenes in Tampa, most of which predated Kevin's homicide. Florence's gaze lingered on the images. She took a deep breath, her thoughts racing with possibilities, as she prepared to dive deeper into the mystery.

"The tarot cards they've been leaving behind are from a specific deck, each with its own distinct symbolism," Alexia explained, her finger tracing the intricate design on the rose gold card. "Take this one, for example," she said, pointing to the image of a man in a wife beater shirt, the Tower Card prominently displayed on his chest. "The victim had a documented history of child abuse and neglect, having been previously convicted of mistreating his own children. When I researched the meaning of the Tower Card, I discovered it represents upheaval, chaos, and sudden change—a theme that seems to mirror the turmoil he had inflicted on his own children."

Florence shook her head emphatically as she dismissed Alexia's theory. "I don't think the tarot card was meant for the victim's eyes," she said, her voice low and thoughtful. "El Cazador is leaving these messages for someone else entirely.A deliberate signal to the authorities, perhaps, or even a rival gang."

Alexia's eyes widened in surprise, her curiosity piqued. "Really? You think El Cazador is sending these messages to law enforcement?" She raised an eyebrow, skeptical. "I doubt it's the other gangs in Tampa. Los Maliciosos has all but decimated them. Since they rose to power, the city has seen a decline in reports of drug trafficking and burglaries from other gangs, but reports linked to Los Maliciosos have persisted, marked by the distinctive rose gold tarot cards."

"We need to get to the bottom of this," Florence said, her eyes scanning the documents as she took a bite of her flaky croissant. She flipped through the next page of Alexia's notes, her expression thoughtful as she sensed the unease growing within Alexia, her gaze holding steady."Does witchcraft bother you?"

"A little," Alexia admitted. "I was raised Catholic, and the teachings about witchcraft being a doorway to darkness and evil have stuck with me. My mom would always warn me about dabbling in the occult, saying it was an invitation for the devil and his demons to take hold."

"That's a common fear," Florence said, her smile gentle. "Witchcraft is complex, often shrouded in misconceptions and tied to deep-seated fears about power and authority." She took a sip of her coffee, her eyes clouding for a moment before she continued, "I had a great-grandmother who was burned at the stake during the Salem witch trials. Her story's been passed down through generations in my family."

"That's horrific," Alexia said, pressing one hand to her mouth. "The Salem witch trials were a dark time in history. I'm so sorry your family had to go through that."

"My family believes the townspeople acted out of fear and ignorance, fueled by the religious leaders' lust for power and control. You should look into the history of witchcraft. I think you'll find it's far more nuanced than most people realize, and it might just change your perspective."

Florence turned the page, her gaze falling on the haunting image of the Ten of Cups. The photo seemed to leap off the page, but it was the crimson stains on its corners—Kevin's blood—that made her breath catch. Tears pricked at the corners of her eyes, and for a moment, her irises blazed with a fierce, otherworldly red, like embers igniting in the darkness.

Alexia noticed the intensity in her eyes as she asked, "Are you a witch?"

Florence's expression softened, and she shook her head. "No, I'm not a witch," she said, her tone measured. For a moment, she hesitated, weighing the risks and benefits of revealing her secret. Then, with a deep breath, she made her decision. "But there's something else you should know about me, Alexia."

Florence's fingers cradled the photo of the Ten of Cups, her gaze lingering on the image as she began to speak. "This card, the one Los Maliciosos left on Kevin, typically represents ultimate fulfillment and happiness – a utopian dream, really." Her eyes met Alexia's, a hint of gravity in her tone. "But when it appears in the reversed position, the meaning shifts dramatically. It can signify the opposite: unhappiness, discontentment, even betrayal."

Alexia's gaze held Florence's, a furrow creasing her brow as confusion clouded her expression. "I see," she said slowly, her voice laced with skepticism as she thought to herself, *"But what does this have to do with your eyes glowing red?"* She shifted in her seat as she said aloud, "Los Maliciosos are now angrier than ever. Xander briefed the team last Friday about a mystical ruby being stolen from them. He mentioned that their attacks may become more brutal until it's found. He asked us to notify him of any leads immediately so he can work with the Tampa police department to stop any future attacks."

Florence's throat constricted as she struggled to find her voice. "The night Kevin was murdered, he proposed to me with this ring." Alexia's expression softened, her eyes filling with sympathy. Florence lifted her left hand, and the red ruby erupted into a fiery, mystical glow on her finger. "I have the ruby," Florence said.

Stunned, Alexia immediately replied, "We must tell Xander you have it." "No!" Florence replied. "Not yet, at least. Can you imagine the danger it would put the entire office in?" Alexia nodded in response, then added, "But what if they kill more innocent people over it?"

"That's why we have to stop them," Florence replied, her gaze falling to her ring, its beauty captivating, yet she knew the ruby at its center could cost more lives. "Kevin had it custom-cut into a pear shape for our engagement ring," she said, her voice tinged with a mix of sadness and reverence. "Los Maliciosos created this ruby, infusing it with supernatural forces from the underworld, but it was meant for their leader, El Cazador. Kevin stole it to give to me because he knew someone like him couldn't be its guardian."

Alexia's eyes sparkled with interest, her gaze intense. "So El Cazador can be all powerful if he harnesses the ruby's energy," she said, her voice filled with a mix of fascination and trepidation.

Florence nodded, a somber expression settling on her face. "Yes, and that's why Kevin was a threat. He was writing a paper on Los Maliciosos, digging deep into their inner workings and planning to expose El Cazador's true identity. He planned to publish his story in the Tampa Bay Sun-Times…but Los Maliciosos silenced him before he could."

Florence felt a sense of trust begin to unfurl within her, like a tentative bloom. Alexia's kind eyes and gentle demeanor had a calming effect, making Florence feel like she was sharing secrets with an old friend. "I think I can trust you, Alexia," Florence said, her voice low and sincere. "I need to tell you something, but you have to promise not to tell anyone."

Alexia's expression turned solemn, her eyes locking onto Florence's. "I promise, Florence. What is it?"

Florence took a deep breath, the words spilling out like a confession."When Kevin gave me this ring, things started happening. I can hear people's thoughts, sense things before they happen…and I think I can fly. This ring is giving me supernatural abilities."

Alexia's gaze remained steady, her voice gentle. "Does anyone else know about this?"

"Just Ryan…he found out accidentally today but I asked for his discretion for the time being. And I'd appreciate it if you and Ryan can both keep it that way."

As Alexia nodded, her attention seemed to shift, her gaze drifting to the photos on the table while her eyes began tracing the intricate design on the back of the tarot cards. "I've been studying these symbols, and I have to say, it's stunning," she said, her voice filled with admiration. "The red six-pointed star, the circle, and crescent moon all blend together in a beautiful pattern. Whoever chose this card has a keen eye for detail and artistry." Florence's eyes widened as she took the photos from Alexia, her fingers brushing against Alexia's as she examined the images more closely.

"The symbols on the back of the card are rich with meaning," Alexia said, her eyes scanning the images. "The red six-pointed star, or Seal of Solomon, represents the perfect balance between opposing forces—a harmony of duality. The red circle and crescent moon on either side of the star symbolize the eternal dance between feminine and masculine principles, or the cycles of life and death. The red symbols at the top and bottom of the star likely represent spiritual growth, protection, and the connection between heaven and earth – a bridge between the material and spiritual realms."Alexia's gaze met Florence's, her expression thoughtful. "And the intricate silver design surrounding the central image…that's a web of interconnectedness, a reminder that every thread is linked, every cycle repeats. It's a beautiful representation of the cyclical nature of life."

"Someone's been doing their homework," Florence said, her tone laced with genuine admiration."I think we're just starting to uncover what Los Maliciosos is capable of." "This could be a key to identifying El Cazador" she added, her voice filled with excitement."Someone who appreciates art and beauty, but also harbors a darker side. And this balance between feminine and masculine principles… Kevin mentioned that El Cazador communicates with his dead sister, Daisy. The crescent moon might symbolize El Cazador's emotional vulnerability, his deep sense of loss, and the nurturing qualities he associates with her." Florence's thoughts spilled out in a rapid flow. "The Seal of Solomon could represent the harmony between opposites, the balance between light and darkness, and the connection between the spiritual and material realms. It's all about unity and balance, the conscious and subconscious, the macrocosm and microcosm."

Alexia's fingers flew across her phone screen as she Googled the Seal of Solomon, her eyes scanning the search results for any relevant information. She paused at the image of a ring. "The Seal of Solomon was a signet ring, a magical object that granted King Solomon power over demons, spirits, and animals. I wonder if Kevin's decision to set the ruby in an engagement ring was more than just a coincidence."

Florence's lips curled into a wistful smile as she thought of Kevin. "I'm sure he did it on purpose. He loved weaving history into his everyday life."

Alexia's smile mirrored Florence's as she shared a memory of Kevin. Her gaze drifted back to the tarot card, her eyes narrowing as she studied the red circle and crescent moon. "What do you make of these symbols?"

Florence's gaze fell upon the symbols, her expression contemplative."They represent the union of opposites, the balance between light and darkness, or the harmony between the conscious and subconscious. The intricate silver design surrounding the central image signifies the interconnectedness of all things – the web of life, the complexity of the human psyche.Given El Cazador's role as the leader of Los

Maliciosos, the masculine principle embodied by the red circle might symbolize his drive for control and assertiveness, but also his struggle to balance his emotional and rational sides." Florence's eyes seemed to bore into the symbols, as if searching for hidden meaning."The Seal of Solomon's representation of balance and harmony could indicate El Cazador's attempt to reconcile his dual identities, but also his struggle to maintain equilibrium between his light and dark sides.I think we're dealing with a sophisticated and calculating individual. The fact that their leader is using tarot cards to leave messages suggests that he's trying to convey a specific message."

"What do you think that message is?" Alexia asked.

Florence hesitated, her brow furrowed in thought. "I think it's a warning—a message that we're being hunted, that our transgressions won't go unpunished. So far, everyone who has received a tarot card has been killed. The message isn't for the victim, but for someone else entirely. Who was the last victim of Los Maliciosos?"

"Ricardo Morales," Alexia replied, her eyes scanning the notes on her computer. "He owned that jewelry store on Main Street."

"What tarot card did they use for him?"

Alexia's expression turned somber."According to the police reports of Sergeant Lopez and Detective Martin, Los Maliciosos used the High Priestess tarot card. It was found sealed in his mouth."

"The High Priestess is a card of secrecy and silence," Florence said. "It's often associated with the subconscious mind and the world of intuition. In this context, it's clear that Los Maliciosos sent a message – silencing him was their goal."

A vision flashed in Florence's mind: Ricardo working on her engagement ring, his eyes sparkling with intrigue as he carefully placed the ruby in the center. "Ricardo was the jeweler who prepared my engagement ring," she said, her fingers absently tracing the band.

Alexia's eyebrow arched. "How do you know that for sure?"

"Because I'm psychic."

Alexia smiled at her response.

"I think Ricardo knew too much, and Los Maliciosos killed him to silence him."

Alexia's gaze drifted to her watch, her eyes narrowing slightly as she calculated the time. "I should get going. I need to head back to the office to meet with Ryan."

"Of course. I'll join you – I need a ride anyway."

They stepped out of the coffee shop, the bright sunlight slapping them with its intensity. Florence notices Ryan's car pulling out of the parking lot across the street, its tires screeching slightly. Suddenly, the air seems to ripple and distort, and Emily materializes in front of her.

The little girl's presence is unnerving, her small face pinched with worry, her eyes wide with a deep concern.Without a word, Emily floats across the street, her tiny hand outstretched, and touches Florence's temples once more, filling her thoughts with telepathic words. Florence's mind becomes flooded with the urgent message: *"El Cazador just sent a death warrant for my sister. Ayudala - help her!"* Florence's feet seem rooted to the spot, her eyes fixed on Emily's ethereal form.

Alexia turns to her, concern etched on her face. "Everything alright?" she asks, her voice low and cautious.

Florence's gaze doesn't waver, her focus still on Emily's ghostly figure. Ryan's car turns right, and Florence's attention shifts to the bus pulling up to the stop. Maria Rodriguez steps in, followed by eight men in leather jackets, their faces cold and menacing. "Go to your meeting with Ryan," Florence instructs Alexia, her voice firm and resolute. "There's something I need to take care of."

14

Chapter Fourteen: The Seal of Solomon

Ryan and Alexia sat in the conference room, surrounded by stacks of files and notes that covered nearly every inch of the table. The fluorescent lights hummed overhead, casting an eerie glow on the pair as they prepared to dissect the case.

"Alright, let's get started," Ryan said, nodding at Alexia. "What have you got on Los Maliciosos and El Cazador?"

Alexia flipped through her meticulously organized notes. "From what Florence and I found, Los Maliciosos is a relatively new gang, but they're making a name for themselves with their brutality. El Cazador—the hunter, in Spanish—is their enigmatic leader, and it seems he's the one orchestrating their calculated moves."

Ryan scribbled some notes on his pad, his brow furrowed in thought. "I wonder what he's hunting for?"

Alexia shrugged, her gaze drifting to the files. "Many of the past victims were individuals who got off lightly on charges like rape, domestic violence, and even involuntary manslaughter. I cross-referenced their files with ours, and it appears we prosecuted all of these cases. My theory is El Cazador is hunting for justice, taking the law into his own hands and targeting those he believes escaped accountability."

"And what about the tarot cards? Any leads on those?"

Alexia nodded. "We've found that the cards are sometimes left at the crime scenes upright, sometimes reversed. It's like they're trying to convey a specific message."

The door swung open, and Xander strode in wearing his favorite pin striped Armani suit, a telltale sign that he was heading to trial later that day. "What's the latest on El Cazador?" he demanded.

"We're still working on it, Xander," Ryan said. "But we did find some interesting connections between the tarot cards and -"

Xander interrupted him , his face reddening."Tarot cards? That isn't new information. You're wasting time. We need to find out where their stolen ruby is. If you don't find anything by the end of the week, I will take you both off this case and find someone else who can handle it. Understood?"Xander stormed out of the conference room, his anger hanging in the air like a challenge.

Ryan let out a deep breath, frustration etched on his face. "Well, that was fun."

Alexia raised an eyebrow. "Damn. What's going on with him?"

"I know he's been pretty upset about Kevin's murder. And… and…" Ryan hesitated as he looked up at Alexia.

"What is it? What are you not telling me?" Ryan took a deep breath. "Melissa was having an affair with Kevin while he was still with Florence. I think Xander knew."

Alexia gasped, covering her mouth in shock. "Does Florence

know?"

"I'm not sure. I don't want to get involved but I suspect that is why Melissa took time off work when we all learned about the murder. I know one thing, though…" Ryan said, pulling out Kevin's briefcase. "I'm not giving Xander Kevin's briefcase until I can trust him with it."

"And why is that?" Alexia questioned.

"There's some things I need to look into first." he replied.

"About Florence's abilities?" she asked.

A smirk crossed his face. "She told you?" he asked.

"She trusts us with her secret and wants to keep this between us, for now at least."

The tension in the room was palpable as Ryan leaned back into his chair, his expression contemplative. "That doesn't give us much time. El Cazador will soon know if he doesn't already that she has his ruby and will hunt her down for it." He paused, collecting his thoughts before continuing,"I did learn something interesting in a recent briefing, though. There's a program called Erebus that allows hackers to create dark networks invisible to law enforcement. I'm going to look into it, see if I can find any connections to El Cazador."

Alexia's interest was piqued. "Really? How does it work?"

"From what I've gathered, Erebus is a sophisticated tool that enables users to create encrypted networks that are extremely difficult to track. If El Cazador is using it, it could explain how he's been able to stay one step ahead of us." He paused, shifting gears. "All we have right now that we can track are those tarot cards he's leaving behind. What else have you found about those cards?"

Alexia pulled out a photo of the rose gold tarot cards from the deck used by Los Maliciosos. "The symbols on the back are really elegant—a six-pointed star, a red circle, and a crescent moon," she said, her fingers tracing the intricate designs. "I think he specifically chose this tarot deck on purpose. Almost as if it resonates with him in some way."

Ryan's eyes narrowed as he studied the photo. "The six-pointed star looks familiar."

Alexia's face lit up with a smile. "It's the Seal of Solomon. But I don't remember reading about the Seal of Solomon in the Bible."

Ryan shook his head. "It wouldn't be in the Bible. Its roots lie in Jewish mystical tradition, in texts like the Testament of Solomon. It's a legendary signet ring said to have been possessed by King Solomon. It's believed to have given him the power to command and control various supernatural entities."

"What kind of entities?"

"Genni, for one. In Jewish mythology and Islamic tradition, genni are supernatural beings created from smokeless fire. They can be benevolent or malevolent."

Alexia's brow furrowed in concentration. "Like demons?"

"Similar, but not exactly. Genni are believed to have free will, whereas demons are often seen as purely malevolent spirits. The Seal of Solomon was said to have been engraved with the Tetragrammaton—the four Hebrew letters YHVH, representing the name of God—and was set in a gemstone, a ruby."Ryan's eyes lit up as the pieces fell into place. "That's it!" he exclaimed. "The Seal of Solomon was said to have been a powerful tool for King Solomon to maintain balance and order in his kingdom. El Cazador, as the leader of Los Maliciosos, might be seeking to do the same in Tampa if he's hunting down criminals who got off on technicalities."

"Wait, you think El Cazador was trying to use the ruby's

power to control the city?"

Ryan's expression turned grave. "I think it's possible. And if that's the case, we need to protect Florence. Her life is in danger now that she has the ruby."

"El Cazador will stop at nothing to get his ruby back. We have to make sure Florence is safe." Alexia's jaw clenched in determination. "I'll take care of Florence, Ryan. I'll prepare her for what's coming and make sure she's protected."

Ryan nodded, trusting Alexia's dedication to Florence. The tension hung in the air, broken only by the shrill ring of Ryan's phone. He glanced at the screen, his eyes widening as he saw Florence's name flashing.

"Hey, what's up?" he answered, his tone light, but his expression shifted to one of alarm as he listened. Florence's panicked voice was barely audible over the sound of crackling flames and the distant wail of fire truck horns blaring in the background, the cacophony of honking growing louder as the emergency responders closed in.

15

Chapter Fifteen: Smoke and Shadows

Emily's gaze floated back through the bus window, landing on her sister Maria, pinned to her seat by the looming presence of Los Maliciosos members, their eyes fixed on her with an unnerving intensity. The worn muffler let out a steady rumble, spewing out a cloud of dirty exhaust smoke that lingered in the air. Seconds ticked by in slow motion before the bus disappeared into the chaotic traffic, leaving Florence feeling even more anxious. She took a deep breath, the familiar surge of anxiety coursing through her veins. She focused on the ruby and its mystical power, but her anxiety seemed to create a discordant resonance that blocked the gemstone's energy, silencing the gift of flight within her. The ruby's gift lay dormant, its power unresponsive to her will.

Frantically, Florence tried to visualize herself soaring through the air, effortless and free, her spirit unencumbered by the weight of her doubts. But her feet remained stubbornly grounded, refusing to leave the pavement. The ruby pulsed softly in response to her desperation, but the gift of flight remained tantalizingly elusive. Anxiety continued to build, sweat forming on her forehead as the seconds ticked away. She couldn't tap into the ruby's energy, and time was running out to catch up to the bus, much less figure out where Maria was headed. Florence's frustration grew, fueled by her own helplessness. Why wasn't it working? She had floated before on a whim, without effort or intent, but now, when her need was greatest, the gift seemed to have abandoned her, leaving her stuck in a frustrating reality.

Self-doubt crept in, whispering cruel truths about her inadequacy, telling her she wasn't good enough, that she would never master her gifts. A vision of flames suddenly flashed before her mind's eye, seared into her consciousness by the image of a street sign emblazoned with the word *Broadway*.

"I know where she's heading," Florence muttered to herself, a surge of confidence coursing through her veins.

With a flourish, she raised her arms toward the heavens, the ruby in her engagement ring glinting in the sunlight. She pictured herself soaring through the skies, a superhero for Tampa, with trumpets blaring a heroic theme and a soundtrack swelling with pounding drums and soaring strings. But instead of soaring into the air, she remained firmly planted on the sidewalk, arms still raised in a gesture of triumph. The patrons of the nearby coffee shop burst out laughing, and passersby couldn't help but stare at the spectacle. A newspaper on the ground near her feet suddenly caught a gust of wind and took flight, soaring through the air with effortless ease. Florence's eyes widened in dismay, her failed attempt at flight mocked by the flying newspaper. It seemed that inanimate objects had better aerodynamic skills than she did.

Florence made one last attempt at flight, raising her left arm toward the sky while keeping her right arm firmly planted at her side, a compromise between dignity and desperation. Just as she struck her heroic pose, a taxi screeched to a halt beside her, its tires mocking her aerial ambitions with a loud, sarcastic squeal.

"You look like you need a ride?" the taxi driver said, his grin stretching from ear to ear like he was privy to a joke Florence didn't know she was in on.

Florence's confidence deflated like a punctured balloon, and she nodded sheepishly, climbing into the backseat with all the dignity of a deflated superhero. "Broadway, please," she instructed, trying to salvage what was left of her pride while wondering if she'd just become the main attraction in a public spectacle.

The driver chuckled, clearly entertained, and pulled into traffic.

Florence smirked at the driver as the taxi lurched into motion, merging into traffic. Her gaze drifted to the ruby on her engagement ring, its fiery glow still illuminating. She turned the band of the engagement ring around on her finger, frustration simmering just below the surface. Why wasn't the ruby responding to her need? She had counted on its power to help her catch up to Maria, but now she was stuck in a taxi, crawling through traffic. The taxi's slow pace was agonizing, and Florence's eyes dropped to her phone. She stared at the wallpaper on the screen, a picture of her and Kevin in last year's Halloween costumes. Kevin was dressed as Zorro, his mask and cape a perfect fit, and she was dressed as Elena, her elaborate gown and beauty mark a testament to her love of Spanish culture. For a moment, she let her gaze linger on Zorro's masked face, a fleeting sense of admiration for the heroic figure she aspired to become someday. She glanced

162

at the time on her phone, her anxiety spiking as the minutes ticked by. Every second counted— Maria's life was in danger, and Florence needed to get to Broadway as fast as possible. The roadwork ahead seemed to be stretching on forever, the taxi inching forward at a glacial pace.

A flashback hit her, the elevator, Maria's worried face, and the ghostly figure of Emily standing beside her, pleading for help. The memory sparked a chain reaction in Florence's mind. Maria had mentioned a meeting with the editor-in-chief of the Tampa Bay Sun-Times: Alejandro, the man who already had a vendetta against Kevin because he blamed him for his sister Daisy's suicide. The coincidence of his sister's name was stark. El Cazador, the leader of Los Maliciosos, was known to communicate with his dead sister Daisy.

Alejandro is El Cazador. How had she not seen this before?

The taxi driver's gaze flicked up to the rear-view mirror, his eyes meeting hers for a brief moment. Florence felt a jolt of awareness, realizing she'd been lost in thought. She caught the hint of curiosity in his expression and quickly composed herself, adopting a more neutral demeanor despite the turmoil brewing inside her.

The taxi turned right onto Broadway, and a thick cloud of acrid smoke enveloped them, choking the air with the pungent smell of charred wood, burning plastic, and electrical wiring. The driver coughed, covering his mouth with his shirt as the smoke stung his eyes. "Wow, what's going on here?" he exclaimed, squinting through the haze.

Florence's eyes widened in horror as flames engulfed the apartment complex, which stood directly across the street from the abandoned warehouse. She noted the proximity, sensing it might be more than just a coincidence. "Call 911," she instructed, already opening the door and handing the driver a wad of cash. "Keep the change," she added, before leaping out of the taxi and sprinting toward the burning building, the heat and smoke swirling around her like a vortex.

The sight before her made her heart plummet. Across the street, a sleek black cat sat like a dark statue, its piercing green eyes fixed on the abandoned warehouse. When Florence's gaze met the cat's, it let out a low, menacing meow, as if warning her away from some unseen truth. The cat's eyes seemed to bore into hers, cold and calculating, before it returned to watching the burning apartment complex with an air of detached interest. The flames devoured the upper floors, casting a hellish glow over the chaotic scene. People screamed and stumbled through the smoke, some crying out for help as others rushed to safety, their desperate faces illuminated by the fiery backdrop.

A young woman's voice cracked with desperation as she clutched her three-year-old daughter tightly to her chest, her eyes brimming with tears. "Someone's still inside!" she cried, her voice trembling. "My neighbor Maria, she's not answering her phone. She must still be in the building!"

Florence's instincts kicked in, but she was grounded, still unable to fly to the rescue. Emily reappeared beside her, her ethereal form glowing in the smoke-filled air, a beacon of hope in the chaos. Without hesitation, Florence followed the spirit guide into the inferno, the heat enveloping her like a suffocating shroud, the smoke choking her lungs, making every breath a struggle as she plunged deeper into the burning building. The stairs creaked beneath her feet, threatening to collapse like a fragile skeleton, the wooden banister charred and splintered. Emily floated ahead, her luminescent form guiding Florence through the flames that danced like demons in the darkness. Florence's eyes scanned the rooms, searching desperately for Maria, anxiety spiking with every step. But as she moved through the inferno, something shifted within her. The weight of her fears began to lift, and her determination took hold. The ruby in her engagement ring ignited, its deep red light pulsing like a heartbeat, and her mystical powers stirred, responding to the crisis.

She stumbled upon Maria, lying on the floor, shawl wrapped around her neck like a noose, the Madrid fan burning in her hand like a tiny, fiery torch. Florence rushed to Maria's side, her hands moving with gentle urgency to loosen the shawl around her neck. The shawl fell away, revealing the Page of Swords tarot card tucked beneath it. The card slipped out and fluttered to the floor, the rose gold surface catching the dim light. Florence picked it up, her fingers tracing the intricate design.The Page of Swords depicted a youthful figure with a sword in hand, standing on a windswept landscape, their gaze piercing and intense.Florence' understood its meaning: a warning, a mockery, a message from El Cazador, taunting Maria for sharing information with the police. The flames surrounding her seemed to grow more intense, casting flickering shadows on the card's surface, but Florence's focus remained fixed on the message.

Emily's voice cut through her thoughts, urgent and insistent. *We need to get my sister out of here at once!* she warned, her eyes fixed on Maria's struggling form. The old woman's breathing was labored, her chest heaving with desperate effort.

With fierce determination burning within her, Florence scooped Maria into her arms, the Page of Swords still clutched in her hand, its rose gold surface glinting in the fading light.

The ruby in her engagement ring pulsed with a fiery light, its flames dancing across her skin like a wildfire, imbuing her with a newfound strength and energy that coursed through her veins like liquid fire. Coughing, she stumbled through the smoke-filled hallways, Emily's ethereal form leading the way through the churning clouds of smoke. The walls and ceiling began to disintegrate around her, pieces of plaster and wood crashing to the floor in a deadly avalanche. A chunk of ceiling detached, plummeting toward them like a deadly missile. Florence raised her arms, her hands instinctively protecting Maria's head, and to her astonishment, the debris froze in mid-air, suspended by an unseen force.

Florence stared, stunned, as she pushed the floating wreckage to the side, her hand moving with a newfound confidence that bordered on exhilaration. The debris crashed to the floor, the sound echoing through the burning walls like a crack of thunder that shook the foundations of the building. Her eyes widened in wonder as she realized she could move objects with her mind, her mystical powers surging through her like a shield that protected her from the chaos. With newfound power coursing through her veins, Florence followed Daisy while carrying Maria through the burning building, her senses on high alert, her heart pounding with urgency and a sense of purpose. They emerged into the smoky afternoon air, the haze still thick with the acrid smell of burning wood and debris. Florence laid Maria on the grass, her neighbors immediately surrounding her to help, their faces etched with concern and worry.

"Is the fire department on its way?" Florence yelled to the bystanders, her voice carrying above the din of the crowd.

"Yes!" a man nearby said, holding up his phone, its screen

glowing with an update on the fire department's estimated arrival time.

The young woman, still clutching her young daughter tightly, nodded vigorously. "Yes, yes, they're coming," she reassured Florence, her voice calm and soothing, a balm to Florence's frazzled nerves.

Maria's pale face was a canvas of pain, her eyes sunken, her skin sweaty and reddened from the burns. "You're going to be alright," Florence murmured, but the sirens piercing the air, growing louder with each passing moment, seemed to mock the promise.

Maria's eyes fluttered open, and her gaze drifted past Florence, fixing on a point beyond, a soft smile spreading across her face like a gentle breeze on a summer day. Her eyes shone a deep love and longing. "Mi *hermanita* Emily," she whispered, her words a fragile sigh. "I've missed you so much."

Florence could see the love and longing in them, the deep connection between the two sisters. Maria's chest rose and fell with shallow breaths, her body weakening with each passing moment. The hand holding Maria's tightened its grip, feeling the fragile thread of life slipping away, leaving only sorrow and loss in its wake. In that moment, Maria's heart seemed to belong not to the one holding her hand, but to the sister who waited for her on the other side.

Chapter Sixteen: The Balance of Chaos

Ryan navigated the car down Broadway, the flashing lights of the fire trucks casting a stark light on the wet pavement. The air was heavy with tension, smoke hanging thick over the scene.Beside him, Alexia massaged her temples, her fingers working to ease the day's built-up tension.They pulled up to the burning apartment complex, where Florence stood speaking with Sergeant Lopez and Detective Martin. Florence's hand extended, her fingers unfolding to reveal a small, rose gold tarot card that glinted in the fire truck lights, catching Ryan's eye. Alexia's gaze followed his, and their eyes met, a spark of understanding flashing between them.

But her attention was quickly drawn to a nearby scene: an elderly woman being zipped into a body bag. "How much more can we take?" Alexia's voice cracked. The past few weeks had been a relentless grind of late nights, endless research, and gruesome crime scenes that haunted her dreams. El Cazador and Los Maliciosos seemed to be perpetually one step ahead, leaving a trail of bodies in their wake like a dark shadow.

Ryan's grip on the steering wheel tightened, his knuckles turning bone-white."We need to find a way to stop them before it's too late," he growled, his eyes fixed intently on the chaotic scene unfolding before them. "And we need to protect Florence and her ruby. It's clear El Cazador is willing to kill for it."

The apartment complex fire loomed ahead, flames devouring the top floor windows like ravenous beasts. Firefighters battled the blaze, their hoses snaking across the ground like metal serpents, straining against the inferno. The sound of shattering glass and the roar of the flames filled the air, a cacophony of chaos that seemed to consume everything. Ryan parked beside Florence, and as he and Alexia stepped out of the car, Alexia rushed to Florence, enveloping her in a tight, desperate hug.

"I'm so sorry you couldn't save her," Alexia whispered, her voice trembling as she held Florence tight. Florence returned the embrace, but Alexia's words cut deeper than she intended. The weight of failure settled heavy on Florence's shoulders, a familiar ache that echoed the bitter taste of defeat.She couldn't shake the feeling that she'd let Maria down, that her gifts had failed her when she needed them most. The what-ifs swirled in her mind, fueling a growing sense of self-blame for not reaching Maria in time.

Ryan's gaze drifted to the commotion between Sergeant Lopez and Detective Martin, where a discussion was unfolding.

"Alright, Martin, start questioning the witnesses!" Sergeant Lopez ordered, his voice firm.

Detective Martin's face scrunched up in confusion, his brow

furrowed in deep thought. "But, Sarge, how can there be witnesses if they were inside the building when it caught fire?"

Sergeant Lopez face-palmed, his round cheeks growing redder by the second. "Just focus on what they saw before the fire, Martin. What they did or saw beforehand might give us a lead.Ask them if they noticed anything suspicious, anyone lurking around, anything out of the ordinary. Just use your common sense, okay?"

Detective Martin nodded, taking a deep breath before walking over to a group of fire victims huddled together. A young lady with a three-year-old daughter clinging to her leg looked up as Martin approached. "Ma'am, can I get your name and your... uh... child's name?" Martin asked, fumbling with his notebook.

The young lady's voice was shaking slightly. "My name is Cynthia, and this is my three-year-old daughter Stacy."

Martin's eyes lit up. "Great, Cynthia and Stacy! Okay, so... uh... what did you see before the fire started?"

Sergeant Lopez, watching from a distance, let out a low groan and rolled his eyes. "This is gonna be a long day."

Ryan watched the exchange, a mixture of amusement and concern on his face as he wondered if Martin would ever get it together.

Noticing him, Sergeant Lopez held out a hand and Ryan shook it. "Glad you're here, Ryan," Lopez said, his voice low and urgent. "It looks like El Cazador's work." He flicked the rose gold tarot card into view, holding it up between them. "Florence mentioned she found this on Maria." He squinted at the card, his brow furrowed. "This card looks to me to mean a young man whipping something away with his sword. Like he whipped away these victims' homes, maybe?"

His expression turned grim as he looked over at the victims. "Detective Martin is gathering statements from the witnesses. These families have lost everything, so we're scrambling to find them temporary housing at local hotels and shelters."

At seeing the Page of Swords tarot card, Florence looked over at the cries of all of Maria's neighbors, their desperate sobs filling the air. The weight of their loss was palpable, a heartbreaking reminder that they had narrowly escaped death yet still, the trauma lingered. Florence's gaze darted around the area, her eyes scanning the crowd for a glimpse of Emily. For a few moments, she held onto the hope that she'd appear, offer some guidance or reassurance. But a subtle shift in her intuition told her that Emily's work was done; her mission as Maria's spirit guide was complete, and Maria has now joined Emily in the spirit realm, their bond eternal. The acrid smell of smoke and char hung heavy in the air, a grim testament to the destruction that lay before them.

Ryan's voice cut through the somber atmosphere. "Thank you, Sergeant, for the update. How many casualties?"

"So far, just one. Maria Rodriguez," Sergeant Lopez replied, his voice somber. "Everyone else who lives at this apartment complex is accounted for. Smoke inhalation seems to be the cause of her death."

"Maria?" Ryan repeated, the name sparking a memory of their earlier encounter at the Tampa Bay Sun-Times.

The realization hit him like a cold wave—the woman had been deliberately targeted by El Cazador, hunted down with ruthless precision. Ryan's sense of urgency spiked; they had to act fast, to find a way to stop El Cazador before he struck again and claimed another victim.

"Yes, did you know her?" Lopez asked, his curiosity piqued.

"Florence and I both met her briefly earlier this afternoon," Ryan replied. "She was on her way to a meeting with Alejandro, the editor and chief of the Tampa Bay Sun-Times."

Lopez's expression remained neutral, oblivious to any potential connections. "I see. Now, Florence tells me this tarot card is the Page of... the Page of..." He turned to her. "I'm sorry, what was it again?"

"Page of Swords," Florence completed his sentence, her voice firm.

"That's right, the Page of Swords," Lopez repeated, his eyes flicking between Ryan and Alexia. "And it was knotted in the shawl that was choking Maria." Alexia's hand flew to her mouth, her eyes wide with horror. "Unfortunately, I don't have my tarot guidebook with me," Lopez continued, studying Florence. "Do you possibly know what this card means?"

"The Page of Swords can signify a message or warning, often from someone young or inexperienced, but in this context, I believe El Cazador left it as a twisted message," Florence said. "Possibly taking Maria's life for talking to the police about Los Maliciosos sightings."

Sergeant Lopez's expression darkened and his jaw clenched. "I wonder if her trying to make a public statement at the Tampa Bay Sun-Times had anything to do with this fire. I promise we'll look into it. Thanks for your insight, Florence. Good day, I'll go speak with Detective Martin." With a nod, he turned and walked away.

Ryan and Alexia turned to Florence, but her gaze drifted away, her eyes haunted by the memories of what she'd endured trying to rescue Maria from the burning apartment building. "I need to go home," she said, her voice distant.

Ryan motioned to Alexia, and together they guided Florence

towards his car. With the engine purring, their attention was drawn to the black cat still sitting at the entrance of the abandoned warehouse, its green eyes fixed intently on Florence.

"Aww, what a cute little kitty," Alexia cooed. Their moment of distraction was short-lived, however; a moment later, Captain Ramone emerged from the warehouse.

"Wait." Florence's brow furrowed. "That's odd. What's Captain Ramone doing inside that abandoned warehouse?"

Ryan paused. It was a good question. He hesitated for a moment before his expression firmed up. "We'll figure that out later. Let's get you home, Florence. You've had a long day."

The silence in the car was oppressive, punctuated only by the hum of the engine and the soft glow of the dashboard lights. Ryan's focus was split between the road and Florence, his concern for her evident in every glance. Florence's mind, however, was already back at the warehouse, wondering what secrets it held. Before long, they arrived at Florence's condo apartment, perched on the oceanfront with the soothing sounds of waves gently lapping against the shore. The ocean breeze filled their lungs, washing away the acrid smell of smoke and fire that still lingered in their nostrils. The salty air and the distant calls of seagulls brought a sense of calm. Florence stepped out of the car, and Ryan lowered his driver-side window.

"Do you need me to walk with you?" he asked, his voice low with concern as he shifted the car into park.

Her smile softened as she met Alexia's and Ryan's concerned gazes. "I'm alright, guys. I'll see you both bright and early tomorrow."

With a quiet click, she closed the car door behind her. Ryan smoothly reversed out of the parking lot while Alexia leaned back in the dimly lit rear seat, her eyes drifting shut in a gentle doze after a long day.

A deep breath filled Florence's lungs as she watched the fading taillights of Ryan's car disappear into the distance. The silence of the evening enveloped her as she turned and walked towards her condo apartment. Her mind turned to the gifts the ruby had awakened within her, abilities that were still raw and unpredictable. The gift of flight had caught her off guard. She recalled how she'd stumbled and faltered, unsure how to control her movements. It was a clumsy, disorienting experience, and she still hadn't mastered it. Training with Alexia, who she now sees as her silent partner, could be the key to unlocking control over these newfound powers, to harnessing them and using them for good. The city of Tampa needed a hero, especially against this villainous El Cazador. The thought sent a thrill through her veins, and for a moment, the weight of her recent losses was lifted. But her attention snapped back to the present as she approached her front door, which was slightly ajar.

Florence's heart skipped a beat.

She pushed her front door open, her eyes widening in shock at the chaotic scene before her. The evening air wafted in, carrying the sweet scent of the ocean breeze, but it was overpowered by an acrid smell of kerosene and sweat that clung to everything. Furniture was overturned, belongings scattered everywhere, and the room seemed to have been tossed upside down. A bouquet of white rose flowers, sent by Xander as condolences, lay trampled on the floor.

Under the roses, an Egyptian oracle card was placed faced down. It was a beautiful yellow-gold oracle card with the

174

front image of the Great Sphinx of Giza, its limestone form depicting a human head with a royal headdress, majestically perched atop the powerful body of a lion, its paws stretched out in serene repose. The Pyramid of Khafre, the second-largest of Egypt's majestic trio, rose behind it, its peak shimmering like a throne waiting to be claimed. She gazed at the card, transfixed by the intricate details, and a vision unfolded.

A hunter stood tall, his eyes gleaming with power and ambition. He reached out a hand, beckoning her to join him, to stand by his side as an equal. In this vision, she saw herself walking beside the hunter while a wolf padded silently by their side, its piercing gaze scanning the shadows as if protecting their every step. She wore a rose gold garment, her hand clasped tightly in his. The image was vivid, and for a moment, she felt the allure of power and the thrill of the unknown. She took his hand, and the vision shifted. She saw herself sitting on her awaited throne, highly elevated and adorned with symbols of power that seemed to balance precariously between mercy and severity. The throne seemed to radiate an aura of authority, and she felt a sense of pride and dominance.

Her hands trembled with anger as she fought against the thoughts of joining El Cazador. An unknown force seemed to be pulling her in, leaving her feeling unsettled and torn. She turned over the oracle card to see the imagery message that she knew was left behind by El Cazador. The golden oracle card depicted Set, the god of chaos, standing over the lifeless body of his brother Osiris. Set's eyes blazed with vengeful fury, as if the desert landscape behind them, barren and unforgiving, had seeped into his very soul.

The image of Set standing over Osiris's lifeless body seemed to hold a deeper meaning. She studied the scene, her mind racing with the implications. El Cazador was drawing a parallel between their own situation and the ancient myth— he saw himself as Set, a powerful force driven by ambition, and her as Osiris, a sacrifice to be made. The ruby, with its dark history and mysterious power, loomed large in this twisted dynamic, binding them together in a way that felt both ominous and inescapable. Visions unfolded before her, like crossroads revealed by a psychic's gaze. She saw herself joining El Cazador, their paths merging in a dance of power and darkness. And she also saw herself refusing his offer, the consequences unfolding like a stormy night. Another vision burst forth, disjointed and surreal—she was flying over Tampa Bay, soaring past the yellow Skyway Bridge as people waved at her from their cars below, their faces upturned and adoring, their voices carrying up to her on the wind. *Rosa! Rosa!* The chant echoed through her mind, a rhythmic call that resonated deep within her. The visions blurred and merged, her mind working to unravel the threads of meaning that bound them together.

A soft breeze wafted through the open front door, carrying a raspy whisper on its gentle currents. The Latin words sliced through her visions like static, distorting the images of power and adoration. "Sequere me, aut omnes quos amas patientur... Sequere me, ne pereas..." The words hung in the silence, translating themselves in her mind: *"Follow me, or all you love will suffer... Follow me, lest you perish..."* The whisper seemed to come from all around her, a female voice that was both seductive and menacing. The tone was hauntingly familiar, and she wondered if it might be Daisy, El Cazador's sister, a face she had never seen, but a presence she couldn't shake.

The voice dissolved into silence, leaving her skin prickling with unease. A presence lingered, its unseen eyes weighing her decision. Her gaze drifted back to the oracle, the message unfolding in her mind like a dark prophecy: *"As Set claims dominion over the realm of the dead, so too will you be consumed by the shadows if you refuse to heed the call. The balance of power shifts, and those who do not align themselves with the forces of chaos will be torn apart by its fury. Join me, and you may yet escape the fate of Osiris. Refuse, and you will be cast into the darkness, forever lost."*

The words seeped into her thoughts, El Cazador's warning echoing through her mind like a dire promise. The shadows around her seemed to deepen, as if the darkness itself was watching, waiting for her decision. The air felt heavy with anticipation, and she wondered if she had the strength to resist the darkness's pull.

17

Chapter Seventeen: The Book of the Dead

The darkness outside her window slowly receded, a hint of dawn creeping into the sky around 4 am. Florence sank into the softness of her sofa, the plush cushions enveloping her like a gentle hug after a chaotic night. Her home was in disarray, furniture overturned, and belongings scattered everywhere, the aftermath of Los Maliciosos' brutal intrusion. They had been searching for something, tearing through her space with reckless abandon, and Florence knew exactly what they were after—the ruby.

The air was thick with tension, and the smell of kerosene lingered. Florence's fingers absently turned the oracle card over in her hands, El Cazador's message seared into her mind: *Follow me, or all you love will suffer... Follow me, lest you perish...* Her thoughts drifted to Kevin, whose life had been brutally cut short by Los Maliciosos' ruthless hands. The ache of his absence still felt like a fresh wound, and she longed for the comfort of his strong arms wrapped around her, holding her close. Tears pricked at the corners of her eyes, her emotions simmering just below the surface. The whispering Latin words *"Amor...vincit...omnia...nocte...sequenti"* echoed in her mind, and she felt herself pulled into another vision. This time, she was sitting on the couch, watching the news about the escalating violence between Los Maliciosos and El Cazador. Kevin stood up, his expression tense, and abruptly left her alone in their apartment. The scene shifted, and she saw Kevin approaching Melissa's door. Melissa opened it, and they fell into each other's arms, passionately kissing. The vision blurred into flashes of them making love, and Florence's heart raced with shock and pain. She was trapped in the vision, her mind reeling with the realization that Kevin had an affair while still with her. She knew she could trust this vision, but the weight of this revelation crushed her, and her grief turned to anguish. Tears streamed down her face, her emotions raw and overwhelming.

After a few minutes, the vision finally released its hold on her, and she dried her cheeks, the darkness of night slowly giving way to the dawn of a new day. The pale light creeping through her windows seemed to bring with it a newfound resolve. The decision not to contact the police had been made the evening before, when the full weight of her situation had sunk in—involving the authorities would mean exposing her own connection to the ruby, and she couldn't risk them digging deeper into her dealings with El Cazador. With that decision firmly in place, Florence focused on the next step, honing her abilities with the ruby to prepare for the challenges ahead. After a long night of cleaning, she sat on her sofa, her body weary but her mind still racing. She picked up her phone and dialed a number, reaching out to the one person she trusted to help her master the ruby's power – Alexia, her partner and ally in this fight.

Alexia answered on the first few rings, her voice groggy from sleep. "Hello?" she said, yawning audibly through the phone.

"Hey, I need your help," Florence said, without preamble.

Alexia's voice snapped into focus, despite the lingering grogginess. "What's going on?"

"I think I know where Los Maliciosos might be hiding. I need you to come over and help me break into the abandoned warehouse on Broadway."

"I'll be right over," Alexia replied, her tone now fully alert.

A short while later Alexia arrived, still rubbing the sleep from her eyes as Florence let her into her apartment. The warm glow of the lamps enveloped Alexia, and she shed her jacket, sighing in relief as she settled into the cozy space. "So what's the plan?"

Florence's eyes glazed over as if her spirit guide was whispering ancient secrets in her mind; visions of worn scrolls unfurled before her, adorned with mortuary texts in crimson ink that seemed to bleed with a fiery intensity. The parchment was aged to a golden hue, and the imagery of the weighing of the heart ceremony danced across the scrolls, Anubis and Osiris watching over the scales with stern gazes. The air around her thickened, heavy with the scent of sandalwood, myrrh, and the dusty whisper of aged papyrus. Florence's gaze snapped back into focus, her voice low and urgent. "I think there's something in that abandoned warehouse that's calling to me. I don't know what it is, but I feel its presence."

Alexia's eyes locked onto Florence, her voice tight with anticipation. "What should we look for?"

Florence's eyes remained distant, her gaze still inward. "I'm not entirely sure. Just anything that might hold the key to understanding my ruby's power. Something that feels… significant." Florence's words hung in the air, and she nodded to herself, as if confirming a decision. "Let's go," she said, already heading towards the door.

Alexia followed, and they slipped into the worn leather seats of her '92 Corolla. The car's headlights cut through the darkness as they pulled out onto the deserted streets. The drive to the warehouse was long, and Florence took advantage of the time to confide in Alexia. "I've been getting these visions," she said. "I don't know what's causing them, but it feels like… guidance, I suppose. Like someone's trying to tell me something."

Alexia's expression was thoughtful as she turned right onto the deserted street, the dimly lit road unwinding before them like a dark ribbon.

"I wonder if I have something like what Maria had," Florence continued.

"What do you mean?" Alexia asked, her eyes fixed on the road as she navigated through the faint glow of streetlights.

"I saw Maria's spirit guide and I spoke with her telepathically," Florence explained. "It was her little sister Emily. She was a ghostly figure, and I realized she was dead. There was something unsettling about her presence, a quiet intensity that lingered in the air. She was asking me to help her sister, warning me that her life was in danger. I watched as Emily moved an artwork on the wall, holding Van Gogh's painting of 'The Sorrowing Old Man' as Maria walked past it. It was like she was trying to send her a message, one that resonated deeply with that piece of artwork."

Alexia's eyes remained fixed on the road ahead, the beam

of her headlights cutting through the fog that swirled around them. A chill crept over her skin, and she could feel the hairs on the back of her neck standing on end. Goosebumps formed on her arms, visible as she gripped the steering wheel tightly. The fog seemed to press in around them, heavy with an unsettling presence. She felt a jolt of fear, her nerves on edge, as if a ghostly figure could materialize in the mist at any moment. "I wonder if everyone has a spirit guide," she gulped, the words tumbling out quickly as if she hoped to distract herself from the creeping dread.

Are spirit guides always relatives, or could they be friends, or even favorite celebrities? she wondered. She recalled her childhood imaginary friend, a little girl with curly brown hair and bright smile, always wearing those iconic mouse ears. Years later, she'd stumbled upon an old TV show and recognized her imaginary friend's face adjusting her Mouseketeer ears.

The warmth of Florence's hand on Alexia's trembling arm was a soothing balm, calming her frazzled nerves. "They're good spirits, sent to guide and support us in navigating our journeys as humans," Florence replied aloud, her voice soft and reassuring.

Alexia let out a sigh of relief, her tension slowly ebbing away. "You can hear my thoughts, can you?" she asked.

Florence smiled and nodded. Her gaze drifted inward, eyes taking on a contemplative quality. "I'm sure everyone has a spirit guide," she murmured, fingers absently tracing the glowing ruby on her hand. "Which means I may encounter more." The thought sent a flutter through her chest, but this time it was tinged with curiosity rather than fear.

Suddenly, Alexia's expression changed "Wait! I read something about Maria's past in her file yesterday afternoon when

I returned to the office," she exclaimed. "Her sister Emily died in 1955 from child abuse at the hands of their mother, who was later able to avoid severe punishment due to her wealth and high-end legal representation. According to newspaper articles in the file, the family sold some of their valuable art collection, including Van Gogh paintings, likely to cover legal fees or as a result of the financial strain. Maria witnessed her sister's death and was taken to an orphanage where she never was adopted. It's clear she had relatives, but none of them remained close to her – probably going to show up now to claim any assets from her estate."

"That Van Gogh painting must have been a warning to Maria about death being upon her, just like it fell upon Emily," Florence said, her voice catching. "Do you recall who presided over the case?"

"Judge Edwin Garcia, the grandfather to Judge Elizabeth Garcia. I guess judgment runs in their family."

How could a judge allow a parent to get off with a crime like child abuse, Florence wondered. *No amount of money could ever sway my judgment.* But another sudden vision flashed before her: she sat tall in a judge's seat, her left hand grasping a gavel, the ruby on her engagement ring casting a faint glow. On the bench in front of her, a small plaque read "Judge Florence Avila". The moment felt heavy with significance, and a stark truth whispered itself in her ear: she would be blood-guilty, having bartered her soul for the power to wield judgment. She emerged from the vision, the air thickening around her, a chill clinging to her skin like damp earth. The darkness lingered, and she felt a growing unease—what if she wasn't immune to corruption after all? The thought sent a shiver through her, and she couldn't shake the feeling that she was staring into the abyss of her own potential downfall.

The turn onto Broadway brought a whiff of smoky charred wood into the car, mingling with the crisp dawn air. Alexia pulled up in front of the warehouse, killing the engine and dousing the headlights to blend into the slowly awakening morning. In perfect sync, they stepped out of the Corolla, the silence broken only by the plaintive meows of a sleek black cat. Florence's eyes met the cat's, and a sudden jolt of telepathic intuition connected them.

I am Gatita, guardian of this warehouse. I am giving you one warning... leave now, the cat's voice echoed in Florence's mind, her green eyes flashing warning. The cat's back arched, her tail twitching with agitation, as if daring them to approach the secrets hidden within the warehouse walls.

"Be careful with this cat," Florence warned Alexia, her voice low and urgent.

Gatita's gaze locked onto them, the air thick with tension. Florence stood firm, flashing the ruby engagement ring. *Let us through. What's in there is mine. I have been given the gift of the ruby and I am its master,* she replied telepathically.

Gatita's response was immediate and menacing. *You stole it from its true master. You will join us or those around you will suffer! See for yourself what we will do.* In a blur of fur, Gatita launched herself at Alexia, claws outstretched. *I'm going to tear off your friend's pretty little eyes, leaving her blind for all eternity.*

Alexia froze, but Florence raised her hands, palms facing Gatita, and the ruby adorning her finger burst into a fiery red glow. The light flashed brighter, illuminating the dim warehouse with an intense, pulsating energy. The air crackled with electricity as the force surged forward, encasing Gatita in a fiery, golden light that seemed to hold her in place. The cat's eyes widened in terror as she felt herself being frozen in mid-air, her paws suspended mere inches from Alexia's face. An orange glow swirled around her outstretched claws, and with a sickening crunch, they fell to the ground, severed from her paws. The force was wild and unpredictable, and Florence felt a pang of horror as she realized the true extent of her powers.

Gatita's terrified voice echoed in Florence's mind. *"What have you done to me?"*

Florence's stomach twisted in a mix of guilt and alarm as she lowered her hands, halting her energy. She hadn't meant to hurt Gatita, but her powers were still a mystery to her.

Alexia stared at Florence with a mix of gratitude and awe."You're getting better with your gifts. Were you communicating with the cat?"

Florence nodded solemnly, her gaze still fixed on Gatita's frozen form. "She doesn't want us here. She's a guardian to this warehouse," she said, her voice low and urgent. "We need to move quickly. We don't know if anyone is here or will be here soon."

With Gatita's frozen form still suspended in the air behind them, they made their way into the front of the abandoned warehouse, walking through broken floorboards and ducking against the cobwebs and dust mites that loomed in the air. The air smelled moldy and dusty, and Alexia began sneezing aggressively from the lack of clean air.

"Shhh," Florence warned, reaching for two flashlights that were left on one of the tables in the center empty room. "Try to stay quiet."

She handed one to Alexia and they turned on their lights, dust dancing through the beams. "How do you know that what we're looking for is in here?" Alexia asked in a hushed tone.

"I'm feeling a pull, like an energy," Florence whispered back. "And I had a vision of what it was. We need to look for pages or scrolls to an old ancient book."

They spread out around the warehouse, searching room after room, but most held nothing more than tables, chairs, and mirrors. At the corner of a back room was an office. Immediately Alexia sensed this was El Cazador's office. It had an elegant ancient chair with a large standing mirror at its corner. At mid center was a Barqueño, a Spanish writing desk with a hinged drop-front that, when lowered, provided a writing surface. Underneath the Barqueño, Alexia's flashlight spotted an old treasure chest sitting elegantly underneath. The treasure chest was made of alabaster, having an ability to diffuse the light coming from Alexia's flashlight.

"Check out this treasure chest," she said, gesturing Florence over and showing her the padlock. "There might be something important inside."

The lock was old and rusted, but Florence could feel that something inside the treasure chest was calling to her. She raised her hands, and fiery red energies emanated from her fingertips. She focused the energy from the ruby to enter into the lock to maneuver its pin tumbler. With a flick of her fingers, the lock clicked open, leaving behind a small trail of smoke.

"Wow," Alexia said, impressed. "Nice trick."

Florence winked at her. "I'm working on it. I'm beginning to figure out I need to stay calm and relaxed when using my gifts," she said, pushing the treasure chest out from under the Barqueño desk and opening its lid.

The chest was divided into four cylindrical compartments. In one compartment, they found crystals; the next compartment held empty glass jars, and the third compartment held herbs, spices, lavender stems, and red rose pedals. At the bottom was a hidden compartment blocked from view with a hardened piece of wood, covering what was hidden underneath. Florence's fingers brushed against the wood, acknowledging the center hieroglyphic image of the eye of Horus. Appearing alongside it was a vulture, which Florence immediately recalled was the goddess of Nekhbet. Raising her hands, she gently called onto her ruby to push it open.

A fiery red glow illuminated from her fingertips, swiping it open like a sliding door. What laid hidden was immediately recognizable to Florence; an ancient Book of the Dead in black with a gold clasp. The golden clasp was also shaped like the eye of Horus, locking away its hidden secrets and spells.

"What is that?" Alexia asked, her eyes wide with curiosity.

"It's the Book of the Dead," she said, as she held it in her hands, immediately realizing that she had held this exact book before in a past life.

The energies from her hands seemed to ignite with its touch, energizing the ruby's gifts. Instinctively, Florence used the enhanced energies from her hands to make a mystical key in the exact shape of the eye of Horus. The energy turned an orange-red, its fiery glow highlighting the stylized falcon eye. The mystical key, forged from the fiery energy of her ruby and shaped like the Eye of Horus, pulsed with an orange-red glow. Her hands moved with deliberate care, guiding the key to the clasp, where it fit with precision, securing the key in place with a subtle vibration of energy settling into the lock. Heat radiated from the key, warming their faces.

With a swift motion of Florence's hand, the lock released. Her fingers trembled with a sense of déjà vu as she pushed the cover of the Book of the Dead open, a gust of wind sweeping through the room, rustling the dust and crackling the yellowed papyrus pages as they unfolded. Words spilled forth in a low, hypnotic whisper of ancient Egyptian incantations. The air echoed with the forgotten rituals: *"Wepet Ra"* - The Opening of the Mouth.

Memories of the Opening of the Mouth ceremony flooded back, and Florence's eyes widened, her past superimposing itself onto her present reality. The Egyptian ritual unfolded before them, a vivid tableau within the golden grandeur of a pyramid. Her lover, a powerful king, lay mummified and still. She reached out to restore his senses and abilities for the afterlife, grief surging through her, the ache of loss and longing almost overwhelming. The Book of the Dead's energy tugged her deeper into the ancient world. She raised her hands, palms outward, and strained against its pull, muscles tensing, breath catching. Every fiber of her being seemed to resist the force that held her, but slowly, agonizingly, she began to pull herself back. With a final, shuddering effort, she wrenched herself free from its hold, the effort leaving her gasping.

The images of Egypt seeped back into the Book of the Dead like ink spreading through papyrus, and Florence felt herself yanked back to the present, where she saw Alexia's shocked gaze fixed on the Bargueño desk, where the mummified king had been laying just moments before. It was now evident to both of them that the Book of the Dead had merged both parallel realities.

Florence's gaze dropped to her own hands, now clutching the Book of the Dead, its papyrus pages secured within a cover of worn, dark granite, as the hidden scrolls and spells stirred, poised to unleash their power into this reality.

Chapter Eighteen: Dancing on Air: Mastering the Ruby's gifts

The pages of the Book of the Dead turned beneath her fingers, ancient words whispering secrets to her as she read. "This book holds mystical truths and dark spells, incantations and prayers," Florence murmured. "It's designed to guide the deceased through the dangers of the underworld and into the afterlife. I remember reading from it before."

Curiosity sparked in the gaze that met hers. "What do you mean you remember reading from it?" Alexia asked.

"In my past life." Her thoughts drifted, lost in those memories. Reading the book was unlocking more and more of her abilities, and with each passing moment, she felt her understanding growing.

The treasure chest lay open in front of the Bargueño, its lid yawning wide to reveal rows of empty glass jars. One of the jars suddenly jerked and rattled, as if an invisible hand had nudged it. Then, with a faint clinking sound, the jar tipped over, its empty interior echoing with a hollow thud.

"What was that? The jar moved on its own!" Alexia

whispered, her eyes darting around the room.

"Let's get out of here," Florence said, tucking the book under her arm.

Creaking floorboards groaned beneath their feet as they traversed the empty rooms, their footsteps echoing off the cobweb-shrouded walls. The dusty air was heavy with the scent of decay, and the silence seemed oppressive. Jittery movements betrayed Alexia's growing unease as she walked, her eyes darting nervously around the deserted space. They reached the front door, its old wooden slats warped and weathered, and pushed it open with a creaking groan. Stepping out into the rising sun, they walked past Gatita, still suspended in mid-air next to Alexia's car, frozen in place by the energy hold.

Gatita's suspended form weighed on Florence's mind as she wondered how to free her from the energy hold. A swirling vortex of fiery red-orange energy circled around Gatita, the colors dancing like flames as they pulsed with a fierce intensity. The air seemed to vibrate with the energy, and the little cat's fur stood on end as she floated helplessly in mid-air.

"You need to let her down before someone sees her," Alexia said, her voice low and urgent.

"I don't even know how I trapped her in mid-air," Florence admitted, a hint of frustration in her voice. She raised her hands, attempting to manipulate the energy, but instead, nearby garbage bins rattled and clattered. Alexia watched anxiously as Florence focused her energy on Gatita again, but Gatita's eyes widened in distress, her body convulsing in mid-air as if the magic itself was causing her pain. Gatita's cries were pitiful, a high-pitched mewling sound. The red-orange energy continued to swirl around her, its fiery tendrils flickering wildly.

"Maybe there's a spell in the Book of the Dead," Alexia suggested.

Florence flipped through the pages reading the intricate Egyptian hieroglyphics detailing Spell 7.

"This is the spell I used in my past life to guide the deceased through the afterlife," she recalled. "It's a protection spell, meant to safeguard against harm from animals." A flicker of doubt crossed her mind: *I wonder if this ancient magic will hold sway in the mortal realm?*

She had to try. The words of the spell began to flow from her lips, her hands outstretched toward Gatita as she channeled the magic. The chanting grew louder and more insistent, her focus fixed on conjuring a shield of protection against Gatita's potential threat. With each passing moment, Gatita's body began to shrink, the swirling vortex of orange-red energy encircling her form seeming to compress her very being. Gatita's size diminished until she was transformed into a tiny newborn kitten, her eyes barely open and her ears folded against her delicate head. Released from the energy's hold, Gatita plummeted toward the ground, only to be caught deftly in Alexia's waiting arms.

"Oh my goodness!" The exclamation was laced with surprise and concern. "You've turned her into a newborn kitten – she doesn't even have any teeth!"

"I... I didn't anticipate this outcome," Florence stammered, "but it makes sense. In this form, she certainly can't harm us." She realized she needed much more practice before continuing any spells.

The tiny ball of fluff, now a miniature version of her former self, let out a surprisingly fierce mental shriek. *Get off me, don't touch me! Ugh, I'm going to gnaw you to death!* The kitten-sized Gatita, with eyes barely open and ears still folded, looked more like a newborn kitty than a menacing cat. Her tiny pink nose twitched, and her miniature paws wiggled as she tried to convey her displeasure.

"She's absolutely precious," Alexia said, kissing the side of Gatita's head, her voice full of affection.

Ugh! Don't kiss me, let me go! Gatita's mental hiss was accompanied by a comical wiggle of her tiny body.

Florence's voice was laced with humor, "You can set her down, she doesn't like the cuddling."

Alexia gently placed the tiny kitten on the ground, where she promptly hopped away like a bunny, her little legs moving in an adorable blur as she made a beeline for the abandoned warehouse. Time was of the essence now—Florence needed to master her magic, and fast, before El Cazador's already simmering rage over the stolen ruby boiled over into full-blown fury upon discovering his once dangerous guardian had been reduced to a helpless kitten.

The sky was ablaze with hues of crimson and gold as the sun began to rise, but the ominous atmosphere clung to them like a shroud.

"Take me back home," Florence requested, her voice low and urgent. "I want to work on my abilities before the day gets underway."

They slid into the car, the engine roaring to life as Alexia reversed. The streets of Broadway blurred together in a chaotic dance, but their tranquility was short-lived. A thick, foggy mist coalesced before them, its tendrils of vapor twisting like skeletal fingers, grasping for the car. Goosebumps erupted on Alexia's skin as Daisy materialized in the windshield, her ghostly form looming like a specter from the depths of hell. Her eyes burned with an otherworldly intensity, black as coal and cold as the grave, while her skin was deathly pale, seeming to glow with an unearthly light in the dim dawn. Alexia's scream was frozen in her throat as she swerved, but her car sliced through Daisy's ethereal form with a chilling ease, as if the very fabric of reality had been torn apart. In a movement that defied human anatomy, Daisy's head twisted, her face rotating a full 180 degrees, her eyes still fixed on them with an unblinking stare. Her gaze locked onto Alexia and Florence, her black eyes boring into their souls like cold, dark drills. The impossibility of the movement was nothing compared to the horror that seemed to sear itself into their minds, as if Daisy's very presence was a blight on their sanity.

"Who… who was that?" Alexia's voice trembled, her eyes wide with fear.

"That must be Daisy," Florence said, the name resonating with a certainty that didn't need explanation. "El Cazador's dead sister," she added, her voice tight with surprise, her eyes locked on the rearview mirror as Daisy's ghostly form aggressively floated after them, passing the warehouse and burnt apartment complex on Broadway.

The morning air seemed to ripple with unease as Daisy chased them down the deserted street. Faint, mournful wails of unseen spirits echoed through the air. The voices grew louder, a chilling cacophony that filled Florence's ears with dread. The sounds were a manifestation of the turmoil Daisy brought in her wake, a dark energy that seemed to seep into every pore. Florence's eyes darted between the road and the rearview mirror, her gaze fixed on Daisy's ghostly form looming larger with each passing moment. The wind buffeted the car with gusts that threatened to send them careening out of control. The wails of the unseen spirits grew more frantic, a haunting chorus that seemed to come from all directions at once.

The steering wheel froze, Daisy's ghostly form grasping for it with an unseen force, her malevolent energy coursing through the car's systems.

"What's going on?!" Alexia screamed. Her voice panicked as she wrestled with the stuck steering wheel. "It won't budge!"

Daisy's eyes blazed with a fierce, unnatural intensity as her ethereal fingers closed around the steering wheel. The tires screeched in protest and the car hurtled forward, out of control, straight towards the massive tree looming at the end of Broadway. The tree's branches reached out like skeletal fingers, promising a devastating impact. Instinctively, Florence raised her hand, the ruby in her engagement ring pulsed with a fiery glow. A beam of crimson energy shot from her finger, striking the passenger rearview mirror with precision. The mirror reflected the energy, and struck Daisy with the force of a blow. Her ghostly form stumbled backward. The steering wheel jerked free, and the car swerved sharply to the left, narrowly avoiding the tree's ancient trunk. Tires shrieked as Alexia fought to regain control. Gatita, struggling to keep up, finally reached Daisy's side, panting heavily. Daisy let out a blood-curdling scream as she realized the tiny creature was now nothing more than a declawed kitten, a victim of the ruby's magic. Her malevolent energy seemed to shatter, her pursuit forgotten. The scream grew fainter, but its echoes lingered, a haunting promise of revenge. Daisy's presence vanished, leaving behind an unsettling silence.

Alexia's hands trembled on the wheel, fingers digging deep

into the leather. "I... I don't think I can do this," she stammered, voice cracking with fear. "This... this is too much!"

The gentle reassurance that filled her ear was a calm contrast to her inner turmoil. "Relax, you're doing great. I need your help, and I don't have anyone else I can trust."

But the words offered little comfort. Alexia's heart pounded in her chest, each beat echoing through her entire body like a drumbeat in a nightmare. Eyes fixed on the road ahead, she sped recklessly, the speedometer needle quivering on the edge of control. Every bump, every vibration of the car felt amplified, her senses on high alert. She couldn't help glancing at the rearview mirror, breath catching in her throat, half-expecting Daisy's ghostly form to materialize, her malevolent presence still a palpable threat.

The car screeched to a halt, the sound echoing off the condos, as they arrived outside Florence's building. Morning sunshine crept over the horizon, the bloody hues of sunrise gave way to soft pinks and blues, a serene beauty that slowly seeped into Alexia's frazzled nerves. The ocean breeze carried the sweet scent of saltwater and the distant calls of seagulls, a soothing balm for her jangled senses. The engine fell silent, and Florence turned to Alexia, her eyes filled with a sense of purpose.

"I have private beach access just down that path," she said, nodding toward a short walkway lined with beach grass and shells. "I was thinking we could work on training my abilities there. The ruby is giving me powers, but I don't know quite how to use them yet. I need your help to learn control."

Alexia nodded, the smile faltering for a moment before she steadied it, a silent promise to help despite her growing sense of unease.

The sound of the waves grew louder as they walked toward the beach, the sand cool and soft beneath their feet. The ocean breeze whipped through Alexia's hair, carrying away some of the tension that had built up during their wild drive. For a moment, the darkness that lurked in every shadow seemed to recede, pushed back by the gentle lapping of the waves and the promise of the approaching sun.

Florence and Alexia shed their shoes, letting the gentle water lap at their feet. A seagull cried out in the distance, its raucous call punctuating the peaceful atmosphere.

Florence gently placed the ancient tome on the sand.

Alexia's brow furrowed in concern. "Are you sure you want to leave that lying there unattended? You know better than to leave valuables exposed at the beach."

"Where did you have in mind?"

"Why not try floating it beside you? Or are you afraid you'll break it?"

Florence's smile grew, and she focused her energy on the Book of the Dead. Her hands swirled, calling upon the ruby's power. A fiery red glow danced around her fingers, casting a warm light on the sand. The flames encircled the book, and the golden clasp shaped like the eye of Horus sprang open, its delicate mechanism releasing with a soft creak. The Book of the Dead lifted off the sand, the red glow forming a sort of magical shelf around it, with the book sitting on top, perfectly balanced and steady. Florence's eyes widened in wonder, feeling the magic coursing through her veins. But in a sudden motion The Book of the Dead fell out of its magical shelf landing hard on the sand.

"Focus on the outcome," Alexia reminded her, her voice calm and reassuring. "Manifest the energy. Believe it's already done, and it will be."

Florence's doubts dissipated, replaced by conviction. She raised her hands once again, the fiery red energy responded, lifting the Book of the Dead off the sand once again and encircling it in mid-air, as if it was its own private bookshelf.

"Wow," Alexia exclaimed, her voice filled with awe.

The heat emanating from the fiery glow warmed her face, and she hesitated to get too close, her hand instinctively reaching out before recoiling.

Florence's eyes sparkled with an idea. "Grab those seashells and toss them into the circling fire," she instructed, her voice steady and focused.

Alexia strode over to collect seashells, some of which were already floating in the air, caught up in Florence's magical currents.

"Now, aim for the book, one shell at a time," Florence directed.

With each throw, Florence's energy responded, deflecting the shells with a burst of power. They careened off in all directions, landing with a soft thud in the sand. Not a single shell came close to the Book of the Dead, Florence's control unwavering.

"Nicely done," Alexia cheered, her voice filled with pride and excitement.

"I want to incorporate my martial arts training with these gifts," Florence declared, her eyes shining with determination.

"You know martial arts?" Alexia's tone was laced with surprise.

"I made it a priority during law school—every Sunday, without fail," Florence said with a hint of pride.

Her dedication to multiple pursuits impressed Alexia, who

admired the way Florence seamlessly blended different aspects of her life. Florence's thoughts drifted to Los Maliciosos, and she imagined herself fighting them off using her martial arts skills. But her thoughts darkened when she pictured Kevin—a pang of grief hit her, and she felt a sudden rush of emotion. Feelings of grief, anger and betrayal flooded her mind, and she felt herself lifting off the ground, her body responding to the intense feelings. She quickly refocused on the training, pushing aside the painful memories that grounded her.

Their training session continued, with Florence practicing a fluid series of maneuvers that blended the disciplines of capoeira and kickboxing while Alexia attempted to intervene..

How do I block these kicks? Alexia thought to herself, watching intently as Florence executed a perfectly timed cartwheel, her feet barely grazing the sand as she transitioned into a swift roundhouse kick.

Florence's foot gently tapped Alexia's shoulder, marking the timing of the kick like a dancer marking a step. "You're doing great, just keep trying to block my moves."

She raised her arms, preparing to dive into a series of flips. Aerobic flips came easy to Florence, but with her aerodynamic gifts, she soared higher in the air than she was used to, making herself doubt her abilities. Landing from her high jump, her foot sank into the sand, and a sudden popping sound filled the air as she crushed a buried beach ball. With a flick of her wrist, she focused her powers, and the deflated ball began to rise into the air. She visualized air molecules rushing into the ball, filling it with a gentle whoosh of sound. The ball began to inflate, its surface smoothing out as it grew larger and more taut. With a swift motion, she launched herself into the air, her wrists bending in a perfect arc as she dove to hit the ball. Her powers surged, and the ball shot forward, flying across the beach to land with a soft thud in the sand.

Alexia watched, noticing how Florence's movements were controlled, almost restrained, as if she was holding back a part of herself. "You're holding back!" Alexia pointed out, her voice laced with a hint of challenge.

"I'm not used to flying, and heights make me nervous," Florence admitted, her cheeks flushing slightly.

"You're doing great, Florence! Keep pushing yourself," Alexia said, her voice filled with genuine encouragement, her smile warm and supportive.

Florence smiled, and they continued their martial arts training. With a swift move, Florence tripped Alexia, sending her stumbling toward the ground. But before Alexia could hit the floor, Florence used her powers to hold her in place, suspending her in mid-air. Alexia laughed, impressed by Florence's quick reflexes.

"I hope you're not this polite when you fight Los Maliciosos," Alexia teased, brushing off the sand from her legs.

"I gave them a few punches and kicks during my first encounter."

"They got what was coming to them, I'm sure. Now let's add complexity with the natural elements," Alexia challenged, kicking up sand toward Florence's eyes.

Florence instinctively raised her hands, and the sand hung suspended in mid-air. She realized her emotions were fueling her gifts, allowing her to control the outcome. With a sudden jolt, she sent the sand swirling back toward Alexia, stopping it mere inches from her face. Then, in a burst of creativity, she envisioned the sand melting away. The sand dissolved into thin air.

"Wow, you made the sand disappear! That's impressive!" Alexia exclaimed, her voice filled with admiration.

"It would be more impressive if I could master flying," Florence said, staring upwards at the seagulls gliding above the shore. "I really need to get the hang of it and get over my fear of heights."

"You think you're ready to fly?"

"I don't know," she admitted. "It's a gift that comes and goes. Usually they're triggered from my emotions, and once I get control of it, I begin to think of what I want to maneuver or do. But flying feels much more complex."

"Do you remember how you felt when you first flew?"

"I was in the middle of telling my fiancé's parents about... the devastating news. It was a painful moment." The words caught in her throat as the painful memory washed over her. Unexpectedly, her feet lifted off the ground, and she felt herself soaring.

Alexia's jaw dropped. "You're flying! Is it... your grief? Maybe the pain you're feeling is lifting you up."

Panic set in as Florence wobbled in the air, her legs dangling helplessly A slight breeze pushed her toward the Bay, and unease crept in about floating above water.

"I can't fly, I don't know how!" she shouted, her body spinning upside down like she was on a roller coaster ride.

"Don't say that," Alexia called out. "Or you'll start to believe it. Imagine yourself as a free-spirited child!"

Florence squeezed her eyes shut, letting the sound of the shore wash over her. Memories flooded back to a carefree time, Saturday mornings spent getting ready for ballet class. Her mother's gentle hands helping her into her pink tutu and ballet slippers. The piano's soothing melody filled her mind – *Pas de deux*, the beautiful piece that accompanied her rehearsals for the *Giselle* ballet. She remembered the thrill of leaping through the floor, feeling freedom and exhilaration course through her body with every turn and pirouette.

Muscle memory took hold, her body drawing on years of dance training. With her eyes still closed, Florence's body reflexively swayed her one way then another, countering the spin and slowly stabilizing her position in the air. Her arms extended, and her core engaged, as if she was executing a perfect arabesque. The familiar sensation of balance and control calmed her racing thoughts, allowing her to focus on the gentle currents of air supporting her body. With each subtle shift, she felt her body respond, her movements becoming more fluid and natural.

"You're doing it now!" Alexia exclaimed, her voice rising in excitement. "You're really flying!"

Opening her eyes, she saw the distant shore, Alexia's figure tiny below, waving enthusiastically as she cheered her on. The sky was painted with hues of orange, the sun's ascent a fiery glow on the horizon, as she shot through the air like a missile, the wind rushing past her as she flew confidently over Tampa Bay.

19

Chapter Nineteen: Buried Secrets

Three weeks had passed since Kevin's homicide, and after the investigation concluded, his friends and family finally laid him to rest. The cold rain drummed against Florence's skin, matching the somber beat of her heart as the minister's voice rang out across the gravesite, directing the mourners to take their seats. Florence walked toward the front row, her gaze drifting to the black metal coffin standing prominently at the center of the ceremony. The polished surface gleamed in the rain.

The mourners took their seats, umbrellas shielding them from the anticipated rainstorm. Melissa chose a seat next to Kevin's parents, Sandra and Kevin Senior, her eyes red-rimmed and her face contorted in a silent scream, her grief intensely felt. Florence sat beside Xander, her gaze lingering on Melissa, anger and resentment simmering beneath her surface. Ryan and Alexia sat on the other side of Florence. A group of journalists and editors from the Tampa Bay Sun-Times, including Alejandro, sat in the row directly behind Xander. The sea of mourners was a gathering of familiar faces, united in their sorrow for the man whose life had been cut tragically short.

Kevin's uncle, minister John, approached the small podium. "We gather today to celebrate the life of Kevin Vega, a man driven by his passion for history and journalism. I remember his love for epic stories of King Solomon and Merlin. I'd scour bookstores for him, searching for new tales of King Solomon's wisdom and Merlin's magic to add to his collection. His curiosity and enthusiasm inspired us all. Let us take a moment to reflect on him and legacy. Please, feel free to come forward and pay your respects to this remarkable individual."

As John motioned to mourners to begin to pay their respects, Florence felt an inexplicable pull, her body rising from the seat. She began to hear an eerie whisper in her mind - the Latin words *"Respice inter rosas"* - *Look between the roses.* She walked toward the casket, her movements almost involuntary, her eyes fixed on the casket spray of white roses. John's voice faded into the background, becoming a muffled noise. Raindrops glistened on the flowers, and a glint of gold caught her attention. A golden Egyptian oracle card had been tucked among the roses. To pull out the card, she had to push her hand through the bouquet, and as her hand touched one, it transformed into a solid black rose. She pulled the card out and took in the image. The card featured an image of Sema-Tawy, the ancient Egyptian goddess, depicted in a traditional pose, uniting the two lands of Upper and Lower Egypt. Her eyes widened, and she gasped, tears streaming down her face as the realization hit her—the message was from El Cazador. Even Kevin's funeral wasn't safe from the menace of Los Maliciosos. Xander noticed her distress and stood up from his seat, walking toward her. Florence quickly tucked the oracle card into her back pocket as he approached.

He enveloped her in a warm embrace, his voice filled with genuine sympathy. "I'm so sorry for your loss, Florence." Xander glanced over at Kevin's casket, his eyes landing on the black rose. "That's odd."

"What is?"

Xander gently plucked the rose from the casket, his gaze fixed on it. "This black rose," he replied, bringing it to his nose to inhale the intensified scent. "I've never seen a rose like this before." He tucked the rose into his coat pocket, evidently deciding to examine it further later, and turned back to Florence with a warm smile. "Flowers are meant to uplift, not somber, especially at a funeral. I'll take this with me. This will be a tough day for you, and I know how hard grief can be. I'm here for you, Florence, for anything you might need."

"Thank you." As Xander walked back to his seat, Florence's gaze fell on Melissa who was sitting next to Kevin's parents, embracing them as if she were their daughter-in-law.

Florence rolled her eyes at the scene, pulling out the golden oracle card from her pocket to distract herself from the uncomfortable display. The card was from the same deck used in the previous message she'd received from El Cazador, featuring the piercing gaze of the Great Sphinx. A familiar voice behind her made her jump.

"What do we have here?" Ryan said, reaching out to take the oracle card from her hands.

"Hey! Do you mind?" Florence snapped, trying to reclaim the card.

"Everyone is staring at you," Ryan whispered, pointing to an empty row of seats where they could talk privately.

Florence walked beside Ryan as they made their way to the empty row, leaving the casket behind. Alexia slipped out of her own row, following them discreetly. Once they were seated, Ryan still holding the oracle card thought to himself, *"What the hell is this?"*

Alexia settled into a seat nearby, her eyes on the card. "Is that another tarot card?" she whispered.

"It's an oracle card," Florence explained, "typically used for guidance and insight. I found it tucked among Kevin's flowers. The message has to be for me. It's energy pulled me toward it."

Ryan's eyes met hers, curiosity burning in them. "Do you think this is a message from El Cazador?"

Florence's response was laced with sarcasm. "Who else would it be from?"

"El Cazador typically uses tarot cards, not oracle cards," Ryan countered.

"He does use oracle cards. When he wants to send a message to someone, but not kill them." Florence bit her lip. "My apartment was broken into a couple of weeks ago. Nothing was stolen, but everything was in disarray. The only unusual thing was an Egyptian oracle card left behind, hidden under white roses. It was an oracle card with an image of Set standing over Osiris's lifeless body." She pointed to the front of the golden oracle card in Ryan's hands with the image of the Great Sphinx of Giza and the pyramid of Khafre behind it. "This card is from the exact same deck."

Alexia's eyes widened in surprise that Florence hadn't mentioned the burglary to her yet. "Was that the night you called me to help you?" she asked, piecing together the timeline. Florence nodded, and Alexia's curiosity turned to concern. "Why didn't you say anything to me?"

Florence fell silent, her gaze drifting away.

Before Alexia could press further, Ryan spoke up, his comment breaking the tension. "Florence, you need to report the burglary to the authorities. We need to track all of El Cazador's appearances, not just the ones you deem fit to pass over." Frustration simmered in his eyes, weeks of dead ends and fruitless leads having taken their toll.

Florence's voice dropped to a whisper. "And let the police know I have the ruby?" Her eyes darted around, as if searching for potential listeners. "I can't do that. They have dirty cops working for them."

Ryan shook his head. "You don't know that for sure."

"I can sense it," Florence insisted. "Especially with Captain Ramone being in that abandoned warehouse the day Maria died in the fire. Come on! They have ulterior motives."

"Well, then what do you make of this oracle message?" Alexia asked. "And how does it tie in with the other one that was left in your apartment?"

Florence plucked the card from Ryan's hand and turned it over to show them its meaning. The oracle revealed the ancient Egyptian hieroglyphic symbol of Sema-Tawy on the back of the oracle card; a windpipe entwined with lotus and papyrus plants.

Ryan studied it for a moment. "I don't know what this means."

Alexia nodded in agreement. "Yeah, me neither."

"It's the Egyptian Sema-Tawy, which means binding of the two lands. It's a symbol representing the unification of upper and lower Egypt. Sema means union, and it depicts the action of binding the two plants together."

Their confusion was evident. "I'm lost," Ryan said. "What

or who are the two parts supposed to be?"

"Don't you see?" Florence sighed. "El Cazador wants me to join him,. The first one represented power, but with a message of death. This one signifies union. He's giving me a choice: join him and gain power, or face death – or worse, harm those I love." Florence's voice trembled slightly. "He's symbolizing himself as the papyrus plant—that's lower Egypt, the swampy plains. And I'm upper Egypt, the fertile valley, because I possess the ruby with its magical powers." Her fear was palpable. "I don't want to give in, but I'm worried."

"Worried about what?" Ryan asked, confusion evident in his voice.

"You're not actually thinking of joining him, are you?" Alexia chimed in, her tone laced with skepticism. "He murders people, Florence."

Florence shook her head firmly. "No, of course not. But... I saw a vision that I did join him."

Ryan's brow furrowed. "A vision?" he repeated. "Like a hallucination?"

"More like a prediction. I was sitting on the bench as a Judge. I felt the power, the pride that came with being an officer of the court, but as I sat on the bench I realized I had guilt... blood guilt."

Fear crept in and in an instant she was transported back to the same vision. The courtroom doors swayed open, and El Cazador stood admiring her, his face obscured. She stood, smirking, eagerly awaiting him, sliding her hands over her judge's robe, smearing away human blood. He had become her partner, and he had helped her take a seat at the bench.

Florence snapped back to reality, fear thrilling through her veins. "This will soon be me," she muttered, pointing to the lotus representing the symbol of upper Egypt. "I'm naive about the court system. Someday I will join El Cazador, and I'll learn the harsh realities of getting ahead." A shiver ran down her spine when she touched the card. The golden image began to shimmer like a heat haze on a summer's day.

El Cazador's voice filled her mind. *Join me, Florence. Kevin's death was not part of my plan. I punished the man responsible for his death and reset the scales of justice.* Another vision entered her mind, and she saw El Cazador hunting down Raul. She watched in horror as El Cazador ended Raul's life.

Ryan's voice broke the vision. "Florence, are you okay?"

Florence's eyes snapped back to the present, the oracle card still trembling in her hand. "Y-yes," she stammered.

Alexia's expression softened. "Hey, visions aren't set in stone."

"You're right," Florence said, rubbing her temple. "Visions can show potential paths. We all have the power to choose the direction we take in life."

She pictured a crossroads in her mind; doors to different futures swung open, each one representing a choice, a possibility, a journey yet unknown. Every decision would lead her down one path, closing others, but the power to choose remained hers.

John's voice continued to drone on, but Florence's mind was elsewhere. She was trapped in a web of El Cazador's making, the image of her union with him still seared into her mind. The service drew to a close, and Florence felt unease settle over her. She knew she wasn't alone in her grief, but she couldn't shake the feeling that she was being watched, that El Cazador was simply waiting for her to join him, and the choice wasn't optional. The mourners dispersed, their voices hushed, offering condolences to Kevin's parents. Florence's eyes met Melissa's, and the two women stared at each other, the tension between them charged.

A spark of fury ignited within Florence, fueled by grief, betrayal, and the ominous presence of El Cazador. Her anger intensified as her gaze fell upon Alejandro, his presence at Kevin's funeral a brazen display of hypocrisy that only fueled her rage. The weight of her unspoken accusations hung heavy in the silence. Without warning, her eyes blazed with anger, the ruby on her engagement ring pulsating with an intense, fiery light that seemed to sense her emotional turmoil. The ring's power coursed through her veins, amplifying her rage. Florence pushed past Alexia and Ryan, her movement swift and decisive as she emerged from the row, leaving them seated and exchanging confused glances. They watched, bewildered, as Florence stormed across the grass, her heels sinking softly into the earth. Sandra looked up, her grip on Melissa's hand tightening in a show of solidarity, as Florence approached, her anger and purpose clear.

Her hand shot out, fueled by the energy of the ruby, her palm glowing with an intense, crimson red glow that radiated heat. With a swift, vicious motion, she slapped Melissa across the cheek, the sound of flesh meeting heat echoing through the somber silence of the gravesite. Rain pattered down, hitting Melissa's ravaged skin and forming tiny plumes of steam where it touched the charred, peeled flesh. A flash of lightning illuminated the darkened sky, casting an eerie glow over the scene. Melissa's skin sizzled and seared, the burning instant and merciless, leaving behind a blistered handprint. Melissa's anguished scream pierced the air, a jarring discordance amidst the funeral's subdued tones.

"How dare you sleep with my fiancé, you filthy tramp!" Florence's voice rang out, her anger and pain palpable, as a low rumble of thunder echoed through the air, underscoring her fury.

The rain intensified, pouring down like a deluge of guilt, as if the heavens themselves were weeping at the secrets kept. Panic rippled through the mourners, and they scrambled to grab their umbrellas, desperate to shield themselves from the torrent. Sandra and Kevin Senior, seated beside Melissa, were shocked into stillness, their faces frozen in horror beneath the umbrella Kevin Senior clutched, its canvas strained against the downpour. They met Florence's accusatory gaze, and their expressions softened. Guilt crept into their eyes, reflected in the rainwater that dripped from their hair and clothes. They had known about their son's love affair but had chosen to turn a blind eye toward his obsession with Melissa, and now the weight of their silence felt crushing, suffocating under the oppressive rain.

Florence's piercing gaze sliced through them, and they turned away, unable to meet her eyes. "You both knew and didn't say anything!" Her words hung in the air, heavy with accusation.

Melissa sprang to her feet, her eyes flashing with defiance as she stood toe-to-toe with Florence. Her hand instinctively rose to touch the raw, exposed flesh on her cheek, where the handprint throbbed with a fiery ache.

"He never was in love with you!" Melissa retorted, her voice low and venomous. "He may have loved the idea of you, but you couldn't even fuck him right. I was the one he always craved."

The two women faced off, their anger and grief colliding

in a maelstrom of emotion. Kevin's parents sat visibly uncomfortable, their faces mortified, as they struggled to process the intensity of the moment.

Alejandro, seated just behind Xander, gazed intently at the scene, a dark thought crossing his mind: *He broke things off with Daisy to date you, breaking her heart in the process. How does it feel, bitch?*

Florence's eyes snapped onto Alejandro's direction, and she pierced the veil of his thoughts, reading the venomous intent. Her eyes narrowed, sealing her resolve. A cold determination hardened her gaze. *I will never join you, no matter how powerful you think you can make me. I can become a judge on my own merit, without your influence.*

Xander swiftly intervened, rising from his chair to separate the women. "Florence, please, this is not the place to make a scene," he urged, his voice a calm counterpoint to the turmoil that surrounded them.

Noticing the peeled skin on Melissa's cheek, Xander turned to look over his shoulder. "Alejandro, can you help Melissa with her injuries?" he asked, his tone neutral.

"Little help over here," Alejandro called out to the funeral director, waving his hand. The funeral director, who had witnessed the altercation, quickly grabbed his first aid kit and rushed over to assist Melissa with her burnt cheek. The mourners stared in disbelief of the burn on her cheek, as if their eyes were deceiving them. "What in the world…" one of them trailed off, while another whispered, "Did she just come straight from hell or something?" Florence's gaze was fixed on the unfolding scene, her eyes cold and unyielding; she felt no regrets. The mark on Melissa's cheek was a testament to her own righteous wrath, a permanent reminder of the judgment she'd delivered with her own hand.

Her attention then shifted to Xander's stern brown eyes, and she began to sob, her body shaking as she buried her face in his shoulder. "I am so angry with him for betraying me and then getting himself killed!" she choked out between sobs.

Xander's arms enveloped her, his hands gently rubbing her shoulders in a soothing motion. "There, there. Let it out," he murmured, his voice a calm balm to her frayed emotions. He stared into her eyes, his gaze lingering on the fiery red glow that still burned within them. "Let me take you home," he suggested gently. "It's been a long day."

Florence's sobs grew more violent, her tears streaming down her face as she wiped them away with a shaking hand. "How could Kevin do this to me?" she wailed, her voice cracking with anguish. "How could he lie to me, deceive me, and break my trust? All for that beetle-headed slut?"

Her eyes dropped to the ground, her thoughts swirling in chaos. She felt lost, alone, and betrayed, the pain of Kevin's infidelity cutting deep into her heart. They turned away from the spectators and walked together to Xander's car. Xander's arm around her shoulders was the only thing that seemed to hold her together, a fragile lifeline in the storm that raged around her. The crowd thinned out, and Florence felt Xander's hand wrap around hers, a gentle reminder of his presence. Her Golden Oracle card slipped from her grasp, fluttering to the wet ground. Xander noticed it and bent down, his eyes locking onto the card, the front of it showing the Great Sphinx of Giza in gold, the color glistening in the rain.

"You dropped something," he said softly, picking it up and handing it to her without comment.

Florence took the card, her fingers brushing against his as

she tucked it back into her pocket. "Not everyone is quite what they seem," Xander replied as he opened the front passenger door of his car to let Florence in.

The black Mercedes with its leather seats was a luxury reminder of what hard work could buy.Xander walked around to the driver's side and settled comfortably into his seat.Since Kevin's passing, Florence had been without a vehicle, relying on others for rides. She pondered a life where she'd have power and status, and the means to afford a luxury lifestyle.

"Let's get you home, okay?"Xander said, turning on the ignition.

Florence nodded, her eyes fixed on the casket as it was lowered into the ground.Her gaze drifted out to the sea of mourners, a world without Kevin laid bare in their tear-stained faces.

20

Chapter Twenty: Rosa Emerges

The sleek Mercedes Benz came to a stop in front of Florence's beachside condo complex, its engine purring softly. Xander put the car in park and turned to Florence, his gaze lingering on hers.

"That was quite a slap you gave Melissa," he said, his voice low and measured as he glanced for a moment at the text message he received from her. "You gave her third-degree burns on her cheeks, don't you think that's rather odd?" He paused, his gaze piercing as he looked straight at Florence, his unspoken question hanging in the air. "Is there anything you want to tell me?"

Florence looked over at him, unable to hear his thoughts. "I was angry, and rightfully so," she replied, her voice firm. "She slept with my fiancé. I wanted to rip her skin off her face."

"Well, your slap will leave a scar on her," he said, a note of pity in his voice. His eyes flicked to his phone, as he sent a quick text to Melissa before meeting her gaze again. "I've asked her not to press charges and she agreed she wouldn't."

A cold, evil feeling crept over Florence as she imagined

Melissa's scarred face. "Maybe it's for the best," she said, her voice laced with malice. "Her face will be ugly now, keeping her away from stealing other women's men."

Xander's expression turned disapproving, his brow furrowed in concern. "I know you two have your differences, but we're a team. We need to work together." His voice softened. "Speaking of team, don't worry about the Gonzalez appearance this afternoon. I'll have Ryan appear on your behalf. Judge Garcia tends to have her own perspective, but I'm sure she'll see things our way this time."

"Thanks, Xander." A flicker of guilt crossed her mind, but she pushed it aside, her thoughts still consumed by the pain of Kevin's betrayal. She smiled faintly and opened the door, stepping out into the warm sunlight. Long shadows stretched out behind her as she walked towards her apartment, the fading light a stark contrast to the turmoil brewing within.

Xander's car idled for a moment, its gentle hum a lingering presence before he shifted into reverse and drove away. Florence stepped into her apartment, the silence a welcome respite from the day's events. Pulling out the Egyptian golden oracle card of Sema-Tawy, she set it beside the initial card she'd received from El Cazador—Set standing over Osiris' lifeless body. The juxtaposition was jarring: one symbolized unity and balance, the other darkness and domination. She stood there, contemplating her decision, her mind weighed down by the conflicting symbols. She had imagined it would be a simple one, but after feeling so enraged today by Kevin's mistress, she had begun to doubt her own integrity, as if something powerful was pulling her to the dark side. The vision she'd had a couple of weeks ago, revealing her suspicions about Kevin's infidelity, still fueled the rage that simmered within her. She'd grown to trust these visions, her powers strengthened by the ruby, and she felt the presence of her spirit guide, an ancestor her family spoke of with reverence, though she'd never had the chance to meet her. She knew that meeting her spirit guide in person would disrupt the natural flow of guidance, undermining the purpose of their connection, so she accepted the distance between them, relying instead on the guide's whispers in her mind and the visions that came to her in moments of need.

But El Cazador's messages only added to her turmoil, leaving her grappling with the darkness that seemed to be calling to her. In her mind, Alejandro and El Cazador were one and the same: a mysterious figure drawing her into the shadows. Both Alejandro and El Cazador shared a haunting coincidence—a deceased sister named Daisy, and both harbored a burning vendetta against Kevin, fueled by a deep-seated anger. El Cazador's offer echoed in her mind, a siren's call to join him on a path of mystery and power. Darkness beckoned, its allure seductive, yet a part of her yearned to remain pure, to hold onto the light. The choice before her loomed like a fork in the road, a decision that would change the course of her life forever. The ruby's power seemed to be playing tricks on her, weaving a web of temptation and seduction.

She closed her eyes, memories of her final moments with Kevin flooding back: the laughter, the whispers, the promise of building a life together. She remembered their last meal together, the lavender in the centerpiece adding a touch of elegance to the table. But the moment the scent filled their lungs, his eyes had drifted away, probably lost in the thoughts of being in Melissa's arms. Florence pulled out her phone

217

and looked at the screen, a photo of them in their Halloween costumes staring back; she, a fiery señorita, and Kevin, a dashing Zorro.

Kevin's admiration for Zorro's bravery and sense of justice sparked an idea in her: this city needed a hero, not another villain. She thought of all those who had lost their lives to El Cazador's cruelty: Kevin, Ricardo the jeweler who had risked everything to prepare her engagement ring, and Maria, the elderly woman who had bravely reported the sightings of Los Maliciosos. They all wanted the same thing: to live in peace, free from fear. The memory of their tragic fates solidified her resolve. Perhaps she could be that hero, fighting for justice and reclaiming her own power. The thought ignited a determination within her, a flame that seemed to burn brighter with every passing moment. Tonight, she'd seek out El Cazador and give him her answer, because her path forward was becoming clearer.

Florence strode to her closet, flinging open the door to reveal an array of clothing. Her hands moved swiftly as she chose black leather pants, the supple material hugging her curves as she slipped them on. A black leather long-sleeve shirt followed, its fitted design accentuating her toned physique. Her feet slid into black boots, the color glinting menacingly in the fading light. She felt a surge of power as she looked at her reflection in the mirror, the black leather transforming her into a formidable force.

Her eyes landed on a black cape with a subtle red lining, tucked away in the back of her closet. A faint smile played on her lips as she remembered the Halloween party she had attended with Kevin while she was in law school. Kevin worn this very cape while dressed as Zorro, his eyes gleaming with excitement as he struck pose after pose with his saber flashing in the light. She wrapped the cape around her shoulders, the black velvet collar encircling her neck as she felt a surge of power and confidence.

Walking over to her closet room mirror, Florence studied herself in her superhero attire, admiring her reflection. She touched her face, her eyes still glowing a fiery red, and wondered if a mask was worth wearing. But her eyes could burn through any material at a moment's notice, rendering a mask useless. She set the idea aside, no longer considering it an option. Abruptly, as if guided by an unseen force, she decided to access her hidden compartment in the closet where she had stashed the Book of the Dead. The number 105 flashed into her mind. Florence turned to that page, noticing a piece of old paper folded between the pages. The paper seemed to be from the 17th century. A spot of blood on it suggested someone had spat on it during a time of their execution. She gently unfolded it, revealing that it was laced with various spells and formulas. Her eyes immediately fell on a spell called "Astral Body."

That's it, she thought to herself. She would manipulate people's consciousness with this spell to separate her face from her physical body. *"But what item would help her do this?"* she wondered.

The collar of her cape—once she cast the spell over the collar—it would forever hold the power to hypnotize those who looked at her, erasing her identity as Florence from their minds whenever she wore it.

Florence removed her cape and laid it out on the bedroom floor, the red lining facing upward, surrounded by the plush edges of her white fluffy carpet. She reviewed the ingredients needed for the Astral Body spell: crushed garlic cloves, basil, cinnamon, and one rose petal. To gather the ingredients, Florence left her bedroom and walked into the living room, where she plucked a single, delicate petal from the dying bouquet on the coffee table. It immediately turned black, the strong scent wafting through the air. Continuing to the kitchen, she collected the remaining ingredients from her cabinet: crushed garlic cloves, basil, and cinnamon. With all the components in hand, she returned to her bedroom and mixed them in a glass jar, the potent scent of garlic and cinnamon mingling with the sweetness of the now black rose petal.

With the ancient words guiding her, she began to mutter the Latin chant inscribed on the yellowed paper: "Astra corpus meum, velo faciem meam, occultare identitatem, solum umbra videam."

A sudden gust of wind swept through the room. The herbs and spices floated up into the air, sprinkling over the collar of her cape and around its center like a gentle snowfall. A glowing light enveloped the mixture, and the herbs and spices dissolved into the collar.

It was done. She thought about how to test it, but a gentle voice whispered in her mind, *'Trust the spell,'* and she knew it had worked."

Now she needed her own signature calling card to instill fear in her enemies and symbolize her fight for justice. Her gaze drifted to the white roses Xander had sent to her home two weeks ago, now wilting in their vase. She picked one up, grasping its stem, and it suddenly revived, the energy from her ruby bringing it back to life. She pondered the magic unfolding before her eyes, then touched the white center. Instantly, it began to darken, transforming into a deep, mysterious black. She repeated the process with the remaining roses, each one undergoing the same transformation.

Recalling the few times she had transformed white roses to black brought back the pain she felt the night Kevin was murdered and just this afternoon at his funeral, when she'd touched the white rose from his casket spray. She looked at the now black rose, her eyes tracing the curve of the petals, the delicate dance of the stem. Her gaze lingered on its thorns, sharp and unforgiving. The rose, a symbol of beauty and strength, also defended itself with fierce determination. The thorns were a reminder that even the most delicate creatures could be fierce and unyielding.

In that moment, Florence knew she needed an alter ego, a symbol of her newfound strength and determination. Her eyes locked onto her reflection in the mirror. "Rosa," she whispered, the Spanish word for rose. The name felt like a promise, a vow to defend herself and others; Rosa would protect the city from Los Maliciosos and El Cazador.

Her mind flashed back to the oracle cards, the messages from El Cazador to join him. She envisioned the union that could have happened and the destruction of her core values that would have followed. She gulped as she remembered envisioning El Cazador's obscured face, his eyes, his smile, his presence. She knew that he was watching her, waiting for her to make a decision. Finally, she had, though it wouldn't be the answer he hoped for. She was Rosa, and she would stop at nothing to defeat him. She had something he wanted—her mystical red ruby engagement ring—but he would never have it.

She had chosen good over evil.

She secured six black roses to her belt, a symbol of her new-found identity."El Cazador likes to send tarot card messages," she murmured, her voice low and husky. "Well, I'll give him my answer with a message of my own."

With a swift motion, she opened the window to her bed-room, the humid evening air rushing in. She stepped out onto the balcony, her heart racing, gazing down at the beach sand far below. Like an actress conjuring emotions for a role, Rosa summoned the now-familiar ache of grief to spark her flight. She thought of Kevin, of the night he was taken from her, and the pain that still lingered. Memories of her parents' tragic death in a car accident flooded her mind, the screech of tires, the shattered glass, the devastating loss. The sorrow welled up, and she felt herself begin to lift. She rose into the air, her body responding to the anguish. To calm her flight movements, she drew upon the discipline that had always centered her: ballet. She focused on the fluid movements, envisioning herself executing perfect pirouettes and arabesques.The familiar rhythms steadied her, and with her arms extended and her movements precise, she glided through the sky. The wind rushed past her, whipping her hair into a frenzy, and the sunset unfolded around her, a kaleidoscope of oranges, yellows, and pinks dancing across the Tampa Bay.

Rosa sliced through the evening sky, the city lights twinkling below her like a scattering of stars. Her destination was the abandoned warehouse, where she had planned to lure El Cazador into a trap. She pondered her next move on the way over, wondering if how she could steal Gatita or his treasure chest. She thought about the warehouse's barren interior—

there wasn't much in the way of valuables there—but she was determined to use it as bait nonetheless. Her eyes scanned the rooftops of buildings with a practiced intensity. A block away from the warehouse on Broadway, a man's scream pierced the air, the sound echoing off the buildings in a haunting resonance that halted her flight.

"Get away from me!" the man yelled, his voice hoarse with fear.

"There's nowhere to run to Marcos," the other man replied.

Rosa's gaze snapped toward the sound, and she saw a young man with a leather jacket and a scorpion embroidery on its back chasing another man, his feet pounding the pavement in relentless pursuit. He threw Marcos against a fence, the metal rattling loudly as their bodies collided.

"Justice is coming for you, compliments of El Cazador!" He shouted, his voice dripping with malice.

From her vantage point on the rooftop, Rosa spotted the struggle unfolding below and swooped down, her cape fluttering behind her like a dark wingspan. She tackled the young man to the ground, sending him crashing onto the pavement, freeing Marcos from his grip. Both of her hands glowed with an intense heat, her fists flying in swift succession as she pummeled him. Every punch landed with a searing impact, his skin sizzling and charring beneath her blows. He let out pained yelps with each strike, his face contorting in agony as the heat from her fists burned him.

"Get out of here!" she shouted to Marcos, her voice carrying above the scuffle, allowing him to scramble to safety. Marcos stumbled away, his eyes wide with fear, his gaze darting back to Rosa as she pinned the young man against the fence, her grip unyielding and her hands still radiating intense heat.

His face was a mask of pain and desperation, his skin scorched and reddened from the relentless barrage.

"Who are you?" Rosa demanded. "Who do you work for?"

The young man's eyes flashed with fear, but he complied, his voice barely above a whisper. "My name is Alex. I work for El Cazador."

"Alex?" she repeated, her voice laced with skepticism. "You seem a little young to be mixed up with Los Maliciosos."

Alex spat blood from his mouth, his eyes gleaming with conviction. "You don't understand. We're vigilantes, righting wrongs. That man you just let get away is Marcos Gonzalez. He raped his ex-girlfriend Brenda and got off on charges today."

Rosa's grip on Alex tightened, her mind racing with thoughts of the case she had been assigned to. She had missed the court hearing due to her confrontation with Melissa, and now she was learning the outcome for the first time. A pang of regret hit her. *I should've handled the case*, she thought. *I would've won.*

Her fingertips dug into Alex's shoulders, making him wince. "I don't believe you," she said, her voice icy. "You kill innocent people, like journalists, jewelers, and elderly women!"

Alex turned away from her, his eyes filling with tears. "The jeweler was my father."

Rosa's eyes narrowed. "Why did El Cazador hunt down your father?"

"He found out that my father worked on the ruby that was stolen from him. El Cazador said he knew too much about its power, that it had to be this way." Alex sounded choked up. "El Cazador has been like a father to me. He's provided for me in ways my own father couldn't. I miss my dad, but El

Cazador... he's been there for me."

Rosa's eyes flashed a glowing red color with anger, her face illuminated by the intense emotion. Alex's eyes locked onto hers, and then dropped to her left hand, where the red ruby engagement ring sparkled.

"Oh shit, YOU HAVE IT!" he exclaimed, wriggling to get away.

Rosa lifted him off the ground, her voice firm. "You know more than you're letting on."

She flew Alex to the police station, the wind whipping through the night sky. She set him down under a street lamp and tied him securely to its silver pole.

"You better let me go!" Alex screamed.

Rosa walked over to him, tapping his mouth shut with her fingers. Her eyes glinted with warning. "Don't worry, you'll have plenty of time to talk." Rosa began searching Alex, as a rose gold tarot card slipped from his pocket, falling to the ground. "A message from El Cazador, I see," Rosa said. "This will be helpful." She picked up the card, her eyes scanning the image - the Ten of Swords. Rosa pulled a piece of paper out of Alex's pocket and found a pen.

Sergeant Lopez,

This is Alex, one of El Cazador's ruthless minions. He was dispatched to eliminate Marcos Gonzalez, accused of brutally raping his ex-girlfriend Brenda. The Ten of Swords tarot card found on him is undeniable proof of his deadly mission. I've intercepted him, but I warn you, Sergeant: El Cazador has many more operatives lurking in the shadows. Be vigilant. El Cazador will stop at nothing to impose his twisted brand of justice.

Rosa

She pulled a black rose from her belt and set it atop El

Cazador's rose gold tarot card, a symbol of her own crusade for justice. With calculated precision, she pinned her note to Alex's shirt. "Sergeant Lopez! Detective Martin!" Rosa called out, her voice sharp and commanding.

The station doors burst open, and the two men rushed out, their faces illuminated by the flashing lights of their own police cars. For an instant, a faint, piercing glow flared from her collar, searing into their eyes. "Here's one of El Cazador's boys for you, hand-delivered," she said with a sly smile, nodding toward Alex. With a final glance, she saluted crisply, her hand brushing against her forehead."Adiós, señores," she said, her voice firm. She lifted her arms to the sky, where the bright full moon hung low, casting a silver glow over the scene. And then she was gone, soaring into the night, disappearing into the darkness.

Detective Martin looked at Lopez, clearly shaken. "Sarge, who the heck was that in the superhero getup?"

Sergeant Lopez motioned for Martin to follow him. "I don't know, but we need to investigate," he said.

Detective Martin gestured toward Alex, who was still bound to the pole, his mouth sealed with tape. "Look, it's that kid again!"

Sergeant Lopez's expression turned sarcasm. "Well, well, well. You never did show up for your 9:00 a.m. appointment three weeks ago. How nice of you to be dropped off now."

They approached Alex, noticing the black rose, the tarot card, and the note pinned to his shirt. Sergeant Lopez ripped the note off Alex's shirt and read it, his expression growing more serious. His gaze drifted toward the note, then back to Detective Martin. The Astral Body spell, cast earlier by Rosa, took hold, imbuing them with a sudden, unshakable clarity.

Sergeant Lopez's eyes locked onto the black rose beside Alex, and he spoke with sudden certainty.

"That was Rosa," he said, a grin spreading across his broad face. "Looks like Tampa's new superhero."

21

Chapter Twenty-One: El Cazador's Rage

El Cazador's face contorted in fury as he screamed in his secret room, the sound echoing off the cold, stone walls. The air was thick with the scent of old leather and smoke. Flickering candles cast eerie shadows on the walls, making it seem as though the darkness itself was moving. Before him, the ornate mirror hung like a window to the soul. Daisy's eerie voice emanated from its depths. Her tone was rough, like the rustling of dry leaves.

"Alex is being arrested by Sergeant Lopez and Detective Martin right now," Daisy reported.

El Cazador's eyes blazed with fury as he watched the scene unfold through the mirror. Alex, handcuffed and helpless, was being dragged away by Detective Martin as the Sergeant reached for, the Ten of Swords tarot card and black rose on the ground.

"What is that black rose, Daisy?" El Cazador inquired, immediately recognizing its transformative state.

"It's a message from Rosa… Florence's alter ego. That's what she calls herself now."

"Calls herself?" he sneered. "What does that mean? You think a simple token like this will deter me from becoming all powerful and doing what needs to be done for this city? I will let nothing get in my way!"

"We have another problem, *hermano*. Alex didn't complete his mission."Daisy's ethereal fingers touched the mirror, showing him Marcos Gonzalez running down an empty alleyway on Main Street and jumping a fence.

Sweat accumulated on El Cazador's brow, his face reddening with each passing moment. "This is exactly what I feared. Now he'll harm his ex-girlfriend again!"

"*Calmate hermano.*"

"Florence doesn't understand what we stand for—our purpose, our mission." El Cazador clenched his fists, pounding one on the desk. "I will make her understand!"

"We are running out of time," Daisy reminded him. "Los Maliciosos failed us. They haven't located Kevin's briefcase which holds the ruby's remnants.And to make matters worse, Florence has now fully bonded with the ruby in her engagement ring with all its power. They have become one. There's no stopping her now. She must join us!"

El Cazador's eyes narrowed, his gaze burning with intensity. "Show me where Florence is right now."

Daisy placed her finger again on the mirror. The surface rippled, and an image coalesced. El Cazador watched as Rosa, now bonded with the ring, flew through the skies of Tampa. "I asked you to show me where Florence is. Not some superhero movie. Who is this?"

Daisy answered, "That is Florence. She is in some superhero costume. Don't you recognize her?"

El Cazador looked again at the mirror of Rosa now soaring above Tropicana Field. He was certain he didn't recognize the woman at all, had never seen her before in his life. "No, I don't. Are you sure that this is her?"

"Do you not recognize her, *hermano?*"Daisy sounded baffled. "I assure you it's her... she's not even wearing a mask!"

El Cazador shrugged. "I trust your judgment, *hermanita*. If you say it's her, it's her."

Daisy looked at him befuddled, as if he had lost his mind.

A cold, mirthless chuckle escaped El Cazador's lips. "So she thinks she can be a superhero for this city, huh? Let's see how long it lasts before this city turns on her." His gaze snapped back to Daisy's image in the mirror. "For now, Daisy, it's time to save my new son."

* * *

Sergeant Lopez leaned back in his chair, his eyes fixed on Alex's cell across the crowded precinct.Phones rang, keyboards clacked, and the murmur of conversations filled the air, punctuated by the occasional shout or slammed door. The air reeked of stale sweat and desperation, the scent of men in cells who hadn't bathed in days hanging heavy over the room. Detective Martin sat beside him, his brow furrowed as he scribbled notes on a pad of paper.

Lopez nodded toward Alex's cell. "Hey, who's he talking to?"

Martin followed Lopez's gaze. "Looks like nobody."

Lopez watched a moment longer, then shrugged. "Maybe he's lost it."

Martin's gaze lingered on Alex, who sat shivering, his lips

moving in a silent conversation, his breath misting in the air. Without warning, the lights flickered and died, plunging the precinct into darkness. The sound of shuffling footsteps and muffled curses filled the air as officers struggled to adjust to the sudden loss of light.

After a few moments, several flashlights, cast flickering shadows on the walls. Lopez's beam landed on a figure in Alex's cell block; not a young man, but a ghostly woman. Daisy's ethereal form was shrouded in a tattered, old-worn wedding gown that dragged across the floor like a mourner's shroud, its veil clinging to her face like a damp, gray mist. The dress, a bitter mockery of the love and joy she was denied in life, clung to her like a shroud of sorrow, its delicate lace and silk torn and frayed, whispering tales of forgotten vows and bitter longing. Her eyes blazed with a wrathful vengeance, the very sight of the living, a reminder of the happiness that had been cruelly withheld from her during her mortal life. She floated toward Lopez, her mouth widened in an inhuman shape as she unleashed a blood-curdling scream that shattered glass and popped light bulbs, plunging the precinct into an even deeper darkness. Officer Fernandez and Patel opened fire, but Daisy raised her hands, and the bullets hurtled back at them.

"Hold your fire!" Lopez screamed as the two officers fell to the ground, struck by their own bullets that had been deflected back at them by Daisy's supernatural powers.

Detective Martin grabbed his radio, desperation creeping into his voice. "We're under attack! We need assistance now!"

Before anyone could reply, Daisy lifted Martin off the ground with an unseen force, slamming him across the room. She shot an energy force toward his radio, making it explode in his hand. Then, her eyes fell back on Lopez, who had ducked for cover.

She grabbed him by the legs, hanging him upside down, and came face-to-face with him. *"Dame las llaves,"* she hissed, her voice low and menacing. "Give me the keys."

"I don't have them," Lopez lied, his voice trembling.

Daisy shook him violently, and the keys tumbled from his pocket. The keys floated in mid-air, dancing on the strings of her supernatural energy, as she sent them toward Alex's cell to set him free. Alex stood with his hands clasped against the bars, a hint of amusement playing on his lips as he watched the spectacle. The keys hovered before the lock, and with a subtle nudge, they slid into place. The lock clicked open and Alex pushed open the cell door. He sprinted out, and Daisy unleashed another blast of energy, sending Lopez and the others stumbling backward. The darkness seemed to swallow her whole as she vanished, leaving behind only the echoes of her unsettling laughter.

Alex burst through the precinct doors into the night. A sleek car waited at the curb, its headlights casting an ominous glow. Captain Ramone sat behind the wheel, nodding curtly toward the passenger seat. Alex didn't hesitate, sliding into the front seat as Ramone's gaze returned to the road. In the backseat, a figure emerged from the shadows—El Cazador, his face obscured by the darkness of the night.

"I'll teach you how to serve justice, *mi hijo*," he said with cold confidence. "Let's pay Gonzalez a visit. After all, we must congratulate him on his win in court today." El Cazador's voice was laced with malice, and Ramone's eyes gleamed in agreement as they shared a menacing laugh, the darkness seeming to grow thicker with their sinister intent.

* * *

The luxury sedan pulled up to Gonzalez's apartment, its sleek design and powerful engine a testament to its high-end quality. Alex slid out of the passenger seat, while El Cazador emerged from the back seat, both men moving in sync. El Cazador was impeccably dressed in a tailored suit. He pulled out a pair of black leather gloves and handed another pair to Alex.

"No fingerprints," El Cazador said. "We don't want to be traced."

Alex hesitated before taking the gloves. "I've never killed a man before," he said, a flicker of uncertainty crossing his face.

El Cazador's expression softened, and he reassured him with a gentle smile. "I'll take care of it, but we need to be quiet. Marcos will be home any minute."

Alex nodded, his eyes darting towards the door as he put on the gloves. El Cazador and Alex positioned themselves on either side of the apartment door, waiting in silence. The sound of a TV drifted from inside.

Marcos stumbled towards Brenda's apartment, drunk and unsteady, his eyes glazed over as he passed by the men hidden in the shadows. With clumsy fingers, he fumbled for his keys, dropping them once before finally picking them up, managing to unlock the door. With a sudden burst of energy, Marcos shoved the door open and stumbled into the apartment, his entrance startling Brenda. The space that had once been shared by them now reflected her newfound independence: the walls, once adorned with his favorite sports team, now showcased her own artwork and vibrant colors. The furniture, rearranged to suit her taste, created a cozy and inviting atmosphere. Every trace of him had been meticulously erased.

His clothes, his shoes, his favorite armchair—all gone. The apartment was a testament to her newfound strength and determination.

But Marcos didn't notice any of this. His eyes were fixed on Brenda, cowering in the corner of the room.

"You bitch!" he screamed, charging towards her and slapping her across the face, sending her crashing to the floor. "I went to jail because of you. Lying, telling everyone I raped you when you know you enjoyed every minute of it."

"Get away from me," she shouted as she backed herself into a corner in the living room. He grabbed her by the hair and dragged her to the dark bedroom, then picked her up and threw her on top of her mattress. "Get off me! Get off me!" she screamed, digging her nails into his arms. He slapped her in the face again, then ripped her shirt. "Please don't do this!" she pleaded.

"I have you right where I want you," he muttered.

The bedroom light flickered to life, illuminating El Cazador's imposing figure in the doorway, his eyes blazing with a fierce intensity. With a swift nod, he signaled to Alex, who sprang into action, charging at Marcos and kicking him off Brenda. Alex grabbed Marcos by the shoulders, holding him in a vice-like grip. Marcos's eyes widened in terror as he recognized El Cazador from the courtroom.

"You!" he yelled, struggling futilely against Alex's hold. "Didn't you hear? I was acquitted."

"Not by me, you're not!" El Cazador shouted, his fist flying towards Marcos's stomach, sending him crashing to the floor.

Marcos doubled over, gasping for breath. El Cazador and Alex stood over him, their movements swift and calculated. Brenda, still on the bed, pleaded with them to stop, her voice shaking with fear. El Cazador looked over at Alex, letting him know it was time to finish him. Brenda ran to El Cazador, tears streaming down her face, as El Cazador pulled out his gun from his holster.

"Please… please… don't kill him.

"This is what you wanted, you bitch!" Marcos snarled.

"I… I still love him! Don't… don't do this please. I beg you!" she pleaded.

El Cazador's expression was unyielding. "It's for your own good," he said, his voice cold and detached. With a swift motion, he raised the gun and pulled the trigger.

Brenda screamed in horror as Marcos's body crumpled to the floor, a single bullet hole to his forehead.

"Justice is served," El Cazador exclaimed, his voice low and even, as he stood tall, his eyes gleaming with a sense of satisfaction.

Brenda screamed again as Daisy materialized beside her.

"Now now, my dear. Don't be alarmed. The way he treated you is not love," Daisy stated, her voice soft and melancholic.

Brenda began to sob looking over at El Cazador with confusion and anger. Realizing she needed to protect her brother's identity, Daisy placed her corpse-like hands on Brenda's temples, erasing her memory of El Cazador. The woman's eyes grew heavy and Daisy gently guided her to bed, tucking her in as if she were a child.

"This will help you forget and will keep my brother's identity safe," Daisy whispered, her breath cold against the woman's ear.

El Cazador watched the scene unfold, his expression un-readable. He reached into his pocket and pulled out a stack of rose gold tarot cards, the metallic sheen catching the dim light of the room. His black leather gloves slid smoothly over the cards as he searched for the perfect message to send to the judge assigned to Marcos's case. He flipped through the cards, his eyes scanned the intricate illustrations, searching for the one that will convey his message. Finally, he came across the Justice card. The illustration depicted a regal figure, seated on a throne, holding a pair of scales in one hand and a sword in the other. The figure's face was serene, yet unyielding.

El Cazador's eyes lingered on the card, his mind absorbing the symbolism. The Justice card presented balance, fairness, and accountability. It was a reminder that every action had consequences, and that those who escaped justice in the mortal realm would eventually face reckoning. He placed the Justice card on Marcos's corpse, the rose gold metallic sheen seeming to mock the lifeless body beneath.

El Cazador stood tall, his eyes gleaming with a sense of satisfaction. He had delivered justice, and the message was clear: those who thought themselves above the law would be held accountable. With a nod toward Alex, he turned to leave, their black leather gloves a stark contrast to the blood-stained floor of Brenda's apartment.

They exited her apartment, El Cazador's expression remained unreadable, his eyes fixed on some point in the distance. He knew that his work was far from over, and that there were still many more who needed to be held accountable. But for now, justice had been served, and the balance had been restored.

22

Chapter Twenty-Two: Betrayal in the Shadows

Rosa landed on the rooftop of the abandoned warehouse, determined to lure El Cazador and deliver her decision. She navigated across the worn surface and slipped into the shadows of the crumbling ceiling, where broken drywall and rusty ducts hung precariously.The city's whispers carried on the wind, but she focused on the muffled voices drifting from within the warehouse.The words themselves were indistinct, yet the tone was unmistakable: cold, calculating, and menacing.

She moved stealthily, her presence seamlessly masked by the shadows that danced around her as she made her way above the gathering. The voices grew louder, and she recognized Victor's tone, his words dripping with malice as he spoke to El Cazador on the phone.

Rosa's realization was instant; El Cazador wasn't here.

The call ended, and Victor turned to face the group, issuing instructions with the gravity of a commander on D-Day. "El Cazador's orders are clear," he said to the Los Maliciosos members encircled around him, his voice echoing off the walls. "We eliminate Judge Garcia tonight, and we make her death look like a suicide."

Rosa's eyes narrowed, and her hands began to glow with a soft red light, the energy building within her like a gathering storm. The air around her vibrated with anticipation.

Gatita, still a kitten, hissed at Rosa, her tiny body puffed out, fur standing on end, drawing attention to her presence. Rosa's gaze softened as she took in the kitten's growth since their last meeting three weeks prior. Gatita's ears, once folded, now perked up alertly, and her eyes, newly opened, shone with a piercing intensity. However, Rosa's attention was caught by the kitten's declawed paws, a lingering effect of her magical nature, and a pang of pity stirred within her.

She's here, Gatita's voice screeched in Rosa's mind. A sharp meow followed, alerting the members that someone was indeed listening in on their clandestine meeting.

Victor's eyes tracked Gatita's piercing green gaze, landing squarely on Rosa as she peered down from her hiding spot. Immediately Rosa's collar flashed, shielding her identity as Florence from the seven members of Los Maliciosos looking up at her.

"Well, well, well," Victor sneered, "Look what we have here. Rosa, the little superhero. We've been expecting you. Your save-the-day routine didn't work with Marcos Gonzalez. El Cazador served true justice and ended his life."

Upon hearing this, Rosa received a vision: Brenda was being interviewed by Captain Ramone, crying hysterically, her eyes vacant as she struggled to recall what had happened.

Rosa's face twisted in fury, her eyes blazing red with intensity. "You call yourselves vigilantes, fighting for justice?"

Her voice cut through the air, laced with contempt, her words echoing down from the shadows of the ceiling. "No, your justice is tainted by bloodshed and fear. You're no better than the monsters you're trying to eradicate. Your cause is twisted, and your methods are wrong!"

With a swift flick of her wrist, she unleashed a wave of energy that crashed into the room, sending the members of Los Maliciosos stumbling backward, caught off guard. Flicking her wrist again, Rosa propelled herself downward, flying through the air with deadly precision, her body hurtling toward the group. Victor drew a gun, but Rosa, anticipating his move, swiftly kicked it from his hand. She raised her hand toward Victor, and a blast of energy sent him flying across the room.

Victor crashed into a stack of crates, the wood splintering beneath his weight with a deafening crack. The sound echoed through the warehouse, a cacophony of crashing and screams filling the air.Rosa moved through the room, her eyes blazing red with power. The other six members encircled her, prepared to fight, but she was a whirlwind of fury. Angel approached her from behind, only to feel her foot connect with his chest with a sickening crunch, sending him crashing to the ground, gasping for breath.

Roberto and Hector lunged at her, but she caught each of their wrists, twisting them with a brutal force that sent them flying backwards, their faces contorted in pain. Mateo, wincing in pain as he gripped the pipe with his taped fingers, swung at her, but Rosa dodged, the pipe whistling past her ear. She countered with a blast of fiery energy that sent the pipe flying out of his hand, leaving his palm scorched and blistered. The intense heat melted the tape binding his broken fingers, and Mateo stumbled backward, his eyes wide with fear, his fingers now dangling at grotesque angles.

Jose and David charged at her, but she raised her hands toward them, lifting them off their feet and swinging them both in the air in different directions. They crashed against the floor, their bodies breaking under their own weight, their screams echoing through the warehouse.The fight raged on, Rosa's powers unleashing a maelstrom of energy and chaos. Rosa stood tall, her eyes blazing with power, her hands aglow with the red energy. Her fists flew, delivering crushing blows that left her opponents reeling, their faces bruised and bloodied. Her energy blasts scorched their skin, leaving burns that seared their flesh. The energy within her built, and Rosa's connection to the mystical forces grew stronger, allowing her to anticipate her opponents' moves. She dodged and wove, her movements becoming almost instinctual. With a burst of speed, Rosa shot upward, her body a blur of motion, until she hung suspended in the air, her fists clenched and glowing with energy. Then, with a fierce cry, she forced herself downward, her body hurtling toward the ground like a comet. The air seemed to ripple around her as she descended, building anticipation for the impact. Her fists slammed into the ground, unleashing a shockwave that rippled outward, shattering crates and sending dust flying. The ground shuddered beneath her blow, and the sound of her fists striking the earth was like thunder. The members of Los Maliciosos were knocked off their feet, sent crashing to the ground as if swept away by a hurricane.

They lay there, unconscious and broken, their bodies battered and bruised. The warehouse fell silent, the only sound the heavy breathing of Rosa standing tall, her chest heaving with exertion, her eyes still blazing with power.

Without warning, a chill ran down Rosa's spine, and her eyes widened as she saw a figure materialize before her. It was Daisy. Rosa's breath caught in her throat as Daisy's ghostly form took shape. She was oddly dressed this time in a wedding dress and veil, the delicate lace seeming to shimmer in the dim light. Rosa glanced at her ghostly attire.

"You like the outfit?"Daisy asked, her voice low and mournful."I like to be a bit theatrical when I make an appearance in the mortal realm. I never did get a chance to wear one during my human life. The man I loved didn't choose me. But I can put my feelings about that aside for now. I know it's you under that costume, Florence," Daisy continued, her whisper sending shivers down Rosa's spine. "Don't fight against us. You're not beyond redemption. You have a score to settle, just like me."

Rosa's instincts screamed to attack Daisy, but she remained frozen in place, unsure how to respond. "What are you talking about? And shouldn't I be having this discussion with El Cazador?" Rosa asked, her voice cautious.

Daisy's eyes blazed with a malevolent energy as she laughed, the sound sending a chill through the air. "My brothers and I, we were wronged by this city. By its corruption, its injustice. Judge Garcia is a tyrant. She rules in favor of criminals, at least for the ones who can buy their innocence. Is that the kind of Judge you want passing judgment in this city? Join us, Florence. El Cazador promises to make you wealthy, powerful, and we'll offer you protection. Join us in our quest for justice. Become our partner. We can show those politicians running this city that we won't be silenced, that we won't be ignored."

Rosa shook her head, her voice firm. "Seeking vengeance

isn't justice, Daisy. It's just more hate, more pain. It's a cycle that never ends."

Daisy's face twisted in a snarl, her eyes flashing with anger. "You don't know what it's like to be wronged, Rosa. To die before you could make a difference in this world and be left in the spirit realm merely to guide humans."

The memory of Maria's face steadied Rosa's resolve, and her eyes blazed with a fiery red glow. "I will never join you," Rosa said, her hands raised in front of her. With a swift motion, a blast of energy shot toward Daisy.

Daisy was unfazed, using her own powers to deflect the sudden attack. "You're getting stronger," Daisy said, "but you're no match for me, not yet at least. Imagine what we can be together if you joined us... we could be unstoppable."

The ghost's words ignited anger inside Rosa, fueling her mystical powers. The air around her began to distort, as if reality itself was bending to her will. "I'll never join you, Daisy. You're just a puppet, a tool for your brother's twisted games."

The two women clashed, their powers locked in a struggle that defied the physical world. The members of Los Maliciosos started to regain consciousness, covering their heads as if nursing a frightful headache. Daisy turned to them, her voice a cold command. "All of you, leave now and get the job done tonight!"

The members scattered, fleeing the warehouse with what little energy they had left. Rosa and Daisy continued their mystical battle, their energies swirling around each other. Rosa's eyes scanned the warehouse, searching for a way to end the fight. She caught sight of the treasure chest that once held her Book of the Dead, the alabaster deflecting the light around it. The air around the chest appeared to vibrate with a malevolent energy, as if it was hungry to trap the evil spirit inside. Daisy stepped up her attacks, forcing Rosa to pay attention. Chairs and tables shattered, the crash and splinter of breaking wood and glass echoing through the space as they exchanged blows. With calculated precision, Rosa maneuvered Daisy towards the area, their battle a deadly dance of magic and malice.

The vacant doorway to El Cazador's office beckoned, devoid of any barrier to block their path.Daisy stormed into the space, her ghostly form standing guard at the entrance like a dark sentinel protecting the secrets within.The alabaster chest beneath the Bargueño desk pulsed with an eerie resonance, drawing the dark energy that permeated the warehouse like a vortex drawing matter from one realm to another. Rosa's eyes narrowed, her mind racing with the implications. The chest's power could absorb the malevolent energy fueling Daisy's spirit, potentially banishing her to a realm beyond their own. With this realization, Rosa's determination ignited, her resolve hardening like tempered steel. Rosa lunged forward, her hands weaving intricate patterns as she summoned her powers."Astra descendo, spiritus obtineo," she chanted, her voice low and commanding. "In alabastro frigido, animus tuus est ligatus."

Stars descend, spirit be bound. In cold alabaster, your soul is trapped.

Rosa's powers surged through her like a tempest, and she hurled Daisy toward the chest, using her magic to force the lid open with a creaking groan. Daisy's ghostly form screamed and struggled against the chest's pull, her ethereal body thrashing wildly before being sucked inside. The alabaster absorbed the dark energy that had fueled her malevolent spirit, its cold, stone heart seeming to devour the shadows that had sustained her. The chest slammed shut, the sound echoing through the warehouse like a prison door sealing its captive. The lid's heavy thud seemed to finalize Daisy's confinement, her struggles against the chest's power having sealed her fate, trapped within the alabaster's icy grasp.

With a subtle gesture, Rosa focused her energy on the chest, lifting it off the floor as if it were weightless. She reached for her belt, releasing the clip that held one of her black roses, and placed it under the Bargueño desk, where the chest had once sat; a deliberate message to El Cazador. The chest floated beside her, its presence a palpable force, as Rosa's powers carried it with her like a shadow.

"Get me out of here or you're going to regret it!" Daisy screamed, her voice muffled but full of rage.

Rosa's eyes narrowed, her gaze piercing the darkness. "You belong in the spirit realm and that's exactly where I will return you," she answered.

Gatita sprang forward, her small body tense with aggression, fangs bared in a hissy fit. *Not so fast,* she telepathically warned, her baby fangs glinting like miniature daggers in the darkness.

Rosa raised an eyebrow, amused by the tiny menace. *Really?* she thought to herself, stifling a giggle.

Without missing a beat, Rosa summoned a furry tidal wave of mice into the office, and the room was instantly overrun with squeaking chaos.Gatita's eyes went wide, and she instinctively gave chase, pouncing on the rodents with all the stealth of a kitten at playtime. Rosa couldn't help but laugh at the absurdity of it all. With Gatita momentarily distracted, Rosa took advantage of the diversion and leaped into the night. The alabaster chest hovered beside her, encircled by her swirling mystical energy, Daisy trapped within its confines. Rosa flew back to her apartment, the chest floating steadily in her wake, its path mirroring hers with precision. She soared through the cityscape, the chest keeping pace beside her, until the familiar outline of her apartment building loomed ahead. The ocean breeze filled her lungs, and the wind whipped through her wavy dark brown hair as she touched down on her balcony, the chest still clutched in her mystical hold.

She swung her bedroom door open and stepped inside, heading for the hidden compartment where The Book of the Dead had lain hidden. The alabaster chest was placed inside, its occupant's screams muffled and fading into the distance, trapped within its stone prison. With the chest locked away, Rosa's thoughts turned to the looming threat: El Cazador would surely come for her, seeking to rescue his sister. Her eyes narrowed, her mind racing with the knowledge that Los Maliciosos still had a plan to assassinate Judge Garcia, and she needed to stay one step ahead.

Determination blazed in her eyes, her grip on her cape tightening like a vice. Time was of the essence; another innocent life hung in the balance, and she had to act fast. Jumping off the balcony, Rosa swooped over Tampa's glittering skyline, the Hillsborough River glinting like a silver snake below, before banking toward Harbour Island's tranquil shores. Judge Garcia's mansion, a waterfront estate infamous among Tampa's elite, came into view, its eight rooms and high ceilings glowing warmly in the moonlight, a beacon of wealth and power. Everyone in Tampa knew the judge's residence, a stunning white home with a private dock and lush lawns stretching toward the beach. Luxurious cars lined the driveway, and a stunning chandelier showcased the grandeur of the wraparound staircase, casting a golden glow across the night.

When Rosa landed on the roof, the glittering lights of Harbour Island stretched out before her, the marina's waters glinting in the moonlight. She tuned into the thoughts of Los Maliciosos, their presence visible even from her aerial vantage point; a black-clad group congregating before the mansion's gate, their faces obscured by the night. The security camera mounted on the gate's pillar shattered under their touch, and with a calculated precision, they deployed a grenade that ripped through the gate's lock, sending shrapnel flying. Victor led the group, now approaching the entrance of the mansion. He pulled out a rose gold tarot card from his pocket and held it up for the group to see. "This is the judge's final message from El Cazador," he said, a sly grin spreading across his face. "The High Priestess, reversed."

Mateo raised an eyebrow. "What's that supposed to mean, Victor?"

Victor's grin widened. "The High Priestess represents intuition, wisdom, and fairness. But when she's reversed, it signifies a severe imbalance."

The group nodded in agreement, their eyes gleaming with understanding.

Rosa watched from above, whispering to herself, "It all makes sense now— the tarot cards were messages meant for Judge Garcia."

She pieced together the sinister puzzle: Judge Garcia's leniency in court, the plea deals, and El Cazador's pursuit of those who escaped justice. The connection was chilling. With her mind racing, Rosa's gaze refocused on Victor.

"Judge Garcia thinks she is the law," Victor continued. "She gets paid off to acquit rapists and murderers and gets away with it. But this corruption ends tonight." Los Maliciosos erupted into a chorus of agreement, their voices filled with venom and hatred. "We're going to make her pay for her transgressions," Victor told them, his eyes glinting with determination. "We're going to show her that justice isn't just a word, it's a way of life. And we're the ones who are going to bring justice to her tonight."

The group continued their cheer, their laughter and shouts filling the night air as they limped forward, battered and bruised from their fight with Rosa, each step fueled by their determination to reach Judge Garcia.

As they approached the front of her mansion, Judge Garcia's two fierce German Shepherds erupted into a frenzy of barking, their furious growls and snarls filling the night air. Before they could attack, Jose aimed his gun toward them. The sound of gunfire cracked through the front of the mansion and the dogs' barks were abruptly silenced, their lifeless bodies crashing to the ground.

Rosa, still watching from the glass rooftop of the mansion, saw a ghostly figure materialize beside the dogs. The figure, a gentle elderly spirit with wispy white hair and spectacles perched on the end of his nose, approached the dogs, calling out to their spirits. The air seemed to ripple as the spirits of the dogs emerged, their ethereal forms taking shape beside their lifeless bodies. The ghostly dogs stood watchfully beside the old man. He turned his piercing gaze toward Rosa.

In a burst of telepathic clarity, he spoke directly to her. *I am Abuelo, or you may remember me as Judge Edwin Garcia, grandfather to Judge Elizabeth Garcia. Please help my granddaughter. Her life is in danger!"*

Rosa nodded as Abuelo and the two canines floated toward the front of the mansion, disappearing from sight. Her gaze fell on Los Maliciosos approaching the front doors of the mansion, their menacing silhouettes stark against the night.

Judge Garcia flung open the front door, responding to the sound of gunshots, and called out to her dogs. "Rocky? Rex? Come inside."

The silence that followed was eerie. Los Maliciosos dispersed, hiding from her view, their momentary stillness a prelude to the impending attack. She scanned her lawn, and her eyes landed on her beloved dogs lying lifeless on the grass. A blood-curdling scream tore from her throat. Judge Garcia sprinted toward them, her feet pounding the ground in desperation. She cried mournfully, placing her hands on the back of their fur, now slick with blood.

"Buenas noches, Juez," Victor snarled.

This is private property," Judge Garcia screamed. "You need to leave now."

"This ain't your chambers, you can't tell us what to do," Angel replied with a smirk.

Victor and Angel charged toward her, grabbing both of her arms as they pushed her back into her mansion. With swift instinct, Rosa burst through the glass ceiling, executing a flawless somersault. The men of Los Maliciosos grabbed their guns, firing at her with precision. Bullets whizzed past her, their close proximity evident in the sharp cracks that pierced the air, but Rosa's agility allowed her to narrowly avoid the shots. She landed on her feet, her mystical powers surging to the forefront. Los Maliciosos closed in. Fists flying, Rosa charged forward, countering their attacks with precision.

Victor sneered at Rosa, his gun raised. "You're a formidable opponent, but you're no match for us."

Rosa snarled, unleashing a blast of energy that sent Victor flying across the room, where he crashed into a priceless collection of Pollock's art, shattering the wall and reducing the masterpieces to rubble. He quickly recovered, his eyes blazing with fury, and charged toward Judge Garcia. Angel still grasped the judge's other arm, but Victor took over, firmly grasping both of Judge Garcia's arms as Angel released his grip. The fight raged on, with Rosa taking down each member of Los Maliciosos one by one. However, her attention remained divided between battling her foes and the growing danger to Judge Garcia, leaving her no opportunity to bring the judge to safety.

Noticing the bruises and burns covering Los Maliciosos' bodies, Victor realized their injuries from Rosa's previous attacks had taken a toll. Their weakened state made them more vulnerable, and he knew he had to end Judge Garcia's life quickly. With cold calculation, Victor positioned the gun to Judge Garcia's head, the barrel pressed against her temple.

With a cruel smile, he made sure the metal pinched her skin, making her gasp in terror. "Can't save her now, can you?" he sneered, pulling the trigger aimed at Garcia's head.

The sound of the gun firing off cut through the chaos, and Rosa's focus snapped to the bullet, which seemed to zoom out of the gun in slow motion, with the help of Abuelo, who was using all his strength to slow down the bullet for Rosa. She was still flying through the air, her cape fluttering behind her, as the members of Los Maliciosos clung to it, trying to distract her. Unseen by the attackers, Abuelo had been hiding amongst the fight, watching anxiously as events unfolded, the canines' spirit beside him. But with his granddaughter's life hanging in the balance, he finally revealed himself, lending his power to Rosa's. Undeterred by the chaos, Rosa focused all her energy on the bullet, and with a surge of power, she narrowly stopped it mid-air. However, due to the lightning-fast speed of the event, Rosa's control wavered slightly, causing her to inadvertently redirect the bullet in the wrong direction. The bullet then ricocheted back toward Victor, striking him squarely in the chest and stopping his heartbeat in an instant.

Victor crumpled to the floor, dead.

Shock widened Rosa's eyes as she rushed to Victor's side. Chaos erupted among Los Maliciosos, with screams of "You killed him!" and "Vamos… let's go!" echoing through the mansion.

Panic set in, and they fled, abandoning their fallen leader. The white carpeted floor was now stained with Victor's blood, and Judge Garcia's face contorted in a mix of shock and rage. "You're responsible for this!" she spat at Rosa, her voice venomous. "You're responsible for the death of my dogs and for the death of this man. For all the witchcraft in this city, I know you work for El Cazador, and you will pay for his crimes."

Abuelo and the canines' departure was swift, walking through the mansion's walls without a word. Rosa watched them go, her face twisted in anguish. "I'm sorry, Judge Garcia," she said, her voice laced with desperation. "I didn't mean for this to happen. I was trying to protect you from El Cazador and Los Maliciosos. He sent them here to kill you!"

The judge's voice rose to a shriek, her anger boiling over. "Don't expect a thank you, because you're not getting one from me. Look at what you've done! A man lies dead in my home. You're no better than the scum of the earth you think you're protecting me from!"

Anger flashed in Rosa's eyes, but her voice remained even. "I saved your life!"

Judge Garcia's laughter was cold and mirthless, a harsh sound that filled the room. "You didn't save my dogs' lives! No, you didn't protect me you've brought chaos into my home. I'll make sure you pay for this, Rosa." The judge's words hung in the air, heavy with malice.

Rosa's eyes narrowed. "How do you know my name?" she demanded.

Judge Garcia's expression turned icy, her voice dripping with disdain. "You think I don't already know about your first appearance with Lopez and Martin?" she said. "You may have fooled them into thinking you're some kind of superhero, but you broke the law. You illegally apprehended a young man, only to have him released from his cell within an hour. You're a vigilante, Rosa, and you don't fool me." Judge Garcia's anger intensified, her words hanging in the air like a challenge. "I know you work with El Cazador. You are all going to be under arrest and will pay for your crimes!"

Rosa's face set in a determined expression. "I don't work for him and I won't let you make me some kind of outlaw," she said. "I won't let you punish me for trying to do what is right."

Judge Garcia's eyes flashed with anger, her voice low and menacing. "We'll see about that. I will have every bounty hunter in this city after you by dawn, Rosa. Mark my words."

With a subtle motion, Judge Garcia pressed a red button hidden under a standing table, discreetly calling the police. Rosa's eyes widened as she realized the police were on their way and the woman she had just saved had turned against her. She knew she had to get out of there fast. Grief washed over her, and with a swift motion, Rosa raised her arms, flying up to the mansion's shattered glass ceiling, leaving the chaos behind.

Within minutes, Sergeant Lopez and Detective Martin arrived at the scene, their faces grim as they took in the carnage. Judge Garcia, still fuming, demanded to know what they knew about Rosa.

"Rosa seems like she's only trying to help," Sergeant Lopez began.

"She's a superhero, not a villain," Martin added, and Sergeant Lopez nodded in agreement.

Judge Garcia cut them both off, her voice dripping with disdain. "I don't care about her motives. I saw her using powers that seemed beyond human control. This destruction is unacceptable. My glass ceiling is destroyed, valuable art pieces have been smashed, my dogs have been killed, and this man lies on my floor dead."

Detective Martin exchanged a concerned glance with Sergeant Lopez. "Did Rosa cause all this?" Sergeant Lopez inquired, confusion etched on his face.

"Yes, and she will be held responsible," Judge Garcia stated firmly. "Someone has to pay for these damages."

"Yes, Your Honor," Detective Martin replied. "But perhaps we should investigate further before jumping to conclusions."

Judge Garcia's expression turned icy. "I won't be swayed. I'm setting a bounty of one million dollars for Rosa's capture."

Rosa lingered near the shattered glass ceiling, straining to hear the conversation below. Her heart felt heavy and sorrowful, and she began to understand why El Cazador might have issues with Judge Garcia.

"I'm in danger," Rosa muttered to herself. "I have to go see

Ryan and get his support. There must be something in Kevin's briefcase that can help me."

Rosa raised her hands, and they began to glow with a fierce red light. The mystical energy emanating from her hands enveloped her body, lifting her off the ground. With a soft whoosh, Rosa rose into the air, her glowing hands propelling her forward as she flew toward Ryan's house.

23

Chapter Twenty-Three: Tears in the Night Sky

Rosa soared through the darkness, the city lights of Tampa twinkling below her like diamonds scattered across the fabric of the night. The wind rushed past her, whipping her hair into a frenzy as she flew over the Hillsborough Bay. The salty scent of the ocean filled her lungs, a bittersweet reminder of the freedom she had once known. Tears streamed down her face, mingling with the wind and the darkness. She replayed the events of the night, her mind reeling with the consequences of her actions. Victor's face flashed before her, his eyes cold and menacing, and then he had crumpled to the ground, a bullet wound in his chest taking his life.

"I didn't mean to," she sobbed, her voice lost in the wind. "I don't know how to control these powers."

She recalled Ryan's address from having glanced at his contact information at work, knowing exactly where to find him. Within a few minutes, Ryan's house came into view—a cozy bungalow with a tile roof and a wraparound porch that seemed to beckon her toward refuge. The porch light cast a warm glow, illuminating the comfortable rocking chairs and the lush potted plants that lined the railing. Her eyes were fixed intently on the rooftop as she descended, her emotions churning in turmoil and making her landing far from graceful. She thudded onto the roof, her feet scrabbling for traction as she struggled to steady herself.

Ryan stepped outside and saw Rosa on his roof, tripping over her cape. "What on earth? Who are you?" Ryan's voice called out from below. Rosa removed her cape, and once the collar was no longer wrapped around her neck, Ryan recognized her.

"You've got to be kidding me," he said, when the spell from her collar released its hold on his eyes, revealing her true identity. "You're the one everyone's been calling me about… you're Rosa!"

Ryan's gaze drifted to her left hand, where the ruby engagement ring sparkled on her finger. A wry smile crept onto his face as he realized she was using the ruby's gifts to be a superhero. It was almost… amusing. But beneath the amusement, a more serious thought took hold.

Tears began to stream down Florence's face as she made her way down his roof. Ryan's expression changed from amusement to concern. "What happened?"

She took a deep breath, trying to compose herself. "I killed someone," she replied, her voice breathless, as if carrying the weight of the world. She paused, the words sticking in her throat. "It was an accident."

"Come inside, quickly," Ryan said, ushering her toward the front door of his house.

They stepped inside, and Florence's eyes adjusted to the warm glow of Ryan's living room. The room was cozy, with a plush couch and a recliner arranged around a large flat screen TV. The walls were adorned with framed photos and artwork, giving the space a personal touch. Florence felt a sense of safety wash over her as she entered Ryan's home. She looked over at the kitchen, and visions of Ryan eating alone at the kitchen table flashed before her eyes. She saw him sipping his black coffee, reading the Tampa Sun-Times on his tablet, his eyes scanning the news with a look of quiet contemplation.

"Tell me what happened," he said, his voice calm and reassuring.

She took a deep breath, and the events of the night spilled out. "The tarot cards are messages meant for Judge Garcia. El Cazador feels she is a corrupt judge and wanted Los Maliciosos to kill her tonight. I went to her mansion to save her. When I got there, they immediately shot and killed her dogs then stormed into her mansion. I intervened and throughout the fight, I was throwing them around, damaging her property. And then Victor, one of the members, held a gun to her head and pulled the trigger. There was a force you wouldn't understand— but there was a spirit guide there."

Ryan's eyebrow arched slightly as he repeated, "A spirit guide?"

"Yes, a spirit guide who held onto the speeding bullet with all its might so I could stop it," she continued, her voice trembling. "And when I did, it ricocheted back to Victor, piercing into his chest and stopping his heart." She began sobbing, covering her face. "I didn't mean to," she whispered. "Now Judge Garcia is going to charge me for the murder of Victor and all of the property damage. She'll have bounty hunters out for Rosa in the morning with a million-dollar reward for her capture."

Ryan's expression darkened, and he let out a low whistle.

"Well, that's a whole new level of hot water. At least it's your alter ego who will be getting chased by bounty hunters." He smiled wryly, trying to lighten the mood.

She let out a laugh, thinking of the irony, and then added with a hint of relief, "At least we've got one less thing to worry about—I captured Daisy today." Her voice was still shaken from the overwhelming stress she was under.

"What? How?" Ryan replied in confusion.

"I had a fight with her at the abandoned warehouse and managed to lock her away in an alabaster stone chest. I locked the chest with a lock made of cold iron."

"Why cold iron?" Ryan asked with curiosity.

"It holds a secret power, one that's been wielded against spirits like Daisy for centuries," she said, her eyes glinting; "It's for protective measures. Cold iron is believed to repel, contain, or even harm ghosts and other malevolent supernatural creatures. I noticed the chest rattling during my fight with Daisy, and I knew I needed to secure it to trap her inside until I could figure out how to return her to the spirit realm. I used the lock's cold iron to my advantage, locking her inside. Now, she is contained, and we can finally breathe a sigh of relief."

"That's quite clever and extremely convenient for you to have," Ryan replied with a smirk, but his expression quickly changed when he saw tears forming again in her eyes. "If Daisy's trapped, El Cazador won't know what's happened yet. That gives us some time to figure out our next move."

"Do you still have Kevin's briefcase?" Florence asked.

Ryan turned from the living room and headed to his bedroom to look for the briefcase. Florence set her cape aside and sank into the plush couch, surrounded by elegant blue pillows with intricate gold embroidery. The soft cushions enveloped her, providing a comforting respite from the turmoil of the night. She ran her fingers over the embroidery, feeling the gentle texture of the gold thread.The pillows seemed to glow in the soft light of the living room, casting a soothing ambiance over the space. Florence waited for Ryan to return, and she felt her eyelids growing heavy, the weight of her exhaustion pressing down on her. She leaned back into the couch, letting the softness of the pillows cradle her head. Suddenly, she heard the sound of papers rustling, and then Ryan emerged with a small Ziploc bag clutched in his hand and a stack of papers from Kevin's investigations about El Cazador tucked under his arm. His eyes locked onto hers, checking to see if she had noticed what he was hiding.

"What are you looking for?"Florence asked, her voice curious.

"Just some of Kevin's notes that I still needed to review on his investigations of El Cazador."

"Is there anything in that briefcase that can help us right now?" Florence asked, wondering if Ryan would try to deceive her.

"I'm not sure, but we do need to get to the office now. We have to find out who else El Cazador is targeting. I suggest you call Alexia it's going to be a long night, and we'll need all the help we can get."

"Ryan, I need to tell you something," she said as she stood up from his couch. "I strongly believe that Alejandro, the editor and chief of the Tampa Bay Sun-Times, is El Cazador."

Ryan halted, staring at her, his jaw dropping. "That's a serious allegation. Are you certain?"

"I've seen it in my visions, heard his thoughts, and there's more that points to him being El Cazador," she said firmly.

"Visions, thoughts, and suspicions are not concrete evidence," he reminded her. "What if you're wrong?"

"I know he is involved, somehow. We'll uncover the truth soon enough," she replied, her voice steady.

Ryan scanned the living room and noticed Rosa's black cape laying neatly beside the loveseat. "You might want to ditch the costume when we get to the office," he said with a hint of amusement as he opened his front door.

A sly smirk spread across Florence's face as she picked up the cape, the fabric flowing through her fingers like a dark waterfall. She wrapped it around her shoulders and secured it into place with a soft whoosh. The collar immediately concealed Florence's identity.

"Wow," he said, staring at her. "I don't know what it is, but when you put on that cape, you don't look like Florence."

"Good. And I'm going to the office as Rosa," she said with a wink. "I'll see you there."

With that, Rosa spread her arms, and the cape billowed behind her like a dark cloud. She took to the sky, soaring into the night with a fierce determination. Ryan watched her go, a mix of awe and concern on his face.

"I'll meet you there," he muttered to himself.

With a thoughtful expression, Ryan pulled the Ziploc bag out of his pocket, his eyes fixed on the ruby remnants inside. A faint glint of curiosity sparked in his gaze, and for a moment, he seemed lost in thought, contemplating the possibilities that these fragments might hold.

24

Chapter Twenty-Four: A Call to Darkness

El Cazador paced back and forth in his secret room, the air thick with tension. The walls, floor, and ceiling were all made of polished obsidian crystal, a deliberate choice he'd made to fortify the space against external threats and malevolent energies, particularly after his obsession with dark magic had grown. This fortress-like sanctuary was designed to shield not just himself, but Daisy as well, from the dangers that lurked in the shadows. The obsidian now cast a dark, mirror-like reflection of his every move. The room was a testament to his growing paranoia, a place where he could retreat from the world and protect himself from those who would seek to harm him.

The soft glow of candles cast flickering shadows on the walls, making it seem the room itself was alive and watching him. El Cazador's eyes blazed with fury, his mind consumed by his inability to reach Victor.

"Answer your phone, you son of a bitch," he yelled. He had been trying to reach Victor for hours, but his calls went straight to voicemail. Suddenly, his phone rang; his younger brother calling.

"Hello?" El Cazador responded cautiously.

"*Hermano*, you need to sit down, the smooth voice said." El Cazador's grip on the phone tightened."I'm afraid I have some bad news. Victor has been killed."

El Cazador's eyes narrowed, his mind racing."What happened?" he asked, trying to keep his tone neutral.

"Rosa used her deadly force against Victor when he tried to assassinate Judge Garcia. Garcia survived, but Victor is now dead."

El Cazador's anger boiled over, and he slammed his fist onto his desk, making candles tremble. Photos of his sister Daisy, younger brother, and him scattered across the floor, the glass from the picture frame shattering into a hundred pieces. Papers he was working on went flying, pens rolling across the floor. El Cazador tried to compose himself, but his mind was racing with the implications. He needed to know what was going on.

"I will find her tonight," he declared. "And we have another problem. Our *hermanita* is lost and not responding to my cries to her. I need you to meet me in my office, pronto."

"I will get there as soon as I can," his younger brother replied before hanging up.

"Daisy," he called, hoping for a response. But there was only silence. El Cazador's eyes scanned the room, his mind racing with implications.Something was wrong. Daisy always responded to his calls.With rage building inside him, El Cazador slammed his phone against the obsidian wall, destroying it completely."I have had it with this incompetence!" he growled, standing amidst the chips from his destroyed phone. "Florence will join me whether she wants to or not! I'm through with these fucking games!"

The candles flickered, casting eerie shadows on the walls. "This ends tonight," he muttered.

With a newfound sense of determination, El Cazador strode out of the room to locate Florence himself.

25

Chapter Twenty-Five: The Red Awakening

The conference room in the DA's office was a sterile, window-less space, the walls lined with bland, beige panels. A long, polished table dominated the center of the room, surrounded by chairs that seemed to march in lockstep. Alexia sat at the table, her brown eyes widening as Rosa entered.

"Wow, Florence, I really didn't recognize you," she stammered. "You weren't kidding on the phone when you told me," she added.

Rosa smiled, her eyes flashing with amusement. "I cast a spell onto my cape so when people look at its collar they are hypnotized into not recognizing me as Florence," she explained. "The spell will protect my identity. I will leave on my cape for now. We need to find out the true identity of El Cazador and we need to do this tonight."

"Why are you calling yourself Rosa?" Alexia asked. "I've already heard about your appearance but I'm curious to know why you chose that name."

"Just like a rose protects itself with its thorns, I too will

THE LEGEND OF ROSA

protect this city from injustices. Together, we'll fight against injustices. Justice…will be ours."

Alexia smiled back at her. "You mentioned Ryan is on his way…do you know when he'll get here? We need to look into Kevin's briefcase and I want to start researching the dark network he was telling me about."

Rosa's eyes narrowed to slits as she checked the clock hanging on the conference room wall. "What's taking him so long?" she muttered, her voice low and husky. "I know I flew over here, but I made a stop at my apartment to get this," she gestured at the alabaster chest, "so he should be here by now."

Alexia shifted uncomfortably, her bright brown eyes darting nervously around the room. "Maybe he's just running behind," she suggested, but her voice lacked conviction.

"We have very little time. I have captured El Cazador's ghostly sister and he will soon notice her disappearance. I need a place to hide this when he starts looking for her. My home will be the first place he will look."

The alabaster stone chest deflected the light around it, its presence ominous. Alexia's eyes flickered toward it, and she could hear faint screams. Alexia's eyes widened. "But how…?"

Rosa's smile was enigmatic. "I cast a powerful spell on the chest. I don't even know how I knew that spell but it was like I had used it in a prior life… it just came to me. No one will be able to release Daisy but me." Her smile was grim. "But I have plans for Daisy."

"What kind of plans?" Alexia asked.

"I want to send her where she belongs, back to the spirit realm." Rosa set the chest holding Daisy at the corner of the conference room. The eerie screams grew louder and louder. "Let's start and Ryan can join us when he gets here," Rosa continued.

They delved into the case files, Alexia pointed out a pattern. "Ryan's been investigating a dark network called Erebus," she said, her brow furrowed. "I think El Cazador might be using it to cover his tracks."

Rosa's eyes narrowed. "Let's take a look." Alexia's fingers flew across her keyboard as she accessed the Erebus site. "Shoot, it's password-protected," she muttered. Rosa's eyes gleamed with intensity. "Try typing in 'Daisy'." Alexia's fingers hesitated over the keyboard before she typed in the name.

"Incorrect," she said, her brow furrowed.

"Try it in all lowercase," Rose suggested.

Alexia's fingers danced across the keyboard again. "Still incorrect."

Suddenly, Rosa's eyes froze, her gaze locked on a document on the table as if someone was whispering to her to notice it. "Wait. Xander's been involved in every one of these criminal cases that Los Maliciosos went after," she whispered, her voice barely audible. Alexia's eyes snapped toward her, but Florence continued, her voice growing stronger. "His name is signed on all these court documents. Plea deals he refused to enter, and later was coerced to enter because of Judge Garcia holding him in contempt."

Alexia's eyes widened."But Xander's sister's name isn't Daisy… it's Marguerite."

Rosa blinked, a horrible realization dawning. "Marguerite is Greek for pearl," she said, her voice low. "But it's also a French name for the ox-eye daisy flower."

Alexia's fingers trembled as she typed in the name 'Marguerite' as the password. The site opened, revealing photos of Xander as El Cazador. Alexia's eyes snapped toward Rosa, her

265

voice trembling in fear. "Oh my God… Xander is El Cazador!"

A round of applause broke their silence, and they both looked up to see Xander standing in the doorway, a smirk twisting his lips. "Am I interrupting something, señoritas?"

Rosa's eyes flashed red with anger, her hands jerking into a defensive motion. "We know who you are now, Xander," she growled, her voice low and menacing. "And you're not going to get away with this."

"Huh, and who is going to stop me? You, Florence?" Xander said, his eyes glinting with amusement.

Rosa was startled at hearing him say her name. She gently touched the collar around her neck, wondering if the spell had faded.

"It's hasn't faded, Florence… Daisy told me," Xander replied aloud to her thoughts. At seeing her stunned face, he added, "And yes, I can hear your thoughts, my dear. I have clairvoyant abilities as well that I've honed. I'm surprised you didn't catch on when you couldn't hear my thoughts," he said as he casually stepped into the conference room. He looked at them both, shaking his head in disapproval. "Oh Florence, you really did it this time. How am I going to get you out of a murder charge?"

"I didn't mean to kill Victor," she protested.

"Oh, I know it was an accident. But you see Judge Garcia doesn't see it that way, and she won't unless, of course, you pay her off, which you can't afford, especially now that you will be out of a job."

"It's you who will be out of a job!" Alexia chimed in.

"Oh Alexia, you will never make it to law school. Your career ends today, I'll see to that. You see, what I value the most from my team is loyalty, but you are just another secretary who will

266

never amount to anything. In fact, I'll end both of your careers today. You don't think with just one phone call I'll have you both in handcuffs? That is unless you join me, Florence."

"You need help, Xander," Rosa snapped.

"Help?"At the thought of therapy, Xander burst out laughing. "I don't think I'm the one who needs the help. I'm not the one dressed in a silly superhero outfit trying to save the day. How long did you think you could play this superhero role before the city of Tampa turns on you? Judge Garcia is already demanding a reward for your arrest."

Rosa's mind began to race as she listened to Xander's reasoning. Xander took a step closer to Rosa.

"Join me… join what I have built. Together we will right wrongs and fight for justice together."

Before Rosa could reply, Daisy screamed again from inside the alabaster chest. Xander's eyes immediately became fixed on the chest with an unnerving intensity. "What have you done? Where is my sister?" he growled.

Rosa's eyes narrowed, her hands clenched into fists. "You'll never have her. She's safe now, and I'll be sending her back where she belongs, where she will never hurt again."

Xander's smile grew wider, his eyes glinting with amusement. "We'll see about that. With a sudden movement, Xander focused on his chest, chanting spiritual witchcraft to release Daisy from the chest.

Daisy shrieked in pain as the chest began to shake and smoke, as if the ghost was being burned inside.

"Stop, stop," Daisy pleaded… "you're hurting me."

Xander reached out to touch the chest in desperation, but as soon as his skin made contact with it, he was thrown backward, his body convulsing in agony because of the cast spell. Rosa's eyes gleamed with triumph, knowing that her protection spell to seal Daisy was working. "You should have stayed away from her," she said, her voice cold and menacing.

Xander struggled to his feet, his eyes blazing with fury. "You're just like me, Rosa," he spat. "A killer, a monster. You're no better than I am."

"I'm nothing like you! I'm fighting for justice, for what's right. You're just fighting for your own twisted desires."

El Cazador chuckled, a cold, mirthless sound. "There is no such thing as seeking true justice, it's all standard procedure," he said, his voice dripping with disdain. "Don't you get it yet? It's money, connections, and favors. That's what practicing the law is really about. Not justice, not fairness. Just procedure."

"You're insane. All those innocent people you killed, including Kevin…"

"Oh, Kevin," he said, his voice turning sing-song. "Your fiance and Melissa's lover. I had one of my private investigators follow him after I learned my ruby was stolen. I believe he was screwing my secretary the night before he was going to propose to you."

Rosa's eyes widen with pain as Xander tossed a photo onto the conference table for her to see. The image showed Kevin and Melissa in bed together, their faces twisted in a passionate kiss. His eyes clearly obsessed with her. At the end of the photo was a red date-stamp of the time and date.

Rosa's eyes glowed red with rage, her hands began to tremble with fury.

"People are deceitful, Florence," Xander reminded her. "They lie, they cheat, they steal to get ahead. You can't trust people but you can trust me. I will make you rich and powerful. I will help you get a seat on the bench," he paused for dramatic effect. "I know that is something you've always wanted. I've seen it in your future," he said with a smile. Together we will become a powerful force."

Rosa looked up at the man she once admired, then down at the photo of Kevin in bed with Melissa.Rosa's anger heightened with the realization that Kevin had betrayed her before his proposal to her. She glanced over at Alexia, who still had innocence in her eyes, and she hoped the paralegal would never face a betrayal like this.

Ryan burst into the room, panting. "Rosa, don't listen to him!" he shouted.

Xander's smile grew wider still. "And you, Ryan. You'll never be working here again. It took you this long to realize I was El Cazador? You're not as witty as I thought."

"You're not going to get away with this," Ryan growled.

"We'll see about that." With a sudden movement, Xander grabbed Ryan, holding him in a tight grip as he raised a gun and pointed it at Ryan's head. "If you don't release my sister right now, I'll shoot him," he snarled at Rosa, his eyes blazed with fury.

Rosa's eyes widened in horror, her hands trembled with fear. "Relax Xander and put the gun down," she pleaded. "You don't want to do this. Killing Ryan was never part of your plans."

Xander chuckled as he cocked his pistol.

"Okay, okay. I will release her!" Rosa said hastily. "Just calm down."

"Don't release Daisy," Ryan said, as Xander edged him closer to the chest.

"I have no choice." Rosa's shoulders slumped under the weight of her decision. "I'm not going to let him hurt you."

With a heavy heart, Rosa reached out and placed her hands

on the cold iron lock. She closed her eyes, took a deep breath, and began to chant:

"Solvo vincla, spiritus libera,

Ferro frigido, animus eximo.

Emergo, Daisy ab tenebris,

In libertatem, redde te."

("I release the bonds, free the spirit,

From cold iron, I remove the soul.

Emerge Daisy, from the shadows,

Into freedom, I return you.")

As Rosa spoke the words to break the spell, the air around her seemed to vibrate with a gentle, pulsing energy. The cold iron lock shuddered, its metal creaking in protest, before it unlocked.

The alabaster chest remained closed for a moment while Rosa chanted in Latin:

"Libera eam, libera eam."

(Release her, release her.")

Daisy's scream grew louder, more urgent, as she emerged from her prison, her ghostly form trembling with rage and relief.

Xander's eyes gleamed with triumph."*Hermana*," he called.

Daisy fully emerged from the alabaster stone chest, her presence filled the room like a dark, icy mist. Rosa's skin prickled with goosebumps as the air seemed to freeze around her. She could see her breath misting in the air. It was visible in the sudden chill.Daisy's eyes blazed with fury, her skin deathly pale, her hair disheveled."You locked me in there," she screamed.

"Enough chit-chat," Xander said, raising his gun toward Ryan's chest. "I want you to join me now and I will force you to join me if you resist. As for you, Ryan… I'll see you in hell."

Rosa's eyes widened in horror as Xander pulled the trigger. The sound of the gunshot echoed through the room which made her ears ring. Rosa and Alexia screamed as Ryan's body crumpled to the ground, his eyes closed, his skin pale.

"You killed him," Alexia shouted as she ran to him in hopes she could check for a pulse.

Upon hearing this Rosa launched at Xander and Daisy, her fists flying, her feet kicking.The three of them clashed, their bodies locked in a fierce struggle. Rosa's knuckles connected with Daisy's ghostly jaw, but the spirit didn't flinch. Instead, she retaliated with a blow that sent Rosa crashing to the floor.Rosa struggled to get back on her feet but Daisy's icy grip closed around her wrists. Her skin felt like it was burning with cold, her fingers numb and unresponsive.

With a sudden movement, Daisy shoved Rosa onto the floor. Xander began stomping on her.

"Stop! Get off her," Alexia pleaded.

Daisy turned to Alex and locked her in place using her spiritual force.Rosa summoned her inner strength, ready to defend Alexia against the looming threat, but before she could react, Xander's swift hand snapped iron handcuffs around her wrists. The cold metal bit into her skin, sending a jolt of shock through her veins.

As the iron made contact with her skin, Rosa felt an unsettling sensation, like a void opening within her. Her magical and clairvoyant abilities, once a vibrant and integral part of her being, suddenly withered and dissipated. The iron handcuffs seemed to absorb her powers which left her feeling drained, vulnerable, and eerily silent. Next, he placed handcuffs on Alexia whose eyes had filled with tears.

Xander's eyes gleamed with triumph as he tightened the cuffs, his grip unyielding. Rosa's gaze fell upon the cold, unforgiving metal, a symbol of her lost freedom and diminished magic. Her heart raced with a mix of fear and defiance, setting the stage for a desperate struggle to reclaim her powers and break free from her captor's grasp.Rosa knelt, helpless and shackled. Her eyes wandered to the lifeless form of the man she had begun to see as her partner, and her soul shattered into a million pieces, her mind screaming in anguish.*Not him too. It's not fair."*

Daisy's energy force locked onto both Alexia and Rosa just as Alejandro walked into the office.

"Better late than never, my brother," Xander said.

Rosa was stunned, but the vision she'd had of the majestic wolf walking beside the hunter came to her mind. Alejandro is the wolf who walks alongside the hunter," she thought. *Both brothers blamed Kevin for Daisy's death.*

"What did I miss?" Alejandro asked, halting at the sight of Rosa and Alexia in handcuffs.

"Time to go home, *hermanos,*" Daisy said as her energy force took hold of both Rosa and Alexia. She lifted them both off of the ground, guiding them to follow her unwillingly.

"*Un momento,*" Xander replied.

He reached into his pocket, and pulled out his rose-gold tarot card deck carefully selecting the death card and placing it on Ryan's chest. The tarot card glinted in the dim light, the image of the death card seeming to mock Ryan and the desperate situation Rosa now found herself in. The grim reaper's skeletal face appeared to leer at her while the two figures bound by chains—a bishop and a maiden, eerily reminiscent of Rosa and Alexia—seem to symbolize the dark fate that awaited them. The chain that bound her appeared to grow tighter, as if closing on Rosa's own freedom.

"Goodbye, Ryan," Xander said, his voice dripping with malice.

As Xander turned away following his siblings out of the office, Ryan's eyes snapped open. His eyes glowed with a fierce, deep fiery red.

TO BE CONTINUED...

About the Author

Jasmine Hernandez writes thrilling stories of heroism and self-discovery. Inspired by classic legendary heroes like Zorro, "The Legend of Rosa" marks her exciting debut in the supernatural thriller genre. Discover more about Jasmine's literary journey, new projects, and events, and explore behind-the-scenes insights on her author website. Don't forget to subscribe to her Newsletter and follow Morpho Butterfly Publishing, LLC on Instagram!

You can connect with me on:

🌐 https://bit.ly/aboutauthorjasminehernandez

🔗 https://www.morphobutterflypublishing.org

🔗 https://www.instagram.com/morphobutterflypublishingllc/?igsh=YnkxaXdicGd3amM1&utm_source=qr

Also by Jasmine Hernandez

A forthcoming memoir that chronicles the author's personal journey through love, loss, and resilience in the face of tragedy. This true story explores the devastating consequences of domestic violence and the failures of the justice system, while advocating for systemic change and victim-centered support. This memoir will be available in English and in Spanish on December 13, 2026.

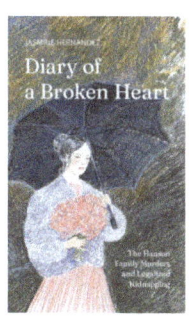

Diary of a Broken Heart: The Hanson Family Murders and Legalized Kidnapping Genre: Memoir

A heart-wrenching exploration of love, loss, and resilience. This memoir is a collection of intimate diary entries chronicling the devastating events leading up to the tragic murder of Jasmine's sister, Jessica Hanson, niece Annika, and brother-in-law Clyde Hanson in their South Dakota home. Through raw and honest accounts, she reveals the horrific domestic violence she endured, and the ultimate failure of the justice system meant to protect her.

The memoir also exposes the corruption and flaws within Child Protective Services (CPS), including the legalized kidnapping that denied her the opportunity to adopt her nephew, the sole survivor of these tragedies. This personal narrative traverses the agonizing grief and resilience that followed, serving as a testament to Jessica's memory and the lessons learned from her story.

By sharing this journey, Jasmine aims to educate readers about the failures of CPS and the need for systemic change, inspire resilience and healing in survivors of domestic violence, and advocate for victim-centered policies and support. The Diary of a Broken Heart is a powerful exploration of love, loss, and the unbreakable bonds of family, offering a beacon of hope for a better future.